TIP AND RUN

Spitfire Mavericks Thrillers
Book Six

D. R. Bailey

SAPERE
BOOKS

TIP AND RUN

Published by Sapere Books.

24 Trafalgar Road, Ilkley, LS29 8HH

saperebooks.com

ISBN: 978-0-85495-405-6

I would like to dedicate this book to my beloved cat 'Miss Kitty'. I've had cats all my life, but she is a special cat. She's my companion, overseer, interrupter of prose but generally cute and a big floof. I am grateful for the sight of her fuzzy face every day and her talkative nature. As Charles Dickens once said, 'What greater gift than the love of a cat'.

CHAPTER ONE

Winter 1942

We were flying a patrol up the coast of East Anglia when we saw it. A Focke-Wulf Fw 190 coming in low and fast, almost skimming the waves.

"Bandit at two o'clock, Skipper," said Pilot Officer Jonty Butterworth.

At the height and distance we were flying, the Wulf was too far away for us to rapidly intercept it.

"What the hell is he doing?" Pilot Officer Willie Cooper interjected.

"I don't know," I said, "but let's try to intercept him. Break, break."

There were six of us in the patrol from M Flight, the others being Flying Officer Tomas Jezek, Pilot Officer Arjun Sharma, and Pilot Officer Dylan Davies. We were part of one of the two squadrons in Squadron 696, unofficially known as the Mavericks. Ostensibly, we were pilots that nobody else wanted, but Fighter Command had recently given us some of the more important top-secret missions.

We made a beeline for the lone Wulf. He continued heading at high speed for Norfolk.

"And what on earth is he about attacking Cromer of all places?" asked Jonty, who had a somewhat scathing opinion of small provincial towns.

"How about we stop talking and try stopping him?" suggested Willie.

The Wulf had now reached Cromer beach but we were still too far away to attack.

"I don't think we can stop him, Skipper," said Jonty.

"We can give it a damn good try," I replied, throttling up to maximum.

It wasn't enough. We were out of striking distance and, besides which, the Wulf was now over the town itself. Even if we could shoot, there was the danger of hitting civilians.

"Hold your fire while he's over the town," I said. "He's too low."

"Damn and blast it," said Dylan. He was an eager young Welsh pilot who had recently joined the Mavericks. He was also very quick. I'd started taking him up on sorties and giving Pilot Officer Jean Tarbon a rest. Jean had been shot down more than once, so he didn't protest.

"Let's try and cut him off," I said.

"He's heading for the church!" Arjun shouted.

"Probably wants to say a prayer," Jonty quipped.

"No, that's not it," said Tomas. "He's dropping a bomb."

The pilot unleashed his cargo and banked away. There was a terrific explosion. Smoke began to billow up into the air.

"Good God," said Dylan. "Whatever next?"

"I'll tell you what's next," said Jonty. "He's going for the main street."

Sure enough the Focke-Wulf, not content with dropping a bomb on the town, now did a fast strafing run down one of the streets.

"Why aren't they shooting back?" Arjun said.

Cromer had a garrison of troops, extensive coastal defensive, and ack-ack batteries. It was odd that they had not opened up on the German plane.

"I assume because he's too low for the ack-ack," I said. "Watch yourselves in case they get trigger-happy."

We were over the town by now and I dropped lower to match the height of the Wulf. As I started to close in, he must have seen me because he turned sharply and headed out to sea at speed.

"He's getting away!" shouted Tomas.

"Tally-ho! The hunt is on," said Jonty, unperturbed.

We gave chase as the Wulf made off over the park at the edge of the town. As he did so, he opened the window of his cockpit and threw something out. I had no time to consider what it was, as he was now over the sand. I was determined not to let him escape.

One Wulf versus six Spitfire Mark IXs should have put the odds in our favour, but he was still ahead. We screamed over the coastal defences of scaffolding and barbed wire, then we were out to sea.

Finally, I saw Dylan get ahead and start to gain on the German, who continued on with dogged determination.

"I've got him in my sights," said Dylan, triumphantly. He fired and the Jerry flicked his plane aside, the bullets splashing on the water. "Damn and blast it," Dylan said, irritated.

The Wulf pulled away to the left, and Willie ended up the closest.

"Now I've got you," said Willie, opening fire, but the Jerry rolled his plane, and the salvo went wide.

"Take that you rotten Hun," said Jonty, cutting loose a hail of bullets. He had followed along with Willie and took a potshot.

None of the bullets hit the mark as the Wulf evaded him too. The enemy pilot was nimble and fast as lightning.

Meanwhile, Arjun had tried a different manoeuvre from above. His plane swooped down, and in what I have to say was a slick piece of flying, the Jerry simply accelerated, flew upwards and passed harmlessly underneath him.

"Ach, this Jerry is too fast," said Tomas. He had anticipated the German's move and came at him from the side. He fired but his shots also went wide, and the pilot kept on climbing.

The Wulf had gained height and he continued heading for home. While all this was going on I had managed to close the distance on him. I had pushed my Spit to the limit to try and catch him. Although he seemed not to notice me, I was sure that he had. I got closer, nevertheless, leaving the others tagging along behind me.

If I could get within range, then I'd have a chance. Then, for a split second, the Jerry was in my sights. It was all I needed. I opened fire.

The German was on the ball; he banked right, then left, weaving this way and that, trying to shake me off. I tried to stay on his tail, firing short bursts and missing every time. I hoped perhaps one of the others would get alongside me, then we would have him, but no such luck.

Without warning, the Wulf pulled sharply skyward. I started to follow, but then I noticed that the cloud was thickening. It would get even thicker the further we flew across the Channel. The next moment he had disappeared. He'd been counting on the cloud for cover, and he'd made it. I had to give him credit for that. I didn't follow but turned my plane away.

"Damn it, Skipper," said Jonty. "What a rotten show. Shall we go after him?"

"No, Jonty," I said. "He'll be long gone. Besides, we are getting too close to the other side."

I knew what that meant. Some of his friends might come out to meet us. We could end up in a firefight with more than one Wulf if we continued, plus the fact we'd get low on fuel and ammo too.

"What a shame," said Jonty sadly.

"Pity you missed him the first time," Willie put in.

"I didn't see you hit him either," Jonty shot back.

"All right, all right, settle down children," I said with a laugh, intervening before they started up in earnest. "Come on, chaps, let's go home."

The others formed up on me and we headed back to Blighty. As we crossed the coastline and looked down over Cromer, we saw that whatever building the bomb had hit was still burning.

"Didn't get the church though," remarked Dylan.

"Divine intervention, perhaps?" quipped Arjun.

"Hopefully nobody was killed," I added.

"Yes, a bad show all around. Can't understand what anyone would want to attack Cromer for," said Jonty. "Dreadfully dull sort of place all told."

"Some people obviously like it," Arjun replied.

We lapsed into silence and to my relief Jonty didn't suggest composing a ballad. Not that I didn't like his ballads, but Willie would inevitably object and the two of them would squabble like brothers all the way home.

It was extremely odd, I thought, for a lone German fighter to randomly attack a town like Cromer, and I resolved to talk to Squadron Leader Bentley about it. Would there be more attacks? There was also the matter of what it was that the pilot had chucked out of the window of his cockpit. I was interested to find out, if it was still there.

We landed at Banley Airfield, and as I taxied to my standing there was the familiar sight of my wife, Section Officer Angelica Kensley, waiting for me to alight from my plane. Immediately after I did so, she hurtled up the field towards me and landed on my chest.

"Oof!" I said, taking the impact. Although I was expecting it, I never did quite get used to her boisterous greetings.

"I'm glad you're home, darling," she said, kissing me before I could reply. I surrendered myself willingly to her ministrations for a few moments until finally, she pulled away.

"Well, Flight Lieutenant Angus Mackennelly, and what happened out there?" she said, smiling.

She would already know the gist, having been on the comms.

"It was a single Focke-Wulf," I said. "He attacked Cromer and then ran off."

"Too fast for you all to catch him," she replied.

"Unfortunately, yes."

There was a discreet cough beside us, and I became aware that Bentley and his adjutant Section Officer Audrey Wilmington were waiting patiently. I let go of Angelica and she stood beside me. Bentley immediately removed his ubiquitous pipe from his pocket and began his ritual of emptying it, scraping out the bowl, filling it with fresh tobacco, tamping it and lighting it. This procedure was as invariable as the sun rising, and we waited patiently until he puffed on his pipe contentedly.

"So, Angus, a lone Wulf, is that what I hear?" he said.

"Yes, sir, very strange indeed for one Wulf to attack Cromer like that. At least I thought so."

"Hmm," he grunted, while puffing out clouds of smoke. "Not as strange as you might think."

"Oh?"

"No, not at all. In fact, come to my office and we'll have a chat."

He seemed in an amiable frame of mind, of which I was relieved since he had quite an irascible temper at times.

"Oh, and you can come too, Section Officer Kensley, since you two seem to be stuck to each other like limpets."

There it was, good old acidic Bentley. I smiled to myself. He allowed me and Angelica quite a lot of latitude, not least because he had encouraged me to propose to her. She also had a much higher security clearance than most personnel on the base, so nothing he said to me could be considered off-limits as far as she was concerned.

"Thank you, sir," said Angelica, smiling at him disarmingly.

"Yes, well, let's not hang around then…" he said, setting off for the main building at his usual cracking pace.

Bentley's office was somewhat spartan. It had an Air Force blue carpet which had seen better days, a few pictures on the walls, some filing cabinets, and a desk for him and one for Audrey, which held a typewriter. The adjutant immediately sat down and began to type. This was her usual style, but I knew she took in every word that was said.

Bentley motioned me and Angelica to sit and then began his pipe ritual once more. I wondered how much tobacco he managed to consume in a month — it seemed like an inordinate amount to me. Although smoking was certainly a common habit amongst many of the others at Banley, I'd never seen the appeal.

When Bentley's pipe was going to his satisfaction, he sat back in his chair and surveyed us for a moment. "These raids," he said, "are happening quite a bit."

"Oh?" I was surprised that this news had not come to my ears earlier.

"Yes, Jerry seems to have started a new tactic of making a damned bloody infernal nuisance of themselves." He sounded most aggrieved at this perfidious behaviour by the enemy. "They're flying in," he continued, "with single fighters or bombers, and in small groups, attacking small towns, and outlying coastal settlements."

"Isn't that rather like —" I began.

"Yes, I know what you're going to say," Bentley interrupted. "Rhubarbs and Rodeos."

The Rhubarb had been an RAF tactic of sending two fighters to France to harass the enemy, and Rodeos were fighter sweeps doing much the same thing.

"Well, yes," I replied.

"It's not the same," he said, brandishing the stem of his pipe at me. "We were attacking military targets, not dropping bombs on civilians and strafing their houses."

I remained silent. I knew that Bomber Command had been attacking areas with civilian populations much as the Germans had been doing since the Blitz. There were guilty parties on both sides in that regard.

"Anyway," said Bentley, electing not to pursue the subject further. "The point is that these raids *are* happening. They've been dubbed as 'Tip and Run' sorties by some bright spark up the chain of command. God knows why, but then who knows what goes through the heads of those jumped-up Johnnies. A parcel of windbags and no mistake. What's more important is that we've got to try and stop them." He subsided and resorted once more to smoking his pipe.

"But how?" I said. "This Wulf came in fast and low, I presume under the radar to avoid detection, so we won't even know where and when they are going to attack."

"Yes, I know all that," said Bentley. "But nevertheless, we are going have to run more patrols up the east coast as a deterrent if nothing else."

"All right," I said. "I'll plan accordingly. Perhaps if Captain Booker's squadron isn't busy, they can run some too."

Captain Sandford Booker was in charge of a USAAF Spitfire squadron which was now accompanying the B-17 bombers from the American base next door on short-range missions. The Mavericks had helped get them acclimatised to the planes, and some of their pilots had also flown a few missions with us. Sandford and I had become friends, and we often visited their base. I was sure he'd jump at the chance to get involved in some more action.

"Yes, do as you see fit," said Bentley. He had encouraged our cooperation with the Americans, which had turned out rather well.

"But why would Jerry attack somewhere like Cromer?" I mused. It had been a question in the back of my mind since the sortie.

"Ah," said Bentley. "Well, Cromer happens to be on the route the Jerry bombers take to the Midlands, and they've dumped a few excess bombs there on their way home. I suppose it's also an easy target."

"Yes, I see, I guess you're right."

Our bombers would have done the same. If they couldn't hit the target for whatever reason, they would dump the payload on the way back to Blighty. It was hard to criticise the Germans for something we'd been doing ourselves.

Bentley seemed to pick up on my thoughts. "This is war, Angus, and as such some terrible things have been done ... on both sides. It's just a matter of who has the just cause. I believe, naturally, that we do. I'm sure you do too."

I couldn't disagree on that point. "Yes, sir, of course. But there is one other thing."

"Oh?"

"The pilot of the Wulf threw something from the window of his cockpit as he was leaving. I'm going to take a trip out to Cromer and find out what it was."

"Hmm," said Bentley, looking pensive. "Out of the window you say? Whatever will these blasted Jerries do next? Yes, go and take a look if you will ... it's a long way, but still perhaps worth the trouble. Let me know if you find anything. In the meantime, get some more patrols going. Let's see if we can't catch the blighters next time."

Bentley turned his attention to the papers on his desk, a sure sign that our discussion was over. I left the office with Angelica, who tucked her arm into mine.

"What do you propose we do now?" she asked me.

"I thought we'd find Fred and take a quick run out to Cromer right away."

"I was hoping you'd say that."

I sent word to M Flight to stand down for the moment. Then we headed to the spot on the base where Sergeant Bruce Gordon, nicknamed Fred, usually parked his jeep. He was batman to those of us billeted at Amberly Manor. He had also become my friend and confidant.

In fairly short order we were heading off to Cromer, with Gordon driving the jeep as usual. It was a fair run and took us a couple of hours to accomplish it. On the way, Gordon enquired as to the purpose of our visit.

"Going to inspect the damage, sir?" he asked me as we bowled along.

"Not exactly, Fred," I replied. "Going to look for something that the Wulf pilot who attacked the town threw out of the window." I elaborated a little more on the episode at Cromer.

"Ah, I see. Sounds rather odd," he said when I'd finished.

"Yes, that's why I'm happy to take this rather long trip to find out what it was."

" I spent a little time in Cromer, as it goes," said Fred conversationally.

"Oh, Fred, go on, tell us — you had a young lady there, didn't you?" Angelica laughed.

"Ah, I'm afraid you're getting to know me rather too well, ma'am," said Fred with a chuckle. "Ostensibly it was to visit my aunt, but she also had a rather attractive neighbour, and so I subsequently found quite a few reasons to look her up…"

I was not surprised to hear this. I had long suspected that Gordon was something of a ladies' man, and he also had travelled quite extensively by all accounts. We spent the rest of the journey being regaled by stories of his rather eccentric aunt, who apparently kept a parrot which was prone to swear. As a result, the time passed quickly enough, and we soon arrived in the seaside town. I directed Gordon to drive us out to North Lodge Park, where I'd seen the pilot throw the object from his plane. We parked and split up to search for whatever it was.

It was a fairly small, well-kept public park set mainly to grass, with flower beds and a putting green. There was a view of the ocean beyond it. A number of people taking the air glanced at us curiously for a moment or two. However, the sight of uniformed personnel must have been quite a common sight in Cromer so they didn't pay us much attention.

After a fairly extensive search, I was disappointed that we had failed to discover anything of interest. There was no obvious object which might have been ejected from the Wulf. I cast around for some reward for our fruitless endeavour. Happily, the park did sport some rather nice tea rooms, and we elected to partake of some much-needed refreshments.

"It's a shame we didn't find anything," said Angelica, as a steaming pot of tea was placed on the table by the waitress. This was followed by crumpets, jam, butter, milk and sugar.

"I suppose it was a long shot, after all," I replied, slightly disconsolately.

"Shall I be mother?" Gordon enquired and after we nodded he began to pour the tea.

I followed Angelica's lead in taking a crumpet and spreading it with butter and jam. I had become rather fond of crumpets since Gordon had introduced me to Annie's Kitchen, a cosy tea room close to Banley. It was our haunt when I needed to have a heart-to-heart. "It's a shame we'll never know what that pilot threw out of the window now," I said, taking a bite of my crumpet and chewing on it with some relish.

"Never mind, darling, as you said yourself, it was a long shot," said Angelica.

Just then the waitress who had served the tea came up to our table. "Excuse me," she interjected. "I hope you don't mind me speaking out of turn, but I couldn't help overhearing that you were looking for something from that German plane earlier today. Is that right?"

I regarded her in surprise. She was a middle-aged woman, with a nice smile, and her hair done up in a scarf. By her demeanour, I suspected I had done her a disservice and she wasn't only a waitress. She most probably ran the place.

"Yes, I was, but we couldn't find it."

"Well," she said. "Just wait a moment, I think I might be able to help."

She bustled off while the three of us exchanged slightly puzzled glances. Shortly after, she returned and placed an object on the table.

"We were watching that German plane when it flew over," she said. "I saw him throw this out, so I picked it up in case someone might want it…" She hesitated. "Were you in those Spitfires chasing him?"

"Yes, that was us," I confirmed.

"Well, I was right riled up. The cheek of him trying to bomb our church. Didn't get it though, just the building next door… Anyway, hopefully that's of use to you."

She looked curiously at the badges on our arms. They were the unofficial badge for our squadron which Bentley had allowed us to wear. On it was the silhouette of a Spitfire, with 'Spitfire' in capital letters written in an arc above the plane and 'Mavericks' in a straight line underneath it. The lettering was coloured in bright yellow, and the Spitfire in light blue with the decals picked out in red.

"The Mavericks?" she said with interest.

"That's our squadron," I replied. "Unofficially."

"Angus here is my husband," said Angelica proudly. "He's a Flight Lieutenant."

"I'm Madge, and don't worry about paying, it's on me."

She withdrew a discreet distance away. I picked up the object she had left on the table. It was a reasonably large stone, onto which a playing card had been securely tied. The card was the Ace of Spades.

"Hmm," said Gordon. "I would say that's his calling card."

"The audacity," said Angelica.

"Yes, indeed," I replied. "If he's throwing something like this out of the window then I imagine…"

"He's going to do it again," she finished for me.

"I wouldn't be surprised if that wasn't the last you see of that Focke-Wulf, sir," said Gordon.

"Unfortunately, I think you're probably right," I agreed.

CHAPTER TWO

The following morning I elected to go and see Bentley. Audrey let me in as soon as I knocked on the office door.

"Ah, Angus," said Bentley when I entered. "Take a seat."

I did so and waited for the pipe of doom to appear, which it duly did. "How did you fare on your expedition?" he asked me at length.

"We did find something, sir," I began. "Or rather, a waitress at the tea rooms in the park found it and handed it over to us."

"I see," he said, taking a few puffs of his pipe. "And what exactly was it that she found?"

"This," I said, placing the stone with the card attached on his desk.

He regarded the object with some distaste, picked it up and turned it over in his hand. "The Jerry pilot threw *this* out of the window of his cockpit?"

"Apparently, sir, yes," I replied.

Bentley began to puff on his pipe at a slightly more alarming rate, which was a sure sign of agitation. "What does he think he's playing at?" he said, suddenly erupting. "This is a bloody war, not a blasted parody. Isn't it enough we've got bloody Jerries coming over here with their blasted Tip and Run raids? Now this?"

He left his chair with alacrity and proceeded to pace the room, waving the stem of his pipe around.

"Bloody Huns playing comic book heroes," he expostulated. "I'm not having it, Angus, not on my bloody watch. This bloody clown of a Jerry pilot has to be stopped at all costs. I'm making you personally responsible for shooting that blighter down."

I stared at him. Even the CO must know what he was asking was a tall order, if not well-nigh impossible. "I'll do my best, sir," I managed to say.

"You'll do more than your best, Angus," he replied in acid tones, before returning to his seat. He said nothing more for a while, but instead opted to refill his pipe. Fortunately, this action seemed to calm him down somewhat. "Of course," he said, in a more reasonable tone, "I understand the difficulties in catching this blasted rogue, but we've got to give it a damn good try."

"Yes, sir," I replied, not feeling at all confident of being able to carry out his wishes.

He took a few more puffs and nodded his assent. "Very well, I'll leave it to you. Get out there and run some patrols … and take this infernal object out of my sight." He pointed the stem of his pipe at the stone in disgust.

I picked it up while he waved his pipe at me dismissively. I took this as a sign to depart, which I did with some relief.

As soon I as left the main building, Angelica accosted me in her usual style. She tucked her arm into mine after soliciting a kiss. "Oh dear," she said. "You look rather down in the mouth."

"Well, so would you if you'd had the meeting I have just had," I informed her.

We walked to the bench at the edge of the airfield where we had spent many moments in the past. It was a haven where we could look out at the fields beyond, and escape the war for a few moments. I told her what Bentley had said to me and she laughed.

"It's no laughing matter," I told her severely. "How on earth am I supposed to catch this blasted Wulf pilot? We only saw him on the off chance as it is."

"Oh, don't be so stuffy," she said, smiling. "It's just Bentley, you know how he is."

"Yes, I do." I sighed and pulled her in closer.

"He doesn't really expect you to be personally responsible for catching him; he was just irate," she said.

"Well, it's a bloody unreasonable request," I told her.

"Look at it this way, if this pilot is determined to play the comic book hero, as Bentley put it, then you're bound to run into him again. Why don't you go and tell the chaps about him?"

"Might as well share the misery," I said.

After I had explained the situation to the rest of M Flight, they broke out into animated conversation.

"What a bloody cheek, that's all I can say. Coming over here and throwing playing cards out of windows," added Dylan.

"I suppose he thinks he's an Ace pilot or something," said Willie dryly.

"I'll show him an Ace pilot," said Jonty, firing up.

"Well, he aced you, didn't he?" Willie shot back.

"He evaded me, yes, and I didn't see you shooting him down either," Jonty told him.

"What are we going to do about it, Scottish?" asked Arjun, who was of a more practical frame of mind. His interjection thankfully prevented the other two from starting an argument.

"I've thought about that," I said. "I think we'll split the squadron and fly patrols with six planes. I will lead one sortie, and Tomas, you can lead the other. If one goes out when the other returns, we can fly two sorties a day. I'm also going to ask Captain Booker if his chaps can fly patrols too."

Tomas was a Flying Officer and also highly experienced. He was a natural choice to lead another patrol. I realised I could not be on every sortie anymore, and I had to accept that.

"Sure, Scottish, but it seems like a lot of work just for catching one pilot," Tomas observed.

"It's not just one pilot," I replied. "The Jerries are running these sorties with other planes too. We might be able to catch them."

"Makes sense," said Jean.

"Puts me in mind of a ballad," said Jonty with a smile creeping over his face.

"No!" cried Willie at once. "Stop him, for God's sake!"

"Go on, Jonty," said Angelica.

Willie made a show of holding his ears, but Jonty ignored him and immediately burst into song. "The Jerry Ace Raider, a pilot with some skill, attacking all our coastal towns, with the hope to get a kill. But the Mavericks will catch him, they'll stop him in his track, and the damnable Ace Raider, he won't be coming back…"

"Bravo," said Angelica.

"Is that the German pilot's nickname now? The Ace Raider?" said Dylan.

"Yes, I suppose it is," said Jonty.

I decided to get things in motion, after all the Ace Raider might be attacking the coastline while we were all sitting around discussing it.

"Tomas," I said. "You take Pilot Officers Clive Roberts, Berek Drabek, Patrick Smyth, Arthur Franklin and Flying Officer Olek Bartnik, up on a sortie while I go over to the

American base to talk to Captain Brooker. Later this afternoon I'll take up another sortie with the others."

"All right, Scottish," said Tomas and he turned to organise his crew.

"Do you want to come with me?" I asked Angelica.

"Of course," she replied. Then she turned to Willie and Jonty. "Boys, try not to quarrel while I'm gone."

Gordon drove me and Angelica to the American base next door. We made our way to Captain Booker's office and found him sitting at his desk. Sandford Booker was older than me and his rank of Captain was the equivalent of my Flight Lieutenant. He stood up to greet us at once, warmly shaking our hands.

"Angus, good to see you, and Angelica too, it's a been a while."

Before I could answer, he shouted out to his corporal to fetch us all something to drink.

"Take a seat," he said, resuming his own.

It was true that our paths had gone somewhat separately since his squadron had been given their Spitfires. They had taken over the escort duties for the bombers when required.

"Thanks," I said. "Sorry we've been a little out of touch."

"Oh, no matter, you're here now…"

There was a slight pause while the corporal placed a bottle of Coca-Cola and a glass containing ice in front of each of us. This had become one of Angelica's favourite soft drinks since the Americans had introduced us to it. Sandford had a good memory for his friends' likes and dislikes.

I took a sip of my Coke, enjoying the flavour. It was also served in our own mess at Banley, along with some other

American fare like hamburgers. We had indeed become more American since their air force had arrived in Britain.

"As much as I'd like this to be a social call," I said, "I've come to ask you a favour."

Sandford raised his eyebrows and smiled. "Oh? Well sure, I'll do my best to grant it if I can."

"We've had a spot of bother with Jerry lately…" I began.

"Who hasn't?" Sandford quipped.

"Yes, but it's not the normal sort of bother," I continued. "It's like this…" I related the tale of the Tip and Run pilot whom Jonty had now dubbed the 'Ace Raider'. Sandford listened with interest until I had finished.

"So, this guy is acting like some kind of winged crusader, is that what you're saying?" said Sandford.

"Yes, that's it. Bentley has asked me to step up patrols along that coastline to try and catch this Ace Raider at it…" I trailed off.

"Asked you or ordered you?" said Sandford with his usual perspicacity.

"Ordered," put in Angelica.

"Hmm," said Sandford. "So, what's the favour? Although I think I can guess."

"I was wondering if you'd care to run some patrols too … if you're not too busy with escort duties," I asked him.

"Sure, we'd be happy to. The guys are sitting around on their butts a lot lately anyways. The targets are moving further away, and we can only escort the bombers so far before turning back. Sometimes we can't escort them at all. The Spitfire is a great plane, but it hasn't got the range."

He was right. The Spitfire range — even with drop tanks — wouldn't be able to match the deep incursions into enemy territory that the American bombers were undertaking. No doubt someone somewhere was going to come up with a solution to it, but that wasn't my problem to solve. I sought confirmation. "So, you'll do it?"

"Of course, it gives us a chance to stretch our wings and will help keep us sharp. Just tell me when and where."

"All right, that's great," I said. "I'll get word to you once I figure out some sort of patrol schedule."

"And what's the plan if we do find this … Ace Raider?" he enquired with interest.

"Shoot him down, that's what Bentley's told us to do."

"Okay, that's good enough for me." Sandford looked at his watch, and I wondered if he needed to be somewhere, but I was wrong. "Look, it's nearly lunchtime, do you want to join me in the mess?"

"Yes, we'd love to," Angelica replied at once.

"Did Fred bring you?" Sandford asked me.

"Yes, he did."

"He can come too."

"I'm sure he'd be delighted."

Gordon had been involved in catching a spy on the American base and Sandford had got to know him. Sandford made sure he was included in any invitations to the American officers' mess. He was quite egalitarian in that respect.

After a rather splendid lunch, we returned to Banley feeling rather full. The American mess had generous portions and fed their troops well. I promised to get in touch with Sandford, but my immediate intention was to fly another sortie.

Gordon dropped us off, and Angelica accompanied me to the dispersal hut. She liked to see me off, and it had almost become a talisman for both of us. M Flight was taking their ease when we entered the hut. Tomas spied me and came over,

"How did the sortie go?" I asked him.

"Ah, there was no sign of this Ace Raider pilot, if that is what we are calling him," he said in disgust.

"I'm not surprised. It's a bit like looking for a needle in a haystack," I said. "I'm just hoping we strike lucky one time."

"Yes, well, good luck to you. Me, I'm going to a haystack to find this needle, it's easier," he said.

We both laughed. Tomas had a sense of humour but was also usually very candid. I could rely on him to give an honest opinion when asked for one.

I rounded up my team for the sortie and we headed out to the Spitfires. Before I left, Angelica wound her arms around my neck. I pulled her into an embrace.

"Take care," she said softly. "Come back safe."

"I will."

We kissed and then locked fingers, gradually letting go as I walked away. Many pilots have their own rituals before taking off, and this was ours. I'm not sure if it was superstition, but it was as if doing something different might somehow unbalance the grand order of the universe, thus setting off a chain of events which, in wartime, could be fatal.

I jumped up onto the wing of my kite and into the cockpit. Leading Aircraftman Dominic Redwood helped me to strap in.

"Good luck, sir," he said.

"Thanks, Techie."

"Hope you get him."

I gave him the thumbs up. The Ace Raider story had obviously found its way around the base, in the inimitable way that these things did.

I fired up the prop and listened with satisfaction to the roar of the Merlin engine as I taxied to take-off position. After clearance from the tower, the six of us took off in formation.

This time I had Jonty, Willie, Arjun, Jean and Dylan flying with me. They were all pilots I could rely on, and Dylan was certainly becoming a stalwart addition to my squadron. Angelica was still watching and waving as we disappeared into the distance. She would go to her comms post and be there when we returned.

I decided to fly the same route we usually took, although I could not imagine the Ace Raider would aim for Cromer again so soon. After all, there really wasn't anything much there to attack. However, there were plenty of other small towns on the coast if he was so inclined, and not all of them were particularly well-defended.

"I wonder if we'll catch the blighter today, Skipper," said Jonty, as we headed for the east coast.

"Let's hope so," I replied, without much optimism.

I set a course for Clacton, as I didn't imagine the Raider would go much further south than that. I figured he would most likely pick on smaller towns further up the coast. That way he could be in and out as fast as possible, after doing as much damage as he was able to.

The flight to Clacton didn't take long, and soon the town was below us. I kept us at a reasonable height because I knew that the Raider would fly close to the ground. There would be less chance of him spotting us if we stayed above him.

We passed over Clacton and flew on to Felixstowe without incident. Then came Aldeburgh, Thorpeness and on towards Dunwich.

"It's no good, Skipper," said Jonty after we had flown past all of these towns. "I don't think we're going to see the Ace Raider today."

"You're going to jinx it by saying that," Willie complained.

"I most certainly will not," Jonty shot back. "Anyway, what pilot in their right mind wants to visit the back end of beyond like East Anglia, I ask you?"

"The Ace Raider obviously," retorted Willie. "He's already been here once."

We had reached Dunwich by now. Jonty was momentarily distracted from his burgeoning quarrel with Willie and gave a cry of alarm.

"Bandit, two o'clock, very low and coming in fast."

I looked over to the right and sure enough, a Focke-Wulf was heading towards the town of Southwold, the next town along the coast, at high speed, just skimming above the waves. We were still at a fairly high altitude, and I hoped he had not seen us.

"Shall we go after him?" said Jonty, spoiling for a crack at an enemy plane regardless of whether it was the Ace Raider or not.

"We'll let him get closer, I don't think we've been spotted yet," I told him. "We'll stay up here for now."

The Wulf kept on his heading for the town seemingly oblivious to our presence.

Southwold had quite a long pier and it looked suspiciously as if the pilot was heading straight for it. We were almost within striking distance of the German now, and I decided not to wait any longer.

"Break, break, let's get him before he does any damage," I said, banking left and dropping down on him out of the sky.

The others followed suit. We screamed down from above, but the Wulf maintained its course. I wondered if we were going to be able to cut him off after all, since he was moving at a tremendous lick.

"That's the Ace Raider," said Jonty suddenly. "That's him!"

"How do you know?" asked Willie at once.

"Well, the Ace of Spades painted on his kite is a bit of a giveaway," said Dylan.

He was right. There was an Ace of Spades symbol painted on each wing and also on the sides of his plane. This seemed a trifle arrogant to me but on the other hand, it made the pilot easy to identify.

"Well, I'll be damned, so he has," said Jean.

"He needs to be stopped," I said.

We were almost within firing range, but the Ace Raider opened up with his guns, strafing the pier before we could do anything about it.

"Tally-ho!" said Jonty, throttling up and pursuing a course which aimed to get behind the Wulf.

The Ace Raider banked away from the pier, seemingly still unaware of us, then flew inland towards the shore. He pulled his plane up sharply, then dived down again, releasing a bomb which landed on the seafront with a tremendous explosion. As he flew away from the town, I saw him hurl a projectile from his cockpit once more.

"There he goes again," said Arjun. "Leaving his calling card."

By this time Jonty had gained enough distance on the German to open fire. I saw a stream of tracers spew out from Jonty's Spitfire. The Ace Raider pulled a tight turn and evaded the salvo.

"He's turning out to sea!" shouted Dylan. "He's trying to get away."

Five of us bore down on the fleeing Wulf and fired simultaneously. I felt sure one of us ought to hit him, but no such luck. The German pilot seemed to bear a charmed life.

We split up and continued to chase after him. However, he was far too quick for any of us. Dylan almost caught up and he fired again, but the Wulf narrowly avoided being hit. Arjun and Jean managed to get onto his tail but suddenly, the Focke-Wulf went straight up into a steep climb. Our Spitfires should have been faster in the climb than his plane, but he had the advantage of a head start. They followed him but were too far behind him to catch up.

I went after him too, and throttled up as fast as my Spitfire would go. It was not enough. On the off chance, I fired off a salvo. It hit nothing but empty air. The Ace Raider disappeared into the cloud bank, so I turned away.

"Leave it, chaps, he'll be long gone in minutes," I said.

"Bad show," said Jonty. "This blasted Ace Raider is starting to annoy me."

The thought crossed my mind that Jonty's irritation would be nothing to Bentley's when he discovered that the German had somehow escaped us again.

"Let's go home, chaps," I said.

We had come for our quarry and our quarry had escaped. There seemed little point in continuing the sortie.

A little disconsolately we formed up and headed for Banley.

"Well, how *are* we going to catch this Ace Raider then?" said Dylan.

"Damned if I know," said Jean. "He's just too quick."

"I think it's going to be more by luck than good judgement," I told him.

"Pretty sure he threw out another calling card," said Arjun.

"I'll go and get it later if you like, Skipper," said Jonty. "The Morgan needs a run." He was referring to his beloved three-wheeler of which he was inordinately fond.

"I'll come with you," said Willie at once. "Can't have you getting yourself into trouble."

Jonty snorted but was probably secretly pleased to have some company. That being settled and saving me a trip, we lapsed into silence until we reached the base.

Angelica hurtled over to me as usual as soon as I alighted from my plane. I caught her and kissed her soundly.

"I heard your chatter about the Ace Raider," she said a little breathlessly. 'You saw him!'

"Yes, but he got away."

"I know, what a shame."

There was a discreet cough next to us. Bentley was standing there going through his pipe routine with Audrey by his side. He lit it and started to puff on it.

"So that blasted scoundrel escaped again," he said, not mincing his words.

"Unfortunately, yes, sir," I replied.

"How the devil did that happen?" he demanded, as if I was personally responsible for allowing it.

"Well, sir, it's like this…" I went on to describe the event in some detail while Bentley listened, patiently smoking his pipe.

"Hmm," he said when I had finished. "And you're sure it was the same raider?"

"Yes, sir, judging by the Ace of Spades painted on the wings and sides of his plane."

"Damn and blast the bloody reprobate! What does he think he's playing at painting playing card symbols on his aircraft? He's taking us for fools and I'm not having it!"

I refrained from pointing out that our planes had the Spitfire Mavericks unofficial badge painted on them. For some reason, this particular German pilot had got under his skin.

"We're running dual patrols," I said. "And Captain Booker will fly patrols too. I'm not sure what more we can do, sir."

Bentley puffed for some moments on his pipe before answering. "No, and that's what makes it all the more irritating," he said. "Well, you can only do what you can do, I suppose. Still, I'd bloody well like to catch that bounder if we can."

"We're doing our best," I said.

"I know, Angus, I know. Don't think I haven't got those tommyrot Johnnies up at Fighter Command complaining about these bloody Tip and Run raids, because I have. Damned if I know what I'm supposed to do about it either. I'm not a blasted mind-reader and we only have access to the same military intelligence they do. Now we've got this damnable Ace Raider pilot taking us all for fools! It's outside of enough."

"Yes, sir," I said. Now that he had revealed the source of his ire, I sympathised.

"Well, I suppose I'd better get back to it," the CO continued. "Keep it up and hopefully one day you'll catch the blighter."

With that, he turned on his heel and left us to it. Angelica slipped her hand into mine and we went to our dispersal hut. The rest of the crew had gathered there and were having a brew.

"A rotten show, Skipper," said Jonty as soon as he saw me.

"Yes, Jonty, and Bentley isn't happy about it at all," I replied.

"Really? Oh blast!"

Jonty had been on the receiving end of Bentley's wrath on numerous occasions. He was always wary if Bentley was on the warpath.

"I don't understand how he can get away so quickly, Scottish," said Dylan, coming up to us.

"Perhaps he's just a good pilot," put in Arjun who had joined the conversation.

"Good pilot or not, we've got to figure out a way to catch him," I said.

Angelica pressed a mug of tea into my hand.

"If we knew when he was going to attack and where, we could set up a giant net," said Dylan.

We all laughed at the idea. It sounded like something out of a comic strip.

"I don't mean an actual net," said Dylan. "I mean a trap; we lie in wait and then boom! Just like we did back home when we went out after rabbits."

"But how could we possibly know where he was going to attack next?" I said.

"Perhaps we might try and predict it," said Angelica.

"Yes, but how? We've only just started encountering him."

"I can go back through intelligence reports," she said. "Look at other Tip and Run raids over the past few months, perhaps there is a pattern."

"Great idea," said Willie, who had remained unusually silent throughout this exchange.

"Thanks, Kiwi." Angelica furnished him with a smile.

"If you're sure," I said. "It sounds like a lot of work."

She nodded. "Of course, I want you to catch him as much as anyone."

"Three cheers for Angelica," said Jonty at once.

I finished my tea while the talk turned to other things. I set up the sorties for the next day before Angelica and I returned to Amberly for dinner. Jonty set off with Willie for Southwold to look for the Ace Raider's calling card.

"Had another run-in with that Ace Raider?" Gordon asked me on the drive home.

"Yes, Fred. Unfortunately, he got away again."

"Ah, yes, sounds like a bit of a cat and mouse affair," he mused.

"I'm afraid so…"

"Then, perhaps the mouse needs some bait … to set the trap…"

"It's a good notion but I don't see how… I mean, what kind of bait could entice him?"

"I'm sure you'll work something out, sir, you always do."

"Oh, Fred, don't be such a tease," said Angelica. "If you've a notion then let us hear it."

"I'm afraid I don't, ma'am," said Fred. "But if I do, I'll let you know."

CHAPTER THREE

The following day after breakfast Gordon drove us back to Banley as usual. He pulled up the jeep in the usual spot and I couldn't help noticing a hive of activity occurring not far from the main buildings of the airbase.

"What are they doing there, Fred?" I asked Gordon. If anyone would know, it would be he.

"I'm not quite sure, sir, it's all been a bit hush-hush. It seems to be some kind of prefabricated house," he said.

"A house?"

"So I've been able to ascertain."

I looked at it again. It had all the makings of a single-storey house being erected in haste. We had no houses on the base, so this was an unusual occurrence. It certainly aroused my curiosity. "Who on earth is it for?" I asked him.

Gordon shrugged apologetically. "I don't know, sir, at least not yet."

"I'll see if I can find out," said Angelica.

Her security clearance would allow her access to information which most of us couldn't get to see. Whether she could tell me if she did find out was another matter.

"All right, well, no doubt all will be revealed in due course," I said.

"I'm sure it will, sir," said Gordon with a smile.

He pulled out a packet of cigarettes and lit one up. He smoked it with evident satisfaction and relaxed back in his seat. I put the mysterious appearance of the house out of my mind. We had sorties to fly, and I needed to arrange a roster for the next few days, including Sandford's squadron.

Angelica and I left Gordon at his leisure and walked over to the dispersal hut. I'd arranged a sortie first thing, and then Tomas would take up his patrol for the afternoon.

"What-ho, Skipper," said Jonty as soon as I walked in. "We've just got back from Southwold."

"Oh yes?"

We hadn't seen Jonty or Willie at breakfast and I had forgotten about their trip to seek out the object jettisoned by the Ace Raider.

"Yes, we stayed over in Southwold at a Bed and Breakfast, it was a bit late by the time we got there. It wasn't as bad as you might think. A tolerable breakfast too," he said.

Jonty's expectations of small seaside towns were evidently not that high. He was used to good living, having come from aristocratic stock.

"I had to share a room with him," said Willie with a sigh. "Your condolences will be gratefully accepted."

"I say!" said Jonty. "I wasn't the one snoring at midnight."

"I was not snoring!" Willie exclaimed at once.

I interrupted them before they began another of their squabbles.

"All right, all right," I said. "So, did you find something or didn't you?"

"We certainly did, Skipper. It was quite easy to spot as it goes," said Jonty.

"We got there just in the nick of time, too," put in Willie. "Some lads were about to make off with it."

"Yes, they didn't want to give it to us at first, but when I informed them it was Royal Air Force property they handed it over at once," said Jonty, looking amused.

"He said they'd be arrested for spying." Willie laughed.

"They scarpered pretty quickly after that," said Jonty with a chuckle.

Jonty felt in his pocket and removed an item from it. I took it from him and examined it. It was another Ace of Spades playing card secured to a stone. There was no doubt about who the pilot was now.

"It's definitely the Ace Raider then," I said, offering it to Angelica.

She examined it briefly and handed it back to me.

"This does rather confirm it, yes," said Willie.

"I'll have to show this to Bentley," I said.

"Rather you than —" Jonty didn't finish his sentence.

"Senior officer in the hut!" said Willie and everyone snapped to attention.

"Show me what, exactly, Angus?" said Bentley, who had arrived unnoticed and unannounced, something he was in the habit of doing.

"This, sir," I said, handing him the stone with the card attached.

Bentley stared at it for some time, hefting it in his hand, and feeling the surface of the playing card. At length he put it in his pocket, electing to keep this one for some reason. "This blasted pilot is playing us for fools!" he said angrily. "The sheer damned impudence of it. Who does he think he is? This isn't a bloody game, it's a war. People are dying and this … this … charlatan is throwing calling cards out of his bloody aeroplane!"

We all remained silent, since interrupting Bentley in full flow was highly likely to draw his fire.

"Well," he said. "All I can say is do your damnedest to catch this ruddy hooligan."

"We are definitely doing our best, sir," I reassured him.

"Good, good, I'm sure you are," he replied in a calmer voice. "Anyway, Angus, a word if you will…"

"Yes, sir."

I followed him outside and we walked a little way from the hut.

"You may have seen that blasted construction being put up on the airfield," the CO said, waving his pipe in the general direction of where the new house was located.

"I couldn't help noticing it, sir, yes."

"Well…" Bentley hesitated and decided to smoke his pipe instead. At length, he continued. "I want you to attend a meeting in a couple of days."

"Yes, sir. May I ask what the meeting is about?"

"About that bloody house," he said crossly, as if it should have been obvious.

"Can I ask who else will be in the meeting?" I ventured, risking another tirade. The response was somewhat unexpected.

"You can … yes … it's those blasted MI6 Johnnies, those two bloody clowns that are the bane of our existence. I can't tell you any more, but just ensure you make yourself available, and bring Section Officer Kensley too, she's got their measure all right."

"Right, sir, I will."

It was the Marx Brothers yet again; the two MI6 spies whom I had nicknamed after the famous screen actors. Since I would never know their real names, the nickname had stuck.

"Audrey will furnish you with the details," he said shortly.

"Yes, sir."

"And before you ask why you need to be there, it's because you're used to dealing with those damnable reprobates and I want you to be present."

"Yes, sir, of course."

I wasn't surprised — there was no love lost by Bentley for the Marx Brothers. In fact, he had rendered his low opinion of them on many occasions. Much of it was justified due to the fact they'd led us up the garden path more than once, only to reveal some completely different underlying purpose to the secret missions we'd been given.

"Good, very good," said Bentley, before turning on his heel and striding away.

As soon as he had gone, Angelica was at my side, brimming with curiosity. She had been standing by the door of the hut talking to Audrey.

"What was all that about?" she asked, tucking her arm into mine and leading me inexorably to our bench at the side of the airfield.

I told her what Bentley had said, and she frowned momentarily.

"The Marx Brothers, coming here ... again?" She was not one of their fans either.

"Yes, apparently."

"I might have guessed they had something to do with it, they have their fingers in every pie imaginable," she said with a tinge of acidity.

"I know, darling, but try to be nice to them."

"Oh, I'm always nice to them," she said mendaciously. "Regardless of what I might be thinking."

I laughed, then said, "The thing is, if the Marx Brothers are involved ... then who on earth is that house for?"

"Whoever it's for," said Angelica, "I doubt it bodes well for the rest of us."

I returned from our bench in a pensive mood; there was much to consider. However, in the meantime, I had to get my patrol up on a sortie. I put the Marx Brothers to the back of my mind.

"What-ho, Skipper," said Jonty when I re-entered the hut. "I do wish Bentley wouldn't sneak up on us like that. He gave me quite a start."

"Never mind; at least it wasn't aimed at you," I said.

"For a change," put in Willie.

"I say!" said Jonty. "He reminds me of old Bagshaw, the History Master, always coming around the corner when you didn't want him to."

Jonty seemed to have spent his boyhood unsuccessfully avoiding the wrath of various schoolmasters at public school. They had apparently left a deep impression on him.

"Yes, well, as interesting as your schoolboy reminiscences are, Jonty," I said. "We've got to get on patrol."

"Jolly good, Skipper," said Jonty, cheering up at once. "Let's see if we can catch that Ace Raider blighter this time."

"We'll see," I replied without much optimism. The chances of us achieving it seemed rather slim. I knew that word had gone up the chain of command specifically to inform us of any coastal raider sightings, but none had occurred today.

Willie, Jonty, Dylan, Arjun and Jean headed for the planes, while I held back and turned to Angelica. We embraced and she kissed me soundly.

"Fly safe," she said.

"I will."

We locked fingers before I walked away. I jumped in the cockpit and Redwood strapped me in. The Merlin engine roared to life, and I taxied onto the runway.

"You're clear for take-off, Red Leader," said the tower.

"Red Patrol, let's go," I said over the radio.

Six Spitfires picked up speed, and we were airborne in short order. This time I elected to fly up to Cromer and then travel southward. It didn't do to be too predictable as far as the enemy was concerned.

It was a clear day, with some cloud cover above us. There was no point in flying above the clouds as it would simply conceal any raiders. The enemy's new tactic of low-flying attacks meant keeping to a reasonable height where we could easily go on the attack if necessary. We had used the low-flying tactic ourselves on our secret missions and had found it to be an effective, if hazardous, method of incursion into enemy territory.

Low flying meant being far more alert to the fact you were often only a few feet off the ground or waves. As a result, the pilot might not be so vigilant for enemy planes, which is why, when we flew a mission, we had an escort above us who were effectively our eyes. These raiders did not have that advantage.

"What's the odds of catching the Ace Raider today?" said Dylan as we reached Cromer, and I turned the flight southwards.

"Perhaps we should start a sweepstake on it," said Jonty. "Winner takes all."

"What do you think, Scottish?" asked Dylan.

"I think we best keep our eyes peeled for the raider," I replied, not entirely wishing to endorse the scheme, although I couldn't see any harm in it. It was typical of Jonty to come up with such an idea.

"We can start one up when we get back," said Jonty, unwilling to give up the notion once he'd thought of it.

"How about we make a sweep on you not singing any more ballads," suggested Willie. "I doubt we'd get any takers though."

"I say!" said Jonty.

"Oh dear, here we go again," said Arjun with a sigh, anticipating yet another argument between Willie and Jonty.

"Let's stay focused on the task at hand, shall we?" I said, intervening.

"Kiwi's just missing his girl, now she's left for another mission. That's why he's so blasted morose," said Jonty.

Olga Zielinska was a Polish national working for MI6. She and Willie had been going steady while she was on the base posing as a chef. However, it was inevitable she would have to move on, and she had left a few weeks ago.

We had passed over Cromer and Lowestoft without incident and were heading once more for Southwold where the Ace Raider had made his last attack.

"I think perhaps we should just —" I was about to suggest we returned to base when I was interrupted by the radio crackling to life.

"Single bandit attacking Felixstowe, repeat Felixstowe."

It was control informing us of another incursion.

"Roger, we'll move to intercept," I said, without much hope. Felixstowe was about fifty miles away. "All right, Red Patrol, let's get to Felixstowe as fast as we can."

I throttled up to maximum and the rest of the flight followed suit. We cut overland rather than following the coastline to shorten the distance. The usual early warning of an attack probably hadn't sounded due to the raider flying under the radar.

"Can we make it before he's gone?" asked Jean as we flew directly towards our destination.

"I don't know," I said, hoping luck was on our side.

Felixstowe came into view, and we were treated to the sight of black smoke rising from where a bomb had obviously just been dropped.

"We're too late," said Arjun. "He's already been."

"But not gone," shouted Dylan. "There he is!"

A Focke-Wulf was banking over the town, and we saw the flash of tracers as he strafed it. We started to close the distance while the Jerry banked for a second run.

"Is it the Ace Raider?" asked Jean.

"Yes, it is! He's got the Ace of Spades painted on his plane," Dylan said excitedly.

We were tantalisingly close but not close enough. The Ace Raider must have seen us heading his way because in an instant, he turned and headed out to sea.

"He's getting away!" said Dylan.

"We'll never catch him now," Jonty added.

"You're right, let him go," I said. "We've no chance of getting him. Let's fly a pass over the town anyway."

I knew very little about Felixstowe other than the fact it had a port and also an RAF base. It was a comparatively small seaside town. The bomb had been dropped near the port and hit some buildings but as we flew over, we could see there was minimal damage. The raider had not been particularly successful. The port was well defended and had ack-ack batteries, plus gun emplacements. Perhaps they had tried to open fire on the raider before we got there. There wasn't much else to see.

"Let's head for Banley," I said. "The Ace Raider's unlikely to be back again today."

"It's a damn shame," said Jonty.

"You can't win them all, Jonty," I said.

We landed in short order, and I received the usual affectionate welcome from Angelica. After she detached herself from my embrace, we discovered Bentley waiting patiently next to us as was his wont.

"I gather you just missed that Ace Raider again," he said without preamble.

"Yes, sir, we could quite catch him."

"Hmm," he said as he puffed out some smoke. I was waiting for a reprimand, but instead he said, "Oh well, better luck next time, eh?" before striding away.

Angelica turned to me and smiled. "I'm glad you missed him, it's one less combat you had to take part in."

"Did you manage to find anything out about … you know?" I asked her quietly.

Angelica caught my meaning at once. It was about the prospective occupant of the house. "I'm afraid not," she said. "Whatever it is, is extremely on the QT."

CHAPTER FOUR

Two days later, Angelica and I were in the main building, sitting in the room where I'd met the Marx Brothers on many occasions. The two MI6 agents were sitting at ease, smoking cigarettes in a lazy fashion. Both men wore dark suits and white shirts, one with a blue tie and the other red. Their trench coats were neatly folded under their fedoras on a nearby table. It was as if they had written the *Boy's Own* manual on what a spy should look like.

Also in the room was Bentley, accompanied by Audrey. Bentley was smoking his pipe, which, along with the Marx Brothers' cigarettes, gave the atmosphere an acrid haze.

The most striking addition to the meeting was a stranger, a woman. She was blonde, blue-eyed and beautiful in the classic style of movie stars. She was well dressed, and I estimated she was perhaps in her mid-thirties. A fur stole lay on the chair next to her, and everything about her looked expensive. Angelica glanced in the direction of my gaze and took hold of my hand possessively.

I had decided to send a patrol to look for the Ace Raider's calling card and it had been successful. One of the soldiers stationed on the port defences had picked it up. They didn't have much to say about the incident, other than they'd opened fire on the Ace Raider but had missed. The bomb damage had not been great, but there were some casualties from the strafing of the town. It seemed callously indiscriminate, but the tenor of the entire war was turning in that direction.

The calling card was the same as the others and the Ace Raider appeared to drop it where it was likely to be found. I tried to rationalise the reason behind this behaviour but couldn't. Perhaps he somehow considered himself larger than life, and the war was all game to him. I couldn't fathom the psychology of such a man. I resolved to ask Gordon, to see if he could shed some light on it.

I was musing on this while we all sat in silence. The Marx Brothers, as usual, were in no hurry at all. There was a studied nonchalance in their air which belied a far darker side to their profession.

Finally, the one I'd dubbed Harpo, who had grey eyes, as opposed to Chico's blue, elected to speak. "You're probably wondering why we are here?" he began.

"The thought did cross our minds, yes," said Bentley acidly.

Unfazed by the CO's tone, Harpo continued. "Let me introduce Maria Von Schmidt, who will be henceforth known as Mrs Smith."

Maria smiled at us, and it was quite dazzling. I began to wonder if she really was a movie star after all. She nodded graciously and said with a German accent, "Charmed, I'm sure."

"I'm sure you would like to know who Maria really is," said Chico, taking up the refrain. They enjoyed revealing their plans almost in the manner of two conjurors undertaking some kind of elaborate trick. It was incredibly irritating and I could tell by the way Bentley was puffing on his pipe that he was not amused.

"I assume that's what we are here for, yes," said Bentley, starting to sound annoyed.

"Maria isn't all she might seem," said Chico. "She's the wife of a prominent nuclear physicist. We can't say who, but he is currently in the United States undertaking very important work."

I noticed a slight tremor pass across Maria's lips as he said this, and a certain sadness in her face.

"So, what's she doing here?" Bentley asked in his irascible fashion.

"For various reasons, they cannot be together," said Harpo.

"And why is that?" Bentley persisted.

"We can't precisely say," Chico told him.

We were all well aware of the Marx Brothers' tendency to obfuscate things, and Bentley was evidently having none of it.

"Can't or won't?" the CO shot back.

There was an ominous silence during which Bentley began to carefully tap out his pipe and begin his routine. This was a sure sign that he was becoming extremely irate.

"It's all right," said Maria, sensing the tension and wishing to break it. "Let me tell them."

Harpo inclined his head in acquiescence and lit up another cigarette. Bentley looked slightly mollified by this intervention.

"I'm German," said Maria. "You probably guessed that, and looking at me, you probably think I fit the German ideal … you know, the Aryan race, the Master Race that Hitler continues to ram down our throats…" There was a certain bitterness in her words. "But I'm not," Maria continued. "I'm not Aryan, even if I look it. I'm Jewish … and as such I am an enemy of the state."

I hadn't been expecting that, nor had Angelica. A swift glance showed her expression had considerably softened towards the woman.

"I'm married to a very important scientist. My husband was employed by the Nazis and because of his work they were willing to overlook my ancestry," said Maria, continuing her story. "But my husband and I don't agree with the aims of Hitler and his thousand-year Reich. He didn't want to work for

49

them. But he did so with reluctance, and I ... I was persuaded ... to my shame ... to act in propaganda films for Goebbels. It was the price I had to pay to be allowed to continue to live..."

"So you see —" Chico cut in, perhaps trying to spare Maria the pain of the explanation, but she waved him away with one perfectly manicured hand.

"No, let me finish, they deserve to know the truth before they give me their protection. My husband was approached by the US Government and began secretly working for them. They got him out of Germany and over to America. They wouldn't let me go with him. I cannot enter the United States because the Americans consider I might be an enemy of their state too, a double agent. It's ironic, wouldn't you say? But I'm not. The pressure they can exert to make you..." She stopped talking and began to cry silently.

Angelica was by her side in an instant. She put her arms around her protectively as Maria's shoulders shook in silent sobs. We were all quiet for a while until she regained her composure.

"I'm sorry," Maria said. "I've done some terrible things ... you deserve to know who you are dealing with..."

"Surely acting in a few movies..." Bentley began, trying to mitigate what Maria obviously felt was beyond the pale.

"They aren't just movies. They are propaganda for the Aryan race, to make the German people feel they are superior to others, to perpetuate a lie, and also to turn them against the Jews."

None of us had any experience of living in Germany under Hitler's yoke. We couldn't know the reality of it.

"Couldn't you have refused?" I asked her.

Angelica shot me a disapproving glance at the question. Maria answered it readily, however.

"I wanted to refuse, but my husband insisted. He didn't want to lose me. They threatened to take me away with all the other Jews. He said I only had to do it for a while until we could escape."

"Take you away?"

"Yes, away to places ... camps ... you don't know about that?"

I didn't know, not precisely anyway. We had heard rumours, speculation, but nothing of what might really be going on in the Third Reich. I changed the subject partly because of my ignorance and partly to spare Maria more distress.

"And how did you escape?" I said, since she had brought it up.

"That was our department, old chap," said Harpo. "We arranged for them to get to Switzerland and then secretly flew them out. We can't really tell you how, as obviously we might want to do it again."

"Yes, I see," I said.

"What you should also see, is that Maria has been through a lot, and no matter what she's done, her husband's work is of vital importance to the war," said Chico.

"We get all that," said Bentley testily. "But it still doesn't explain what she's doing here. No disrespect to Mrs Smith, naturally."

Maria gave him a watery smile. "None taken," she said. "I completely understand your reluctance."

"It's not reluctance," Bentley said to her in a softer tone. "I simply want to know the truth."

Harpo held up his hand in acquiescence. Bentley was not a person to be trifled with, and the two agents had done exactly that more than once. "We need you to keep her here for the moment, in secret, for her own protection," he said. "Hence the reason that a house has been built on your airbase."

Bentley puffed on his pipe for a few long moments, digesting this information. "And why this airbase?" he said. "Why not a safe house somewhere, I'm sure you have them."

"Because it's not somewhere anyone would suspect. They also wouldn't imagine us putting Mrs Smith on an RAF base and this base, in particular, is very secure, it's got a perimeter fence, guards and so forth. It's well protected."

"That's all very well," said Bentley, brandishing the stem of his pipe at Harpo. "But we can't be with her night and day, my chaps have jobs to do, a war to win."

"We know that," said Chico, getting up from his chair. "That's why we've engaged someone for Maria's personal protection."

We watched with curiosity as he went over to the door and left the room. Moments later he reappeared with a woman who I recognised at once.

"Olga!" said Angelica as soon as she entered the room.

Willie's girlfriend was standing on the threshold.

"Nice to see you, Angelica, and Angus too," said Olga, before turning to the others. "Audrey, Squadron Leader Bentley."

"So, Olga will be Maria's bodyguard?" said Bentley unnecessarily.

"The very same," said Chico. "She will be with Maria night and day. They will live in the same house. Everywhere Maria goes, she will go too. Although, we don't expect Maria to go off the base for any reason, and we certainly would not advise it."

The War Office would spend money on things they felt were important, as Olga evidently was. No doubt Mrs Smith's safety was paramount to her husband continuing to cooperate with the Americans.

Olga walked over and sat down next to Maria. Maria smiled at her, and Olga said something in German to her. They were obviously already well acquainted.

"So," said Harpo. "What's the verdict? Can she stay?"

"Do I have a choice?" asked Bentley, surprised.

"There are always choices," replied Harpo.

"Well, since a blasted house has already been built for her, it wouldn't make any sense for her not to stay now, would it?" said Bentley.

"Nevertheless, we want to be sure you're comfortable with it," said Chico blandly.

Bentley appeared to be controlling his temper with an effort.

"It's not a matter of comfort," said Bentley with barely suppressed fury. "There's a war on. If I wanted to be comfortable, I'd be at home with my feet up in front of the fire. Instead of which I'm running two squadrons to which the RAF seems happy to send every unwanted reprobate in the force. So, on that basis, comfort doesn't come into it. Duty, however, does, and Mrs Smith here evidently requires shelter. Since we've been chosen to give it to her, then we'll do our damnedest to keep her safe. Does that answer your question?"

"Perfectly," said Harpo. "It seems we are all in accord."

"Is there some kind of cover story for Mrs Smith's presence here?" I asked. Practically speaking she couldn't stay out of sight forever, and people were bound to discover she was staying on the base.

"You can say she's working for the government, which in a way is true," said Chico.

"Doing what exactly?" said Bentley, not entirely persuaded by this answer.

"Interpreter, translator, something like that. Tell people it's all very hush-hush, she's from Military Intelligence, you know … they'll think she's working for us then … which again, is perfectly true," Chico told him smoothly.

"That will probably do the trick," I agreed.

"Yes, well, if that's all, I'll leave you to settle Mrs Smith into her new home. I've got things to do," said Bentley, getting to his feet.

"By all means," said Harpo.

"Mrs Smith," said Bentley, addressing himself to Maria. "Welcome to the Mavericks."

With a nod to the rest of us, the CO swept from the room with Audrey following behind. I had no doubt he didn't want to spend any more time with the Marx Brothers than he had to.

"He's a kind-hearted soul really, it's just his way," said Angelica to Maria.

"I understand. I'm not exactly anybody's favourite person right now. I'm sure the Germans will be happy to see me killed if they can."

"Which is exactly what's *not* going to happen," put in Olga. "Not on my watch."

"Come on, why don't we get you two moved in?" suggested Angelica, taking charge.

"Thank you," said Maria. "You are all too kind."

The three women departed, leaving me alone with the Marx Brothers. The two spies seemed in no hurry to go.

"How's things, Flight Lieutenant?" said Chico conversationally.

"All right, I suppose," I said warily.

"Don't worry, we've not come here with another mission," said Harpo with a laugh, picking up on my suspicion.

I breathed a sigh of relief. It was their habit to arrive with one apparent purpose and then surreptitiously reveal quite a different one. Since they were here, the thought occurred to me that perhaps I might be able to pick *their* brains for once.

"There is one problem we are grappling with," I said to them.

"Oh? Do tell," said Chico, blowing smoke into the air and watching it rise up to the ceiling.

"There's this pilot, in a Focke-Wulf, carrying out stealth attacks. Tip and Run raids. You've probably heard of them," I said.

"We have indeed," said Harpo.

"There's one particular Jerry causing us problems. We've dubbed him the Ace Raider. He's carried out three Tip and Run raids that we know of and probably more. What's unusual about it is that he seems to work alone, and every time he carries out a raid, he throws a playing card tied to a stone out of his window. The card is the Ace of Spades, which he also has painted on his aircraft."

Harpo took a drag on his cigarette. "We'd heard something about this; sounds rather theatrical," he said. "But how can we help?"

"We'd like to catch him," I said. "But he has evaded us every time. He's a very quick and agile pilot. We've managed to come upon him by chance each time so far but, obviously, we don't know where and when he's going to strike. Angelica has tried looking at patterns in the recent coastal attacks, but there doesn't appear to be too much logic in it."

"Hmm, I see the problem. Perhaps he's just sticking a pin in a map?" said Harpo, a little facetiously.

I ignored this unhelpful suggestion. It didn't seem like the sort of thing Jerry would do. The Marx Brothers had previously insisted how precise and organised the enemy were. Instead, I pressed on with my theme, hoping they might be able to assist in spite of Harpo's flippant comment.

"I just wonder if we might be able to discover his intended targets, then possibly lie in wait, that sort of thing."

The two of them sat back in their chairs, smoking for a few moments.

"You're wondering if we have any intelligence about this … Ace Raider. Is that it?" asked Chico.

"Well, yes, I just thought perhaps…" I trailed off. It didn't sound hopeful after all.

"We haven't. But that doesn't mean we can't find out. Of course, resources are committed to things that our superiors consider are important."

"How is this not important?" I said, annoyed. I stood up and started to pace the room. "This pilot is attacking seaside towns, dropping bombs on innocent civilians and then strafing the streets, killing God knows how many people."

"You know that Bomber Command is doing exactly that to civilian populations in Germany and Axis cities — dropping bombs indiscriminately," said Harpo quietly.

I had not thought that the Marx Brothers had a conscience, but perhaps I was wrong.

"It's a matter of degree," said Chico. "We have spies in the field, obviously, but we seek to obtain the intelligence that will do the best for the war effort."

I sighed, this was getting nowhere. I made one more attempt. "All right, but what if we could set a trap instead."

"Go on," said Chico, lighting up another cigarette.

"Well, what if we could tempt the Ace Raider out, on our terms. When he appears, we would be waiting for him."

"Yes, I see," said Chico. He and Harpo were silent for a while, puffing on their cigarettes and filling the room with smoke.

"It's possible we might be able to plant the information or leak it through our sources," said Harpo eventually.

"If you can come up with a suitable plan, that is,' added Chico. 'We can't guarantee it will work, or that the Ace Raider will take the bait, but if you can shoot him down, or, better still, capture him, then that might be a propaganda coup of sorts, and *that* would appeal to the higher-ups."

"All right," I said. "I'll discuss the idea with Bentley and the chaps and see if we can't come up with something which might actually work. Capturing him will be a tall order though."

"Oh, I'm sure a man of your calibre can figure it out, Flight Lieutenant," said Chico.

"Okay, I'll let you know," I said, then hesitated.

"Something more on your mind?" asked Harpo.

"Maria," I said, taking the plunge. "What she said about, you know, the camps ... being taken away ... I mean, are they true? And how do you know she isn't a German spy?"

Chico nodded grimly. "The camps are real. We are hearing some things which are not for the general public. Better you don't know, not just now. Suffice it to say it's bad, very bad indeed, which is why we have to win this war sooner rather than later.

"As to whether Maria is a spy ... she's not,' Chico continued. 'She has been very helpful and informative. We've learned a few things we didn't know about before, particularly where Mr Goebbels is concerned. A despicable character if ever there was one. She has been thoroughly debriefed. We were lucky to get her and her husband out of Germany. It was touch and go."

"And if you hadn't?" I asked him.

"Then we would have had to eliminate any chance of him working for the Germans," Harpo replied without hesitation.

There it was. The ruthless streak that ran underneath it all. The stock-in-trade of being a spy. The answer had been obvious perhaps, but it was chilling to hear it spoken out loud.

"All right," I said. "We'll do our best to protect Maria."

"We are counting on it," Chico said.

I left them each smoking yet another cigarette, seemingly without a care in the world. But I realised now that, contrary to appearances, they were carrying a very heavy load, and I felt a little more benign towards them than I had on previous occasions.

CHAPTER FIVE

I decided to go and see how Maria was settling into her new house. I set off for the corner of the airbase in which it was situated. From the exterior, it looked rather nice, although the original whitewashed walls had been painted dark green in order to make it less conspicuous. It had been put up in haste, but no doubt had all the facilities needed. It was surprising how quickly things could get done in wartime. I went up to the front door and knocked. It was opened by Angelica.

"Hi," she said, smiling.

"I came to check on things," I said. "How is everything going?"

"All right," said Angelica. "Come in."

Inside, the house was naturally very new, with white walls, and very much like any other bungalow. The living room was furnished with chairs and a sofa. Maria and Olga were seated drinking tea.

"Hello," I said. "I thought I'd pop by to see how you were settling in."

"How kind," said Maria. "Please join us."

I did so and accepted a cup of tea from her. Angelica sat down beside me.

"Is it all to your satisfaction?" I asked her.

"Yes, it's very nice, more than I could have expected. You can have a tour if you like? Angelica can show you around. I've nothing to hide."

I have to admit I was a little curious to see the rest of the house, having never been inside a prefabricated home before. Apparently, many such buildings were being erected around the country to house those displaced by bombing. God only knew how long they would have to live in them.

"Squadron Leader Bentley doesn't really want me here, does he?" said Maria candidly.

I hastened to reassure her.

"The CO has a lot on his plate, that's all," I said. "And he isn't particularly fond of the Marx Brothers…" I trailed off.

Maria looked puzzled for a moment, then she let out a peal of laughter.

"The Marx Brothers? Is that what you call them?"

"For my sins, yes, but don't tell them, for God's sake."

"My lips are sealed," she said, still laughing. "But my word that's so very apt."

Her laughter was infectious. We couldn't help but laugh too.

I finished my tea, while Maria told us a little more about life in Nazi Germany. It sounded rather dire unless you happened to be one of Hitler's 'chosen people'. I was shocked to learn of the insidious propaganda that was being perpetrated in that country. Maria's shame at being even a small part of it was evident.

I set down my cup and stood up. "If there's anything you need, do let me know, otherwise I'll leave you to it."

"Thank you," said Maria.

"I'll show you around before we go," said Angelica.

The bungalow had a kitchen, bathroom, two bedrooms, dining room and a living room. It was adequately if sparsely furnished, but it was, nevertheless, a place of refuge. I wondered about heating, and Angelica pointed out the stove in the living room. I was sure that Maria could make the place more homely, were she to be staying for long. That was something none of us knew.

We said our goodbyes and made our way back to the dispersal hut. Angelica tucked her arm into mine as we walked.

"I feel sorry for Maria," said Angelica. "Or anyone forced to live under the Nazis."

"Then you should feel sorry for the whole of Europe," I said.

"I do, very much so, darling. I'm just glad we're here in Blighty and not there."

"A fortuitous accident of birth for sure," I quipped.

"That house isn't bad, either. I wouldn't mind something like that myself."

I forbore to say that as heir to a large estate in Scotland we didn't need a house like that. I could tell that she wanted something that was exclusively ours, hers and ours. Living with my parents probably wasn't an option. However, until the war was over, I wasn't going to think about that or anything other than surviving it.

Back at the dispersal hut, there appeared to be some sort of commotion taking place. The first thing I heard on entering was a loud squawking noise, and on further investigation discovered a large cage had been put in the corner of the hut.

Inside the cage was a large, yellow and blue parrot which immediately fixed me with a beady eye and said, "Hello, hello, stranger, hello, hello ... hello."

"Oh my God," said Angelica. "It's a parrot."

Before I could make any further comment on the unexpected arrival of the exotic bird, Jonty was by my side.

"What-ho, Skipper," he said. "Do you like the parrot?"

"I might have guessed you had something to do with its appearance, Jonty," I said with a sigh.

"It's a legacy, Skipper," said Jonty beaming at me.

I stared at Jonty a little incredulously at this statement, but before I could ask any questions we were joined by Willie.

"I told you bringing it here was a bad idea," said Willie. This was quickly followed by a very loud, "Senior Officer in the room!"

Everyone snapped to attention. My heart sank. It could only be Bentley, and now I was going to have to explain why there was a parrot present when I didn't fully understand why it was there myself.

"All right, all right, at ease," said Bentley in his usual testy manner. Then his eyes narrowed.

He walked up to the cage before stopping and staring at it as if he could not believe his eyes.

"What," he said, pointing at the parrot, "is that?"

"It's a parrot, sir," Jonty supplied helpfully.

"I can see it's a bloody parrot, I'm not blind," said Bentley, firing up. "What the hell is it doing on this airbase?"

"Sir," said Jonty, "I can explain..."

"Really?" Bentley replied, at his most acidic. "Do tell, I cannot wait to hear it."

While he waited, Bentley took his pipe from his pocket, tapped out the tobacco, and then scraped out the bowl. The parrot watched this procedure with great interest. Bentley tamped in the tobacco and lit it while we remained silent.

"Ooh, smoking a pipe ... he's smoking a pipe..." said the parrot, unaware of the solecism it was committing.

Bentley studiously ignored this and said, "Well?"

"The parrot, sir, it belonged to my Uncle Eric. He left it to me in his will."

"He did what?" said Bentley.

"He left it, sir, in his will ... a legacy ... sir..." Jonty trailed off.

Bentley's expression didn't bode well for Jonty, nor for the parrot.

"His name is Percy, sir, Percy the parrot," Jonty added.

There was an ominous silence while Bentley took some furious puffs on his pipe. I regarded this procedure with foreboding. I wasn't wrong.

"So, you thought that the best thing you could think of was to bring this blasted Percy the parrot to Banley Airfield, did you?" Bentley suddenly erupted. "Of all the bloody places in the world that you could find to put it, the dispersal hut came top of the list, hmm? As if it's not enough of a bloody circus around here as it is, you thought you'd add to it with a tropical bird. I'll have you know this is not a blasted aviary, Butterworth. In case it hadn't escaped your notice there's a war on and nowhere in the RAF manual does it say anything regarding keeping parrots on RAF airfields. What the hell do you think you're playing at?"

Faced with this tirade, Jonty was rather lost for words. It was left to Percy the parrot to intervene on his own behalf.

"Who's this bloke, who's this old bloke, this old bloke..." Percy started saying.

Bentley turned towards Percy and barked, "That's Squadron Leader Bentley to you!"

Unperturbed, Percy took up the refrain, evidently being a fast learner.

"That's Squadron Leader Bentley... Bentley, Bentley, Bentley..."

"Enough!" shouted Bentley, brandishing the stem of his pipe at the parrot in a menacing fashion.

Percy decided discretion was perhaps the better part of valour and subsided. However, it seemed as if this little performance had somewhat cooled Bentley's ire. Beside him,

Audrey was desperately trying to conceal a smirk on her face which threatened to turn to laughter at any moment.

"Can't we keep it, sir?" said Jonty, noting a softening in Bentley's demeanour. "It's not doing any harm. It might do wonders for morale."

Bentley puffed on his pipe, eyeing the parrot with misgiving. When he spoke, it seemed as if he might have had a change of heart as regards the unfortunate bird.

"Well, it's highly irregular," he said at length. "But I will defer to Flight Lieutenant Mackennelly, since he's in charge of this hut. If he says it can stay, it can stay."

All eyes at once turned to me. I cursed inwardly at being made the final arbiter in the parrot's fate.

"Can we keep it, Skipper?" said Jonty, in a manner which was hard to resist.

"Well…" I began, not sure which way to jump. On the one hand, I couldn't see the harm in it, and on the other, I wondered if Bentley wanted me to be the killjoy, as it were.

Fortunately, Angelica, seeing my hesitation, stepped into the breach.

"I think it's rather droll, don't you?" said Angelica. "It would be fun."

That more or less clinched it for me. I thanked Providence for the practical nature of my wife.

"All right, fine," I said. "The parrot stays on condition that you take care of it, Jonty, and don't allow it to get into any kind of mischief."

"Thank you, Skipper," said Jonty, beaming. "I promise that Percy and I will be the soul of discretion."

Bentley snorted. "We've heard that before, Butterworth. Perhaps you can try to stick to it this time."

"I will, sir, I promise," said Jonty, at his most convincing.

Having dealt with the question of Percy satisfactorily, Bentley turned his attention to me. "Angus, a word, if I may?"

"Yes, sir," I said, following him outside.

As the door to the hut closed behind us, I heard Audrey burst out laughing. I glanced at Bentley, but if he had heard it too, he was pretending not to notice.

"This ... erm ... Mrs Smith," he said, when we were out of earshot of the hut.

"Yes, sir?"

"What do you think?"

"Well, sir, I don't think we've much choice in the matter of keeping her here, and you know what the MI6 chaps are like."

"Oh yes," he said caustically. "I know exactly what they are like, all right. A blasted pair of reprobates, that's what they are. In any case, the orders have also come from the War Office, so there's not much we can do about it."

"No, sir," I said, wondering what he was really getting at. I did not have long to wait.

"My point is, can we keep her safe?" he said. "We've had far too many spies on this airbase already. I'd have thought there were safer havens than this one."

Bentley was nothing if not a realist. He was correct on all those counts. Far from being a haven, we'd had quite a bit of trouble instead as part of our lot.

"I suppose they had to weigh it all in the balance. I mean, someone would have to know she was here in order to threaten her life..." I trailed off.

"Well, then we'd better make sure nobody ruddy well finds out," he replied shortly.

By this time, Audrey had joined us from the hut and waited patiently a little to the side. She had recovered her composure and was looking suitably serious.

"Anyway," Bentley continued. "I want you to keep an eye on things regarding our new addition, all right?"

"Yes, sir," I said. It seemed that with my recent promotion came more responsibility. Even then, it was probably only a fraction of what Bentley had to deal with.

"Right, well, carry on, and keep me posted," said Bentley, saluting and striding away.

As soon as he was out of sight, Angelica appeared.

"Isn't it fun, darling, the parrot?" she said, clapping her hands together with delight.

"I'm not sure I'd exactly designate it in that fashion," I replied.

"Oh, don't be so stuffy, come and tell me what Bentley wanted."

We made our way to our bench, and I gave her a precis of Bentley's fears. She listened patiently.

"It's understandable," she said at length. "He's right that we've had more than our fair share of spies."

"Let's hope there are no more, then," I said.

"Yes, let's hope so." Her face took on a sly look and she adroitly turned the subject. "So … what do you think of Maria?"

I was at once suspicious in case she was laying some kind of trap. Knowing her quite well by now, it would be just like her to test me.

"What am I supposed to think of her?" I shot back.

"Well, do you think she's pretty?" she said, seemingly without a trace of guile.

I wasn't buying it, so I gave a non-committal answer.

"I mean, I suppose so…"

"Oh, go on, darling, you can be honest with me, we're married after all. What do you really think?" Angelica fluttered her eyelashes just a little.

She was incredibly beguiling when she wanted to be. I unwisely dropped my guard.

"Well, if you must know, I think she's a very striking woman … in my opinion," I told her candidly.

This was evidently what she had been fishing for.

"More than me?" she said, moving closer.

"No, not more than you," I said at once, realising I'd been fooled.

"That's the right answer," she said with a smile, her lips now touching mine.

"You know I've only got eyes for you," I said.

"Oh, I know… I'm just checking… And it's all right, as far as Maria goes … you can look … but you better not touch," she whispered.

"Is that so?" I whispered back.

"Oh yes…"

I kissed her, unable to resist her as always. She was simply harking back to my past, which she hadn't quite forgotten, even though I might have been forgiven.

We'd spent a while communing on the bench when something else occurred to me. Angelica was snuggled into me with my arm around her. I was beginning to learn how fulfilling simply being with someone, in their presence, could be. Despite my initial reservations, married life seemed to suit me after all.

"Willie," I said.

"Willie?"

"Does he know Olga is here?"

Angelica sat bolt upright.

"Oh, I hadn't thought of that. Perhaps we should tell him."

"Yes," I said. "Yes, we should."

He was going to find out sooner or later. The Marx Brothers knew about his relationship with Olga, and hadn't said anything against it. So, I decided it was better to tell him.

We returned to the hut. Willie was playing chess with Jonty. They usually had some lively games with plenty of banter, as opposed to the impression I previously had that chess games were supposed to be staid affairs.

I interrupted them in mid-altercation about a bishop.

"You moved it, so you can't move it back," Jonty was complaining.

"I had *thought* about moving it and then I changed my mind," Willie replied.

"You took your hand off it."

"No, I didn't."

"Yes, you did."

It reminded me of a child's pantomime and before it could degenerate further, I coughed discreetly.

"Skipper?" said Jonty, looking up.

"Sorry to interrupt your … erm … game … but I need to speak to Kiwi," I said.

"It's all right, Scottish," said Willie. "I'm done with his cheating for the moment."

"Well, that's rich!" said Jonty, firing up.

"If we might?" I said, interjecting before they could start arguing in earnest.

Willie stood up and followed me out. I glanced over at the cage where Percy resided, but he seemed to be quietly taking stock of his new surroundings. I wondered how many other airbases had parrots on them and I suspected there were none.

"I demand a rematch!" Jonty called after us and Willie just laughed.

Outside the hut, Angelica was waiting.

"What's this all about, Scottish?" Willie asked expectantly.

"Come with us," I told him. "There's someone I'd like you to meet."

Willie glanced at me curiously but didn't say any more. As we walked, I thought I would better impress upon him the need for circumspection.

"Kiwi," I began. "I hope I can rely on you to be discreet…"

"You know me, Scottish," he said. "Why? Is this something to do with spying?"

"Not exactly, no. It's just, well, you'll understand when we get there."

"I'm sure Kiwi has plenty of common sense, don't you?" said Angelica brightly.

"Usually yes, but I wish the two of you would stop talking in riddles."

I laughed and said no more. He didn't suspect a thing. We were in sight of Maria's house in any case. Willie regarded it curiously but made no comment. We reached the house and Olga opened the front door.

Willie stood stock still, as if he could hardly believe his eyes.

"Olga?" he said.

"Willie…"

The next moment, she was in his arms.

After letting them have a few moments, I asked, "Nice surprise?"

"Yes, Scottish, very," said Willie. "But I don't understand, what is Olga doing here?"

"I'm protecting the person staying in this house," said Olga. "You can come in and meet her, it's probably best."

I was sure Olga would come up with a suitable story; she was a spy herself, after all. Willie was also highly reliable and I had no doubts about him on that score. Besides, Maria's presence would become known on the base, one way or another.

Angelica and I elected to go to the mess for lunch. Olga had originally been a chef there as a cover for her counter-espionage duties, and had laid some groundwork in terms of cordial relations between our mess and the Americans next door. This meant that our mess was able to augment their provisions from the Americans. I wasn't sure what we gave them in exchange, and I didn't like to ask.

We were eating some rather nice fish pie with mash when Olga, Willie and Maria came into the mess and sat down beside us.

"Maria wanted to get out of the house," explained Olga. "She was feeling a little claustrophobic."

"But should she be in here?" I asked concerned.

Glancing around, I saw there were some curious eyes turned in our direction, but they soon lost interest.

"I'm sorry, I can go," said Maria.

"No, please stay. I just want to be sure you're safe, that's all," I replied in a low voice.

Maria was rather conspicuous in her mink stole. We didn't usually have such glamorous people on the base. She would certainly attract some attention. I resolved to suggest to Olga that perhaps Maria should dress down a little. I wondered what Olga had told Willie about Maria, but didn't like to ask. As long as there was a consistent cover story, that was all that mattered.

Maria and Olga also opted for the fish pie, while Willie ordered a hamburger with chips on the side.

"This is rather good," said Maria. "I will probably eat here more often, if I may."

"Why not?" said Olga. "Although I am happy to cook for you."

"She's an excellent chef," added Willie.

"I wonder where they got this fish from," Angelica mused. "It's trout, isn't it?"

I had no idea, but trout was certainly hard to come by unless it was from a country estate. It certainly wasn't from Amberly. They had a lake, but it was only inhabited by several carp.

"Horse trading, I imagine," I replied, taking another forkful.

"Well, as long as there are no actual horses involved," Maria quipped.

We all laughed and the conversation mellowed. Maria was a good sport and once her guard was down, she was rather witty. Obviously, we could not talk about her time in Germany as you never knew who was listening. After the main course, we opted for dessert. The mess served a rather good apple pie and custard. Having done this justice, we left the mess hall together.

We accompanied Olga and Maria halfway to her house and were just about to split off to go our separate ways when I caught the sound of a plane in the distance. Ordinarily, I would pay it no mind. We were on an airbase, after all; planes came and went quite frequently. However, there was something about it which got my attention. It wasn't a Spitfire, nor a German plane. I could tell by the hum.

Curious, I turned in time to see the plane in question approaching us at high speed. It was painted black, but I thought I recognised the shape.

"That's an American plane, isn't it?" Willie asked me. "A Curtiss P-40 Warhawk?"

Regardless of where it had come from, I didn't like the way it was angling or the speed it was flying. It also had no markings. The whole thing was highly suspicious. Then, suddenly, it headed straight towards us.

Instinct kicked in. I knew we were out in the open, but there were some storage buildings nearby. I acted at once to get the others to safety.

"Run!" I shouted to Olga. "Get Maria out of here!"

Olga didn't need telling twice. She grabbed Maria's hand and sprinted with her for cover.

"Come on," I said to Angelica and Willie. We started running together in a different direction to Olga and Maria, in order to confuse the pilot.

Even as we did so, the plane opened fire. Bullets kicked up the dirt as the aircraft passed over where we had been standing. We managed to reach a sheltered spot just in the nick of time. I pulled out my sidearm and emptied my revolver in the plane's direction. It was a futile attempt, but I had to try.

The plane banked around, as if it was going to come at us again, but by then the air-raid siren had sounded. Shortly afterwards one of the ack-ack batteries opened up, firing at the plane, although it was too far away to do any real damage. However, this action put the pilot off their attack. The mystery aircraft banked away and took off at full throttle. I turned to Willie.

"Look after Angelica," I said. "I'm going after it."

"Angus!" Angelica shouted after me, as I started to run. "Be careful!"

I pelted down to my Spitfire, jumped into the cockpit and fired it up. I was up and away within a matter of moments. As I gained height, I searched the sky for the offending aircraft, but it was nowhere in sight. I was just considering which direction to go in when I discovered I was not alone.

"What-ho, Skipper!" The radio crackled to life. It was Jonty.

I looked over, relieved to see his Spitfire and one other beside me.

"I am here too, Scottish," said Tomas. "We saw you running. I said to Jonty, "Scottish will need our help, come on," so here we are."

"Thanks for that," I said. "Let's split up and search for that plane. It may have landed somewhere."

We flew several passes over fields and wooded areas, places which might afford a suitable landing for an aircraft, and shelter. We went quite far in several different directions, but to no avail. The plane was nowhere to be found.

In the end, I decided to give it up.

"Let's got back to base, there's nothing here," I said. "They're long gone."

"Damn and blast it!" said Jonty, sounding annoyed.

"This was an American plane, no?" said Tomas, as we closed up in formation and headed for the airfield.

"Kiwi said so, yes," I replied.

"Ah, well…" He left the rest of it unsaid.

Surely our allies wouldn't make such a blatant attempt on Maria's life? She had not even been at Banley a day. How could this possibly have happened? These questions and more were uppermost in my mind as we landed.

We were met, unsurprisingly, by Angelica, Bentley and Audrey. Bentley looked grave and was smoking his pipe rather furiously.

"Did you find him?" Angelica asked, putting her arms around me briefly.

"No, there no sign of him at all," I said with a sigh.

"This pilot ... this raider ... has disappeared," Tomas put in.

"I say, Skipper," Jonty began. "You don't think it was the —
"

"The Ace Raider?" I interrupted him. "No, I don't. For a start, the plane wasn't a Focke-Wulf."

"But what if it was a double bluff?" Jonty wondered. "Some new form of subterfuge?"

"Possible, but highly unlikely. Where would he get such a plane from anyway?" I reasoned.

"But the plane has disappeared," Jonty persisted. "So couldn't he have flown back to enemy territory?"

I considered this. Could it really have been the Ace Raider? It was certainly the kind of stunt someone like him could pull. If it was him, then that meant the Germans knew that Maria was here.

"Yes, thank you, Butterworth and Jezek, for your timely response," said Bentley impatiently, "but I need to talk to Angus — in private."

Jonty and Tomas took the hint and left for the hut. Once they had gone, Bentley emptied his pipe and went through the routine of refilling and lighting it. I think this was as much to calm his nerves as anything else. He was certainly agitated by the unexpected attack.

"That was a blasted rum do," he said, puffing on his pipe once more. "No sooner does this woman turn up on the base than somebody comes along and tries to assassinate her."

"It certainly poses quite a few questions," I replied.

"Indeed it does," said Bentley, his voice rising. "Not least that someone already knows she's here when this was supposed to be the safest bloody place for her in the whole of England. So much for those two MI6 scoundrels fobbing me off with a poppycock story like that. I'll be having them down here *tout de* bloody *suite* to give an account of themselves!"

"I'm not sure it's entirely their fault, sir," I said, trying to be fair, as much as the Marx Brothers weren't my favourite people.

"Not their fault? Well, who brought her here, I ask you? They did! And now we've got a bloody security breach the size of the Nile Delta. What kind of clown show are these people running? A circus, that's what, a bloody circus!"

Having vented his wrath sufficiently, Bentley simmered down with a few more puffs on his pipe. He turned his attention to more practical matters.

"Firstly, we need to get some further protection for that house. I want to get an ack-ack battery in place nearby and a machine-gun post on watch twenty-four hours a day. If that blasted would-be assassin turns up again, we're not going to be caught napping, no by Jove," said Bentley. "Secondly, as I said, we're going to get those two clowns down here from MI6 and see what they've got to say about it."

It seemed like a good plan. I thought that the presence of an ack-ack battery next to the house might deter the pilot from trying to strafe it, or worse. A machine-gunner would also be a deterrent. At low level, any plane was vulnerable to small-arms fire. However, there was an issue I needed to raise.

"There is one other thing, sir," I said quietly.

"Which is?"

"It was an American plane, sir, a P-40..." I trailed off as Bentley looked fit to explode once more.

"What? An American plane? Well, we'll be off to the American base once those two Johnnies get here to demand an explanation!" the CO thundered.

"It doesn't mean it came from the American base, sir," I said, trying once more to be reasonable.

"Oh, it doesn't? Well, we'll soon find out. I knew there was going to be trouble, the minute that house was built," he said irascibly. "We're going to get to the bottom of this farrago and no mistake! In the meantime, I'm going to see to the new defences."

He marched off with Audrey in a determined manner.

"Oh dear," said Angelica, coming over. "Looks like Bentley is truly on the warpath now."

"With good reason," I said.

Another thought occurred to me.

"It might be a good idea for Maria to wear something else, you know, to try and blend in…"

Angelica agreed with this suggestion at once.

"Yes, you're right. I will suggest it next time I get a chance."

I walked with her as far as the dispersal hut, and then let her go. I still had to see to the rostering of our patrols in spite of this latest diversion.

Bentley would no doubt want me to be present at whatever meetings were convened about the assassination threat. In the meantime, I decided to get Tomas to lead one patrol and Willie the other. I had yet to include Sandford's squadron, and now matters were complicated by the fact that the would-be assassin had been flying an American-built plane. I wondered again if it could be the Ace Raider. But could the Germans be that devious? It didn't seem very likely, and yet I could not entirely dismiss it. Surely, if the Germans wanted to kill Maria, they'd send an entire squadron of bombers and not just one plane. It seemed unlikely that anyone other than Maria was their target. Which meant it was highly likely that whoever it really was would be bound to try again.

CHAPTER SIX

That same afternoon brought the Marx Brothers up from London. Shortly after they had arrived, I found myself once more ensconced in the mission room with them, along with Angelica, Bentley and Audrey. As usual, they had discarded their trench coats and hats on a table and lit up cigarettes. Bentley was regarding them with a jaundiced eye while carrying out his pipe ritual. When he was finally smoking it, he elected to tackle the subject at hand.

"You received my message no doubt?" he said to them in a deceptively mild tone.

"Indeed, which is why we are here as you perceive," said Harpo laconically.

I should have expected no less from Harpo, I suppose. They never seemed to be surprised by anything, and the attempt on Maria's life was no exception.

"Well, and what do you make of it?" Bentley asked him.

"It's rather an unfortunate turn of events to be sure," said Harpo, taking a drag on his cigarette.

This was definitely the wrong thing to say. Bentley, who had obviously been simmering close to the boil like a kettle on the stove, jumped out of his chair and started to pace the room.

"Unfortunate? I'll bloody well say it's unfortunate! No sooner does Mrs Smith arrive here than someone tries to kill her and you describe it as unfortunate? You don't find it rather alarming that your supposed top-secret bloody plan isn't top secret after all? It doesn't cause you any concern that her presence here has been discovered? Well?"

He stopped and puffed on his pipe in the most alarming fashion.

"Naturally, we are concerned about the situation, yes," said Chico, in an attempt to mollify the CO.

"And what are you bloody well going to do about it? Tell me that!" Bentley demanded.

"We have set some investigations in train internally, to ascertain if there's a leak."

"A leak? A leak? It's more like a burst pipe than a blasted leak!" said Bentley, not in the least placated.

I could see that this was getting us nowhere and decided it might be wise to intervene.

"If I might suggest, sir," I began. "Perhaps we could apprise our friends from MI6 of the circumstance of the attack, as it might be of assistance."

"What?" said Bentley. "Oh … oh, yes. Good idea, Angus. At least somebody is on the bloody ball."

The Marx Brothers took the barbed comment in good part as Bentley resumed his seat in what appeared to be a slightly calmer frame of mind.

Angelica squeezed my hand and shot me a smile of encouragement.

"All right, the events unfolded as follows…" I began.

I told them in detail of the attack which had taken place, and also the fact it was an American-made plane. They showed a considerable amount of interest in this piece of intelligence.

"Hmm," said Harpo when I had finished. "And you're sure it was a P-40?"

"As sure as I can be. Pilot Officer Cooper is pretty good with aircraft identification and I trust his judgement. It certainly wasn't a British-made plane, or German … at least not one that we know about."

"I think perhaps we should pay our American friends a visit," said Harpo, coming to a decision.

"Exactly what I was thinking myself," said Bentley, pleased that they seemed to be finally tracking along the same lines.

"Do you really think the Americans could be behind the attack?" I asked Harpo.

His answer was not encouraging.

"Unfortunately, in this game, you can't rule anything out. What the motive could be, I couldn't possibly guess at, but it's certainly where we should start."

Angelica and I glanced at each other. It was a bad state of affairs if the Americans were going to assassinate the wife of one of their scientists.

"We will get in touch with the Military Intelligence chaps over there, arrange a meeting pronto," said Chico. "In the meantime, how well protected is Maria given what's just occurred?"

"I've got an ack-ack emplacement set up outside the house, as well as a machine gun," said Bentley. "They will be manned around the clock. In addition, there's a searchlight for possible night raids. That's the best I can do for the moment, other than housing Mrs Smith in some sort of bunker, and I'm sure she would not be amenable to that."

"No," said Harpo. "Thank you for taking such swift action, Squadron Leader. We shall make sure the Ministry arranges for you to get some additional equipment and personnel to replace those you've had to redeploy on defending Mrs Smith."

"I'm obliged to you," said Bentley. "But you should also thank Angus, here, whose swift thinking very probably saved her life."

I didn't really want to be thanked, since it was all part of my duty.

"Yes, indeed, Flight Lieutenant, your sterling work does not go unnoticed," said Chico.

The meeting broke up, and the Marx Brothers departed to make the necessary arrangements with the Americans.

"Bloody reprobates those two," Bentley growled as he left for his office. "Absolute bloody clowns."

Once we were alone, Angelica turned to me.

"Do you think it *was* the Americans?" she asked me.

"I don't know what to think, but I can't see what they could possibly gain from it," I replied.

"It's one less problem for them, though, isn't it?" She gave me a tight smile. "If Maria is dead, I mean."

"True," I agreed. "But on the other hand, her husband might refuse to keep working for them if they fail to keep her safe."

"Yes," said Angelica. "Good point."

It wasn't long before Angelica and I were sitting in a meeting room at the American base, along with Bentley, Audrey, Sandford, the Marx Brothers, and two officers from American Military Intelligence. Major Jim Foster was the younger of the two, in his early thirties. Lieutenant Colonel Eddie Thompson was slightly older. Both sported a moustache, but Jim had black hair to Eddie's grey. I had met them before, when they had been involved in a hunt for a spy on their base. The room was also the very same room in which we'd met them the last time.

Jim was a smoker, along with Bentley and the Marx Brothers. All four of them were engaged upon filling the room with a pungent cloud of smoke.

Sandford Booker was involved as he seemed to be something of a liaison between the two bases, as well as running their Fighter squadron. In addition, he'd been involved in the spy hunt too.

"You are aware, I'm sure, of our guest at Banley," said Harpo, as the meeting convened. He didn't name Maria directly, but since her husband was working for the US Government, it seemed highly unlikely her presence at Banley wasn't known to their intelligence forces.

"Yes, of course," said Jim, watching a trail of smoke curl up towards the ceiling. It was a habit of his that I had noted on prior occasions.

"Are you also aware that an attempt was made upon her life?" asked Chico.

"No, we were not," Eddie put in. "What sort of attempt?"

"The sort of attempt that almost got her killed," said Bentley, annoyed already at the obtuse manner in which all spies seemed to behave.

"I assumed that was the case," said Eddie smoothly, "but how?"

"Flight Lieutenant Mackennelly?" said Harpo. "Perhaps you'd like to elaborate."

I did so while they listened without comment, during which Jim extinguished one cigarette and immediately lit another. He was in good company with the Marx Brothers in that respect.

"So, Mrs Smith was attacked using a plane," said Jim. A statement, not a question.

"Yes," I said. "An American-built Curtiss P-40 Warhawk. Painted black and without any markings."

There was a short silence while this information was digested. I noticed that Angelica was watching the Americans closely. If she was expecting a reaction, she didn't get it. However, as they were in Military Intelligence I assumed acting deadpan was part of their training.

"I get it," said Eddie, breaking the silence. "You've come here because you think that plane somehow came from us."

He was nothing if not blunt. An accusation couldn't be directly made, but it had been all but mooted by virtue of holding a meeting in the first place.

"Did it?" said Harpo and I noticed his voice took on an edge. It was a tone I'd not heard from him before. He was normally rather insouciant, if not flippant. This indicated to me that he might suspect American involvement after all.

"Not to our knowledge, no," said Eddie blandly.

"Not to your knowledge, but it could have, is that what you're saying?" said Bentley, cutting in.

I was sure that Harpo would have preferred to do things his own way, but Bentley was a tad more impatient. It pushed the point home in any case.

"As I said, not to our knowledge," said Eddie, unruffled. "However, I would be surprised if it had come from our side. I would be sure to know about it if it had."

I glanced at Bentley. I wasn't sure if he quite believed him. The CO was suspicious of intelligence operatives and with good reason.

"So, you're saying it categorically didn't, or that it's unlikely?" Harpo asked Eddie, attempting to take back control of the conversation. His voice still carried the hint of steel I'd heard in it just a moment before.

"I'm saying it's unlikely, but I can't give you a categorical answer because I simply don't know for sure," said Eddie.

His tone was neutral and not at all defensive. However, the response wasn't good enough for Bentley. The Major's rank was equivalent to one above Bentley, but that didn't stop the Squadron Leader from expressing his extreme irritation.

"Good God," he said. "A woman's life has been threatened and for all we know likely to be so again. She could have died. We've been given the charge of protecting her, and we need answers, not riddles. If something happens to her it falls on us. You understand our concern, I'm sure."

Eddie held up his hand to acknowledge Bentley's frustration.

"We are just as concerned as you," he said. "Make no mistake about that. The problem is that I don't know. I can't imagine why anyone on our side would want to assassinate … Maria Von Schmidt, is that her name?"

"Yes, that's her name," I said.

"It doesn't make any sense to me why anyone would want to kill her from our side," he continued. "However, that being said, the machinations of those in higher positions in the USA is something you would not believe, and so I can't completely rule it out without asking some questions internally."

"I would believe it," said Bentley, "because we have the same blasted machinations on our side of the fence. I can bloody well vouch for that."

Eddie laughed.

"Then it looks like we're all in the same club. Every organ grinder is also a monkey to the organ grinders further up the chain of command," he said.

The tension eased considerably with this statement. However, I still had some questions and decided to broach them.

"If this attack did not come from your side," I said, "then where did the plane come from? How would someone have been able to get hold of a military aircraft like that?"

"Fair point," said Eddie. "And one which again I can't immediately answer."

Jim, who was now on his third cigarette, chimed in.

"Happens I know something about planes," he said. "This P-40 was developed around 1938, and other forces including the RAF have some of them. There would also have been prototypes. So, it might be possible for one to have fallen into the wrong hands."

"Could the Germans have one?" I asked him, thinking about the Ace Raider.

"I don't rightly know," said Jim after a moment's thought. "They could if one had been captured."

"Is that likely?"

"I can check records, see if any have been shot down," Sandford put in, "or lost in action. Why would you think it was the Germans?"

"The Ace Raider," I told him.

"You think it could be him? In an American plane?" Sandford sounded surprised.

"We can't entirely rule it out." I shrugged. "Admittedly it seems highly unlikely, but we've seen some very unlikely things happen during the course of this war."

"Rest assured we shall be exploring all avenues," said Harpo. "That includes known sympathisers in this country."

"Known sympathisers who happen to have an American P-40 in their possession, know how to fly it, and somewhere to hide it?" I asked, incredulous.

"Admittedly it does seem far-fetched," said Harpo. "But then again, you said yourself…"

He was right. We couldn't rule anything out. The attacker could be exactly that. A person as yet unknown somehow in cahoots with the Germans. Not all citizens of Britain were loyal, as we knew already to our cost.

"Could it be someone from your side?" asked Jim.

It was a question that needed to be asked.

"Categorically not," said Harpo. "I can say that with a high level of certainty."

In the following silence I decided to broach an idea which had been forming in my mind. It seemed as good a time as any.

"Should we keep a couple of planes and pilots on standby in case the would-be assassin attacks again?"

Bentley grimaced.

"We don't exactly have spare capacity," he said. "Two planes set aside just for that purpose, and two pilots means three shifts a day, so really that's six pilots."

"Yes, I see," I said. "Perhaps not."

"Let's talk about this later," said Harpo. "We might be able to help you out."

Bentley nodded. No doubt Harpo didn't like to discuss all of our business in front of the Americans. There seemed no more to be said.

"How about some chow? An early dinner," said Sandford, ever practical. "We can go to the officers' mess, I hear they might actually have some beefsteak today."

"Why not?" said Bentley.

The others agreed without demur, and we followed Sandford down to the mess. Angelica tucked her arm into mine and smiled up at me. The American officers' mess was currently her favourite place to eat.

The meal was convivial, and we returned to Banley in good spirits. I went to check on Maria. All seemed to be well and the defensive guns were in place. There was nothing more to be done except return to Amberly, where I finally managed to put my concerns to the back of my mind, at least for a few hours.

CHAPTER SEVEN

The following day I checked in with Tomas and Willie regarding their patrols.

"We didn't see the Ace Raider, Scottish," said Tomas. "We didn't see any Germans."

"Nor did we," said Willie.

I was surprised to hear this, since the Ace Raider had seemed to be waging a campaign single-handedly. The fact that he hadn't appeared brought back my doubts as to whether we could really rule him out of the attack on Maria. He couldn't be in two places at once.

"We will get him, Scottish," said Tomas. "These people, they always make a mistake, sooner or later."

I didn't entirely share his optimism, as the Raider so far had proved more than capable in evading us.

"Come on, Scottish, come on. Everything will work out, you will see." Tomas clapped me on the back and then wandered away to get himself a brew. He was quite happy-go-lucky in many respects. He'd seen a lot before escaping from Czechoslovakia before the Nazi occupation, and I suppose he was more phlegmatic about the fortunes of war than I was.

As he departed, Jonty sidled up to me in a manner which made me think that he wanted something.

"What-ho, Skipper," he said.

"Hello, Jonty."

"I heard a funny story, Skipper…" Jonty began.

Willie rolled his eyes. He had no doubt heard the tale already.

"What story, Jonty?"

"One of the bomber crew next door ... an American. He's got a dog..."

"And?" I prompted him.

Then came the rather unexpected punchline.

"He takes the dog up in the bomber with him, it has an oxygen mask and everything. I think that's rather droll, don't you?"

"Yes, it's most amusing," I replied. "Perhaps the British aren't the only eccentric nation after all."

"It got me thinking, Skipper."

Jonty was intent on pursuing whatever point he was making in a roundabout way.

"Did it?" I said, suddenly suspicious.

"Yes, Skipper. I mean, if the Americans can do it..." He trailed off.

"I don't really see what you're getting at, Jonty."

Jonty flicked a glance at Percy's cage. The parrot was preening himself. It all suddenly made sense.

"Jonty," I said firmly. "That parrot is not going up with you in your Spitfire!"

"I say!" said Jonty, looking abashed. "But he's never been in a plane, Skipper. He might enjoy it."

"And he's not going to find out if he enjoys it either," I said firmly. "I absolutely forbid it. What on earth do you think Bentley would have to say about it?"

"Say about what?" It was Angelica, arriving at the tail end of the conversation.

"This idiot wants to take his bloody parrot up in his plane, that's what," said Willie.

"Oh, Jonty, you are such a silly boy," said Angelica, laughing.

"It's a ridiculous notion," I said.

"Well, I didn't think you'd be quite so much against it, Skipper," said Jonty, sounding aggrieved. "It was just a bit of fun, after all."

"Your idea of fun has got you — and me — into more hot water than I care to recall," I told him. "The last thing we need is another carpeting from Bentley because you've taken that parrot up for a spin."

Jonty put his hands up in mock surrender.

"All right, all right, I get the message."

"Loud and clear I hope," said Willie.

Jonty sighed theatrically.

"I'll just have to make up a ballad about it instead."

"No!" Willie said emphatically.

"Spoilsport," said Jonty.

"Come and play chess, and put these stupid ideas out of your head," said Willie placatingly.

"It wasn't a stupid idea, it was rather a splendid one I thought," said Jonty, as they turned away and walked over to the table where the chessboard had been set up.

"That's your trouble, you don't think," said Willie.

"I say!"

Angelica giggled and tugged my arm lightly.

"Come on," she said. "Come for a walk before your sortie."

"Yes, all right."

Now that the immediate danger to Maria had passed, I had decided to resume leading one of the sorties. I had also arranged with Sandford that they would fly one sortie a day when they weren't on escort duty.

"You don't think Jonty will really take his parrot up in his plane, do you?" Angelica asked as we headed for our bench.

"He'd better not," I said. "Bentley would be apoplectic and that wouldn't be good for any of us."

"Let's hope Jonty doesn't do it then."

"Yes, let's hope," I replied, having very little faith in that hope being fulfilled.

Before we left for our sortie, I decided it would be wise to check that Percy was still in his cage. He fixed me with a beady eye.

"It's a rum do," he squawked. "A rum do, a rum do."

"Jonty's been teaching him Bentley's sayings," explained Dylan.

I felt a pang of regret in having allowed Jonty to keep Percy in the hut. I was certain the parrot and Jonty were going to get us into trouble one way or another. There was nothing to be done about it now, however.

Angelica was waiting to say goodbye. As always, we held hands until the last moment.

"Fly safe," she whispered. "Come back to me."

"I will, I promise."

It was a promise we both knew I might not be able to keep. If today was the day that a bullet had my name on it, it would be all over.

Angelica waited steadfastly, watching Redwood strap me in. I fired up the kite, waved and she blew me a kiss. I taxied out onto the runway with the rest of the flight.

"Red Leader, you're clear for take-off," said the control tower.

"Red Patrol, here we go," I said, throttling up.

In short order the six of us were in the air and flying towards the east coast. I decided to head for Harwich this time. There was a fair wind on our tail, and the sky was clear. It was a sunny winter's day and the landscape sparkled in the sun.

"Do you think we'll see the Ace Raider today, Skipper?" asked Jonty.

"Who knows," I replied.

"I told you, we should run a sweep on it," Jonty continued.

"And perhaps we shouldn't," Willie said at once.

It seemed he would almost always take the opposite view to anything Jonty suggested. Most of M Flight had become inured to their squabbles.

"It might be inviting fate," said Dylan, entering the fray.

"I hadn't thought of that," Jonty said, sounding much struck by the notion.

"That's the trouble, you don't think. I've said it enough times after all," said Willie with some acidity.

"All right, settle down. Let's keep our eyes peeled for bandits."

I intervened before the two of them had a full-blown argument while we were on patrol. It had happened before, and as flight leader I was determined to keep a tighter rein on them.

There was silence for a while, as we approached the outskirts of Harwich. It was a small yet significant port in that it had a number of naval vessels sheltering in its harbour. There were barrage balloons, mines and more to deter attacks, although it had its fair share of those. I thought it might be a prime target for the Ace Raider, but it seemed as if he shied away from the heavily defended towns and went for easier prey.

I turned the patrol northwards to head up the coastline. We flew on without incident, past Aldeburgh, Thorpeness and Sizewell, and then onwards to Southwold.

Lowestoft came into view. It was a comparatively large town to others on the east coast and had been targeted by bombing raids more than once during the year. Hopton was next, with a sizeable military training camp. This seemed a more likely target.

"I don't think we're going to see the Ace Raider today," said Jonty with a sigh.

"Must you persist in doing that?" Willie complained.

"Doing what?"

"Every time you say that we won't see him, the next moment, there he is!"

"Surely not!" protested Jonty.

However, it seemed as if Willie was right.

"There he is! It's the Ace Raider!" shouted Dylan.

"And he's not alone," said Arjun. "There are another two planes."

Sure enough, the Ace Raider was streaking in across the water, and right behind him were two more Focke-Wulfs. We would have a fight on our hands, that was for sure.

"Break, break, let's get them before they reach the camp," I said.

I throttled up and headed straight for the three Germans, who had not yet seen us. Even so, we would not reach them before they made landfall.

As we got closer, the three planes split up and went on a pincer attack against the camp, still keeping low. We had to get lower and we did. There was small arms fire coming from the camp, and men in uniform ran for cover as the Focke-Wulfs continued their relentless approach.

On my right, Willie had managed to get behind one of the Jerries. It hadn't seen him, and Willie opened fire. The shots peppered the German's wing but did no real damage. The Wulf banked away sharply. Willie gave chase.

"Tally-ho, Kiwi, I'm on my way," said Jonty, gunning his plane toward the two of them.

The Wulf was weaving left and right, flying away from the camp and trying to avoid Willie.

I put my attention on the other two planes. They strafed the camp as they flew over, then turned back for another pass. The Ace Raider was in the lead. I made a beeline for him, hoping to stop him before he dropped any bombs. The pilot seemed, as usual, completely unperturbed by the fact that he was outnumbered by four Spitfires.

Arjun came in from the left of the two Germans and fired a salvo. The second plane broke off his attack and pulled a tight turn. Arjun pursued, with Jean following.

It was left to me and Dylan to continue attacking the Ace Raider. We were almost head to head when he suddenly pulled up and dropped his bomb, before flicking his kite hard over. Dylan and I both fired, but the bullets passed him harmlessly by.

I cursed inwardly. Somehow, we had to bring him down to earth. He turned tightly and headed for the sea once more.

"Let's keep on him," I said to Dylan as we set off after him.

"I'm with you, Scottish. Never fear, he's not going to get away this time."

I admired Dylan's optimism but, judging by the speed at which he was going, I doubted we could stop him.

In my rear-view mirror, I saw the almighty explosion as the bomb went off. I was wondering what was happening with the other two German planes when another explosion occurred.

"I've hit him! I've hit him!" cried Jonty gleefully.

"Nice shooting," Willie acknowledged.

"Ours is doing a runner," said Arjun.

A glance to my left revealed the Wulf being hotly pursued by Arjun and Jean.

In front of us, the Ace Raider started pulling up towards the cloud cover.

"He's doing it again," complained Dylan.

"Leave him, we won't catch him," I said. "Let's try and get the other one."

Dylan banked left towards the final raider.

The last plane spotted this new attack and turned away, still over the town. As luck would have it, tracers streaked up from a machine-gun emplacement towards the German plane. It scored a lucky strike and smoke began pouring from the engine.

The next moment, Dylan got within firing distance of the German. A stream of tracers sliced into the Wulf amidships, shattering the cockpit. The pilot slumped forward and the plane dived earthwards, exploding into flames upon impact.

We circled around to check the damage. It didn't seem as if the Ace Raider's bomb had hit anything vital in the camp. Some of the soldiers were waving at us. Two smoking Focke-Wulfs were left, having made their impact in the fields rather than on some unfortunate resident's house. There was nothing more to do. The Ace Raider had eluded us yet again.

"Come on," I said. "Let's go home. There's no point in hanging around."

"We got two Jerries, that's something to celebrate," said Dylan, full of enthusiasm.

"But we didn't get the Ace Raider," said Jonty.

"Ah well, two out of three is not a bad score," said Dylan.

The flight formed up on me, and I set a course for Banley. It seemed unusual for the Ace Raider to come with two compatriots, and I mused that perhaps he wouldn't do it again in a hurry since he seemed to be far more successful on his own. One thing he hadn't been able to do was leave his customary calling card. I wondered if that meant he might be back. Perhaps Gordon might be able to shed some light on it. He was fairly well read and understood a lot about the psychology of people. I decided that a visit to Annie's Kitchen was in order.

We landed at Banley to be met by the usual reception. Angelica pelted over to meet me and hurled herself onto my chest.

"Oof!" I said, enveloping her in an embrace. "Nice to see you."

"It's marvellous to see *you*," she said, planting a kiss on my lips.

"I wasn't away *that* long," I teased.

"Too long for me," she teased back.

My attention was claimed by Bentley, who appeared beside us with Audrey.

"I gather you encountered that bloody scoundrel the Ace Raider again, and two of his blasted compatriots," he said.

"Yes, sir," I replied. "Unfortunately, the Ace Raider got away, but we managed to bag the other two. Well, one of them was initially hit by small arms."

"Good, good, at least that's two damn Jerries we don't have to worry about," he said. "But what do we do about this Ace Raider?"

This had been on my mind for some time, and it was probably as good a time as any to mention my idea.

"I've been thinking about that, sir, and I think that we need to set a trap," I said.

Bentley raised an eyebrow at this.

"And how do you propose to do that?" he said.

"I haven't thought it through yet, sir," I admitted. "But it would perhaps involve putting out some false intelligence to lure him in."

"No doubt using those blasted reprobate spies, I take it?"

"Yes, sir, that would be the idea. I've asked them about it and they said they could give it a go."

"Right, well, when you *do* think of a plan run it by me first, if you would."

"Yes, sir."

"Jolly good."

"Any incursions on the airfield here?" I asked him tentatively.

He knew at once that I was referring to Maria.

"No, thankfully," he said. "And long may it stay that way. However, on that subject, those MI6 Johnnies have pulled some strings. We'll be getting one or two extra pilots and two more planes to keep on standby as you suggested. You can sort out a rota with your chaps."

"That's good news," I said.

"I suppose there has to be some good news coming out of this bloody farrago," he said acerbically. "Anway, carry on, Angus, carry on."

With that, he left as rapidly as he had arrived.

"What now?" asked Angelica, as we watched Bentley stride away with Audrey.

"I will check the next sortie is going up and then we are going for tea."

She looked surprised.

"For tea?"

"Yes, with Fred."

"Oh, my goodness." Her eyes sparkled. "You don't mean you're actually inviting me to your special tearoom?"

"Yes, as a matter of fact, I am. There's something I want to pick Fred's brains about. You might as well be in on it too."

Annie's Kitchen was not exactly sacrosanct, it had just become a place I had come to regard as *our* tearoom.

"I take it you're not picking his brains about *me* this time," Angelica said with a laugh.

"What makes you think I was doing so before?"

"Oh, you know, woman's intuition," she said.

"Well, you're not wrong," I sighed.

Angelica caught hold of my hands and looked at me a little more seriously.

"Was I really *that* bad?"

"You were something of a conundrum at times, yes."

She laughed again and her voice resumed its teasing tone.

"A conundrum? I've never been called *that* before."

She was smiling at me in an amused but not mocking way. The problem was she looked quite charming and completely irresistible.

"Oh, you're incorrigible," I said with a laugh.

"Better than being a conundrum." She let me go and tucked her arm into mine.

"All right, impossible, that's what you are," I said, as we set off to find Gordon.

"Always," she shot back at once.

We both laughed and I gave it up. She would invariably have the last word and I was happy to let her.

Gordon, Angelica and I were soon seated at a table in Annie's Kitchen. Gordon had not demurred at Angelica's inclusion, rather he welcomed it. In the past, we had gone to the tearoom when I had needed to consult his wisdom, and today was no different.

"So, this is where you two have been going all this time," Angelica said, taking in the charming surroundings.

"I wouldn't exactly characterise it as 'all this time'," I said.

"More when the need arises, ma'am, for a civilised cup of tea," said Gordon.

Annie brought a pot of tea, milk, sugar, hot crumpets, butter and jam.

"These look delicious," Angelica observed, surveying the spread.

"Wait until you try them," said Gordon with a wink. "The best crumpets this side of London."

On that recommendation, Angelica carefully spread butter and blackberry jam on a crumpet while I poured the tea. Gordon and I waited expectantly as she took a bite with her eyes closed.

"Well?" I asked her, once she had finished her first mouthful.

"Well, I'm perfectly cross with you that you didn't bring me here sooner," she said with a smile. "I feel utterly deprived of all the missed opportunities to have such delicious crumpets."

Gordon and I laughed.

"Don't worry," I said. "I will bring you more often from now on."

"I shall insist on it," she informed me.

"Is this a pleasure outing, sir?" asked Gordon, sipping his tea. "Or is there something on your mind?"

"A bit of both really," I said. "I rather wanted to pick your brains."

"Pick away. I'll do my best to help, but do eat your crumpets, sir, while they're hot."

"It's about the Ace Raider," I began, ladling jam onto a crumpet.

"Yes?"

"It seems that he has a certain pattern of behaviour, or at least he does the same things repeatedly. I wondered if perhaps, given your knowledge of Freud, psychology and so on, you might be able to shed some light on it."

"It's funny you should mention it," said Gordon, polishing off his first crumpet. "I was musing on that very subject only the other day."

This didn't surprise me at all. Gordon was something of a deep thinker by all accounts.

"Go on," I encouraged him.

"Freud talks about the three parts of the unconscious mind which control a person's behaviour and is to all intents and purposes outside of their control."

"Oh, I see," I said, not seeing at all.

He took another sip of tea and continued.

"There's the Id, which is the most primitive part and acts according to the 'pleasure principle'. It's perhaps best characterised by needs, wants and impulses. Then there is the Ego, which is the rational part of the mind and attempts to moderate the impulses of the Id, if you like. Then there is the Superego, which is the supposed moralistic conscience that strives for socially acceptable behaviour."

He paused to butter his second crumpet. Angelica was regarding him with some fascination. She hadn't really heard him talk like this before.

"I had no idea you were such a fount of knowledge," she said.

"Hardly that," Gordon demurred. "I've read a lot."

Gordon wasn't one to puff up his accomplishments.

"Anyway," he continued. "With respect to your Ace Raider. What Freud says is that sometimes the Ego and Superego are subordinate to the Id. Those primaeval urges, as it were, override their civilising influence."

"Right, so you think the Ace Raider is somehow satisfying some subconscious urge?" I asked him.

"In a manner of speaking, yes. It would appear that he's driven by some kind of obsession which manifests itself in performing the same things over and over again, in very specific ways, as you've noticed."

"Gosh," said Angelica, looking impressed.

Gordon paused to finish off his second crumpet, and I did the same. Angelica poured us all out another cup of tea.

"If that is so, then how would we go about tempting the Ace Raider to go after, let's say, a specific target?" I asked.

Gordon regarded me shrewdly.

"Ah, so you want to set a trap and you're looking for the right sort of bait. Am I right?"

"Perfectly," I replied.

I signalled Annie to bring us another round of crumpets and replenish the tea. Gordon sipped his tea, considering the matter.

"You have to appeal to his sense of ego. He is, after all, quite the showman, isn't he? He has the Ace of Spades painted on his plane. He leaves a calling card in an ostentatious fashion. To some degree, he believes himself bulletproof, invincible even. After all, he's got away with it many times already without being caught."

"You certainly have the right of it," I said.

"If you think about it, he's a man playing to the crowd," said Gordon, warming to his theme. "He likes an audience; perhaps it makes his pyrrhic victories all the sweeter."

Angelica, who had been listening intently, suddenly spoke up.

"What about a fete or a celebration of some sort?"

"A fete?" I said in surprise. "But it's winter, aren't those normally held in summer?"

"So?" she countered. "It could be some kind of commemoration; with lots of people there, it would be very tempting for him to come and attack it."

Gordon looked thoughtful.

"You're right, that's exactly the sort of thing which might appeal to his sense of vainglory."

"And if," Angelica added, "there was someone famous attending it..."

"Such as?" I asked

"What about Churchill?"

I was slightly flabbergasted at this suggestion.

"Churchill?"

Angelica was undeterred.

"Yes, why not?"

"I hardly think Churchill would come out for something like that," I objected.

"But he might, you haven't asked him."

"I don't know Winston Churchill," I protested.

"Ah, but the Marx Brothers do."

Gordon smiled and intervened.

"Nothing ventured, sir..."

"Nothing gained," Angelica finished triumphantly.

I thought about it more seriously. Perhaps we could get Churchill to come to Banley, or, rather, the Marx Brothers could. It was worth a shot.

"Well, I suppose there's no harm in it. I mean, it's a good notion. We just need to think it through."

"Indeed," said Gordon.

"You could be lying in wait nearby, squadron ready to scramble once the Ace Raider appears," said Angelica, warming to the theme.

Her enthusiasm was infectious.

"Yes," I said. "With hidden flak batteries too, and machine-gunners. Shoot down the blighter once and for all."

"That's the spirit," said Gordon.

"Oh, Fred, you're a treasure," said Angelica. "I can see why Angus comes to you for advice."

"You're too kind, ma'am," said Gordon, blushing slightly at the unexpected praise.

We talked a little more about the idea, and then more generally about the war. Gordon furnished us with his opinion that it was far from over. This was a depressing thought, but I tended to agree. In spite of the bombing campaigns, the Germans did not look like a nation — or an army — about to be defeated. It was going to take a superhuman effort to dislodge them from Europe.

I paid Annie's bill, after which we made our way back to Banley. I wanted to be sure all was right and tight before we went home for the evening.

The evenings were drawing in and it was twilight when we arrived back at the airbase. The afternoon patrols had not encountered any bandits, and certainly not the Ace Raider. It would have been something of a surprise had he perpetrated a second attack on the same day.

I went with Angelica to check on Maria. Hopefully, the two extra Spitfires and pilots would soon arrive so that we could have them on standby in case of another attempt on her life.

"It all seems quiet," said Angelica as we approached Maria's abode.

"Yes," I agreed.

A few yards from the house stood the new ack-ack battery, and also a machine-gun emplacement. Next to those was a searchlight. All of this to protect the life of one woman. I wondered if her husband hadn't been a famous scientist, if anyone would have cared. These were the fortunes of war and the accidents of birth. So many civilians were now dying in bombing raids and by all accounts, even worse things were happening to those of Jewish descent under the Nazi yoke. There was an irony in it somewhere, but since we were charged with Maria's safety, we'd carry that duty out to the best of our abilities.

As we approached the door, I heard the hum of an aircraft. It was a recognisable hum even from a distance. I had heard it before, the last time the would-be assassin had attacked.

"Do you hear that?" I said to Angelica urgently.

"What?"

"That plane…"

It was louder and I was now absolutely sure that it was the would-be assassin's aircraft. I scanned the skies anxiously and could just make out a black shape crossing the perimeter fence.

"The light. Hit the light!" I shouted at the searchlight team.

The searchlight beam came on, piercing through the gloom, a bright shaft of light moving desperately to locate its quarry. And there it was — the black P40, heading straight for us.

Fortunately, the sergeant in charge of the battery was on the ball.

"Open fire!" he shouted.

There were barked orders to the gun crew as the gun barrels were rotated towards the intended target. Within seconds the ack-ack was pumping out flack in the direction of the incoming plane. I was torn between getting under cover and having a better look at the plane. In the end, I pulled Angelica away from the house, so that we were standing to the side, out of the direct line of fire.

The air-raid siren was now sounding and then the machine-gun emplacement opened up. A stream of tracers erupted from the muzzle. The pilot banked the plane to avoid being hit.

At that moment, the wings were lit up by the searchlight.

"Look!" said Angelica.

I looked in the direction she was pointing. Painted on the underside of each of the wings in white was the symbol of the Ace of Spades.

"Good God," I said. Were the would-be assassin and the Ace Raider the same person? Having ruled out the idea, I was now having to quickly reconsider it.

The pilot flew away as rapidly as he had arrived, disappearing into the encroaching darkness.

"Are you going to go after him?" Angelica asked me.

"No point," I replied. "It's too dark and he's already got a head start. I couldn't find him in the daylight, let alone now."

"Thank goodness for the ack-ack. He certainly wasn't expecting that."

"Yes," I agreed. "Without that, it might have been a different story altogether."

The searchlight went off as the plane disappeared, and the hum from its propellor grew fainter and fainter.

"Well done, Sergeant, you were commendably quick off the mark," I said to the NCO in charge of the battery.

"Thank you, sir," he said. "Shame we didn't hit him."

"Never mind. You put him off, that's what matters."

He saluted and returned to his duties, getting the gun ready in case it was needed again.

Angelica and I went up to the house and knocked on the door. It was opened by Olga.

"Are you and Maria okay?" I asked her.

"We're both fine," said Olga. "Was that another attack?"

"Yes, I'm afraid so," I replied.

I hesitated but she gave me a broad smile.

"Do you want to come in?"

"For a few minutes, why not?" I replied.

Angelica and I entered the house. Maria was sitting in the living room, looking a little shaken. Angelica immediately went to sit beside her.

"It's hard living with this constant threat," said Maria. "I'm afraid to go out."

"You're safer now than you were, particularly with the new defences," said Angelica, ever practical.

Maria sighed.

"When I was brought here, I never expected to become such a target."

"I'm sorry," Angelica replied. "I wish there was more we could do."

"It's okay. Others are worse off than me. I'm grateful to you all … for protecting me."

"You're welcome," I said.

"We worked out a strategy for an attack," Olga informed me. "The safest place is the main bedroom, under the bed. I've also asked for the walls to be reinforced."

The walls were not bomb-proof, however. So far, the would-be assassin hadn't attempted it. This time the gunnery emplacements had kept him at bay.

"I'll make some tea," said Olga. "If you'll stay for a cup?"

"Yes, all right," I said.

As Olga disappeared into the kitchen, there was a knock at the front door. I went and answered it. It was Bentley with Audrey beside him.

"Angus," he said. "Is everything all right?"

"Yes, sir. Why don't you come in? Olga has just offered us tea."

"Don't mind if we do," said Bentley.

While tea was in preparation, Bentley went through his pipe routine. I told him what had transpired.

"Hmm," he said at length. "So, either this *is* the Ace Raider, or it's someone imitating their *modus operandi*."

"Yes, that's the thought I had too," I admitted.

"Whichever way it is, they are a confounded nuisance."

Olga brought in a tray with tea and fruit cake. She proceeded to serve it to each of us.

"Very nice," said Bentley, trying his slice of cake. "Been a while since I've had a decent fruit cake."

"I made it myself," said Olga with a smile.

"Ah, yes. I had forgotten you were a chef last time you were here. I imagine you spies can turn your hand to anything."

"It goes with the job."

"If there's anything else you need, then let me know," said Bentley.

"Some reinforcement for the bedroom walls might be helpful," Olga told him.

"For protection?"

Olga nodded.

"Right, I'll get someone onto it tomorrow. In the meantime, the gun battery should do the trick. We'll have some pursuit planes on standby soon too."

A thought occurred to me about the would-be assassin, and I voiced it. There seemed little point in hiding these conversations from Maria. She was, after all, the target.

"If it is the Germans behind this," I said, "then I would have expected a more robust attack than just one plane. Surely, they would send a flight of bombers, or similar?"

Bentley puffed on his pipe for a moment before answering.

"Yes, I see your point. It also doesn't make much sense to attack using an American-built plane, as opposed to the Focke-Wulf the Ace Raider normally flies. We are very much aware of the German's position on Maria here, so subterfuge seems unnecessary."

"Yes, sir," I agreed.

"Perhaps someone is trying very hard to put us off the scent?" he continued. "The question is, who?"

"No doubt these planes have quite a range, sir," I said. "So, on that score, it could have come from outside of Britain, or within."

"Flying under the radar, so not easy to spot either."

"No."

Bentley sighed.

"Given this was the second attack, I've no doubt there will be another. We just have to remain vigilant," he said.

"Yes, sir."

He finished his tea and stood up. Audrey did too.

"No point in speculating any more tonight. I must be off; I'm glad it's all right and tight."

After they had left, Angelica and I had another slice of cake and some more tea, at Olga's behest. Angelica broached another issue which had been on her mind.

"Maria," said Angelica. "We've been thinking. You should probably dress down a little. If you're out on the base you would be less easy to spot."

"It's a good idea," said Olga. "I will see to it that Maria starts wearing an RAF uniform, that way she will blend in."

"Yes, exactly," said Angelica.

We took our leave and walked arm in arm to the jeep, where Gordon was waiting, enjoying a quiet cigarette.

"Ready to go, sir?" he asked.

"Yes, let's go back to Amberly," I told him as we climbed in.

"Was that another attack, sir, by the would-be assassin?" Gordon asked me as he drove.

"It was indeed," I said, and told him about the Ace of Spades painted on the wings.

"I see," said Gordon, looking pensive.

"Any thoughts, apropos what we discussed earlier?"

"My thoughts are, sir, that given the likely psychology of the man, he's unlikely to have resorted to subterfuge. No, if he was the person carrying out these attacks he'd do it in the Focke-Wulf, just like before. He's trying to make something of a statement by his actions. Playing the hero, or whatever it is that's compelling his actions."

I pondered this for a moment.

"Do you think he's compelled? I mean, isn't he just fighting the war like the rest of us?"

"I think it's more than that. It seems to be more like a game to him. Also, how is this would-be assassin getting their information?"

"The Marx Brothers are looking into that," I said. "The Ace Raider business is most likely common knowledge by now."

"That's true, of course," he acknowledged. "I'll keep my ear to the ground, shall I?"

"By all means, Fred, thank you."

We relapsed into silence and soon we were bowling up the driveway to Amberly Manor.

"Thank God," said Angelica. "I'm glad to be home."

I couldn't help but agree. I was looking forward to a hot meal and relaxing in Angelica's company. At least for one evening, we could put our problems aside.

CHAPTER EIGHT

The following day I arrived at the M Flight dispersal hut with Angelica to be greeted by Dylan. He seemed quite excited.

"Scottish, look," he said, holding something out for me to see.

I took the object and examined it. It was a playing card depicting the Ace of Spades tied to a stone. It was very similar to the others we'd found. The would-be assassin had no doubt thrown it out of the plane. However, following yesterday's conversations, I was no longer convinced of the veracity of the origin of this particular calling card.

"It's the Ace Raider's — he's been here," said Dylan. "That was him last night, wasn't it?"

"It might be, and it might not," I said to Dylan.

"But, Scottish, I heard that the plane had the Ace of Spades painted on the wings. It's surely got to be him," he persisted.

"Pah!" said Tomas, who had joined the conversation. "Just because something looks obvious, doesn't mean it is."

Dylan regarded him with a puzzled expression. Tomas took the stone from me and turned it over in his hand. Then he held it up in front of him.

"This looks like the Ace Raider's stone, yes?" he said.

"Well, yes, it's obvious that's what it is," said Dylan.

"You've seen a magician, no? Making magic?" Tomas continued.

"Well, yes..."

"That was obvious too, the magic trick? Except that it was just a trick. You understand what I'm saying?"

I half expected Tomas to make the stone disappear, but conjuring tricks were not in his repertoire.

"So, you're saying that was not the Ace Raider?" said Dylan.

"I'm saying," said Tomas, "that someone wants us to believe something, perhaps. Just like the magician."

"Oh!" Dylan finally cottoned on. "Then it might have been someone pretending to be the Ace Raider, yes?"

I was pleased with Tomas' intervention. Not much got past him. However, I decided to say something to the flight as a whole.

"All right everyone," I said. "Listen up."

The hut fell silent, which I still found rather remarkable since I wasn't really one to particularly exercise my privilege of rank.

"I don't want it going outside of this hut that we suspect the would-be assassin in the P-40 isn't the Ace Raider, understood? So, for the moment, as far as anyone outside of M Flight knows, we think it is. I hope that makes sense?"

There was general laughter at this since what I had just said did seem rather convoluted.

"A sort of a double bluff, Scottish, is that what you mean?" asked Dylan.

"Yes, something like that," I agreed.

"So, Skipper," said Jonty, joining in, "we've got the Ace Raider and now we've got the Ace Assassin, who might or might not be the same person."

"Oh Jonty," said Angelica. Her eyes twinkled mischievously. "I hope you're not going to make up another ballad..."

"No he's damn well not!" Willie fired up at once.

"I jolly well might. It's a rather spiffing notion," Jonty protested.

"No, it bloody well isn't!" said Willie.

"Here we go again," groaned Arjun.

I grabbed Angelica's hand and we rapidly exited the hut. I didn't want to hang around for another of Willie and Jonty's squabbles.

"Let's leave them to it," I said. "I don't have a sortie until later. Tomas is taking the first one up."

"Shall we go and get some tea in the mess?" Angelica asked.

"Why not? I could use a cuppa."

After we'd spent a pleasant half hour in the mess, I suggested we might check on Maria. With that in mind, we wended our way towards her house.

As we approached, the sergeant at the ack-ack battery saluted me.

"One of the ladies is round the back of the house, in case you were after her, sir," he informed me helpfully.

"Around the back of the house?" I said, surprised.

"Yes, sir, with a gentleman. I mean a pilot officer, sir … the Kiwi chap."

"Thank you, Sergeant," I said, as we moved away from the gun battery.

As we made our way around the side of the house, I heard the sound of raised voices. It was Willie and Olga. It sounded very much as if they were having a quarrel.

"So, you won't marry me, is that what you're saying?" said Willie.

"I didn't say I won't, I just said that I can't marry you *yet*."

Olga was speaking a little more softly, perhaps trying to placate him.

"You mean you won't, that's what you mean isn't it?"

Willie obviously wasn't in the least mollified.

"No, darling, I just said that I cannot marry you now, not until after the war," said Olga.

"And when will that be? When is the bloody war going to end?" Willie shot back.

"I don't know, nobody knows."

"Exactly! So, it doesn't make any sense."

"Maybe not to you, but it does to me."

I glanced at Angelica, unsure whether we should intervene. She shook her head, and we stayed put.

"I love you. Doesn't that count for anything?" Willie said hotly, evidently trying a different tack.

"Of course it does, and I love you too. I've told you many times."

Olga's tone was earnest, but I could hear the frustration in her voice. Willie was evidently deeply in love with Olga and unwilling to be thwarted. I was certain Olga felt the same, but no doubt the exigencies of her duties weighed heavily upon her.

"Do you? Well, you've a bloody fine way of showing it!" Willie shot back at her.

"Oh, you are impossible. I've explained it to you before. Because of what I do and what you do, I just … can't."

I wondered where this argument was going to lead. Unfortunately, the next moment things took a turn for the worse.

"Is it that, or is it … because there's somebody else?" Willie demanded suddenly.

"What?"

From my own, admittedly often inexpert, handling of relationships, I knew this was probably not a wise thing to say.

"Is there somebody else?"

Olga finally, and unsurprisingly, lost her cool at this accusation.

"Oh, you are stupid, you are so stupid. You don't understand anything. There isn't anyone else, just you. And now you're making me cry."

I heard Olga half choke on a sob. Angelica squeezed my hand. I knew her impulse would be to go to Olga, but we couldn't get in the middle of it. It didn't seem right. We'd also have to admit that we were eavesdropping on their conversation.

"I'm sorry, I didn't mean…" Willie was contrite at once.

"No, you didn't mean. Well, this is what *I* mean. I don't want to speak to you just now. Go away!" Olga shouted.

"Wait, no… I'm not going, I said I'm sorry, Olga, can't we just…"

"Then I will go, damn you!"

"Olga. Olga, wait!" Willie called out.

A moment later we heard the door to the back of the house slam shut. I assumed Willie had been left standing alone.

"Should we go to him? See if he's all right?" Angelica whispered.

"Perhaps not just at the moment," I whispered back.

One thing I knew about Willie, he was quite a private sort of man. He wouldn't want to feel embarrassed by us knowing what had happened. Hopefully, he'd be sensible enough to leave and lick his wounds, then come back to fight another day.

A little sheepishly, we hurried away before either Willie or Olga saw us. We didn't speak until we were some distance from the house.

"Perhaps getting them back together wasn't such a good idea after all," Angelica mused.

"Oh, I don't know," I said. "We managed to get through *our* ups and downs."

"We were never as bad as that though," Angelica persisted.

"Well, now you come to mention it…" I teased.

"Oh, you're perfectly beastly!" she said crossly.

I stopped at once and caught her in my arms.

"And you are perfectly beautiful."

"Really?" Her lips curved into that smile I knew so well. "Then show me."

Neither the Ace Raider nor the would-be assassin were seen for a few days. We continued with the sorties and didn't encounter any bandits, let alone the Ace Raider.

"Do you think, the gun battery scared off the Ace Assassin?" Angelica asked me as we sat on our bench. We had started using the nickname Jonty had assigned the raider.

"I doubt it," I replied. "I imagine he's just biding his time."

"Lulling us into a false sense of security?"

"He might think that, but the gun battery seems to be very vigilant."

"No doubt he'll attack when we least expect it."

I turned my head just then, as I heard a distant thrum. I relaxed when I recognised the sound of a Merlin engine. Two Spitfires were approaching the airfield at a steady pace.

"Those must be the standby planes," I said. "Come on, let's go and meet them."

We walked back to the edge of the runway. The Spitfires landed and taxied to a stop a few yards away. They were painted black and had the night fighter flare screens in place. These would prevent the exhaust flares from blinding the pilot at night. We had used them on one of our missions and they had been very effective.

Bentley strode across with Audrey as we watched the two Air Transport Auxiliary crew get out of the cockpits. Now that women pilots were delivering planes with great regularity all over the country, their arrival had ceased to attract much interest. Redwood went over to them and effected the handover. His team would be looking after the new planes.

"Jolly good," said Bentley, puffing on his pipe. "Now those planes are finally here you can set up the rota, Angus."

"What about the pilots we were promised, sir?" I asked him, since they were not yet in evidence.

"Pencil them in, but in the meantime fill in with the others, all right? I want round the clock protection for Mrs Smith."

In true Bentley fashion, he brandished his pipe and waved it around for emphasis.

"All right, sir, I'll get it sorted," I said.

"Splendid," he said.

He seemed to be in a rather benign mood, so I took the opportunity to ask another question.

"Have MI6 made any progress on how the Ace Assassin is getting their information, sir?"

This was a dangerous gambit since any mention of the Marx Brothers could set the CO off.

"What, those blasted popinjays? Chance would be a fine thing. Haven't heard hide nor hair of them," he said, without losing his good humour.

"Perhaps I should enquire…" I began, but he cut me short with a wave of his pipe.

"The last thing we need is those two clowns coming up here unless it's absolutely bloody necessary. We've got everything under control for the moment, I'd say, so let's just hang fire … unless of course, they contact us."

"Yes, sir."

He puffed ruminatively on his pipe for a moment and then decided he'd seen enough.

"Right, well, I'll leave you to it, Angus. Got things to do and all that."

He gave me a perfunctory salute and left with Audrey beside him.

"Come on," said Angelica. "Let's go and introduce ourselves to those pilots."

Susan Bell was tall with blonde hair, while Linda Harris had red hair and was the shorter of the two. They were both Second Officers in the Air Transport Auxiliary. Their uniforms were a darker shade of blue than the RAF ones but just as smart. We offered to take them to lunch at the mess, something they were more than happy to accept.

"We don't always get such hospitality," said Susan as we sat down to eat.

"Oh?"

I was surprised to hear it, considering they were providing a vital service to the war effort.

"Not everyone thinks women should be flying planes," Linda added.

Angelica gasped in annoyance.

"It's true," said Susan. "Some think it's an exclusively male preserve."

I didn't hold with such views and considered them somewhat outdated. The prevailing attitude of society was that the roles of men and women were subject to certain expectations; however, the war had changed all that. The war had proven that women were perfectly capable of doing jobs which many once considered traditionally male occupations.

"You'll find us a bit different here," I told her. "We are the Mavericks, after all."

"So I'd heard," said Susan, laughing. "What have you all done that's so ... maverick?"

"Well, everyone is here for a different reason," I said. "It started out as a squadron where those who didn't fit the mould were sent. Some of us have blotted our copybooks in other ways…" I trailed off.

Neither of the women could have failed to notice the glance which Angelica shot me. She knew all about my chequered past. She had read my file.

"Mavericks by name, and mavericks by nature," Angelica said.

Linda changed the subject adroitly.

"This is a rather spiffing mess," she said. "The food is excellent."

"It's augmented somewhat by our compatriots next door, the Americans," Angelica replied.

"Well, this is delicious," said Linda, biting into a hamburger. "I must try one of these more often."

"What's it like in combat?" Susan asked me suddenly.

This was not an easy question to answer. Combat was such a jumble of high-speed actions and reactions.

"It's a few moments of adrenaline that seem to go on forever," I said. "Kill or be killed. You don't have time to think; you're just trying to shoot the other fellow down before he shoots you."

"And I sit on the comms worrying if he's going to come back or not," Angelica added with a light laugh.

"You're lucky you can be together," said Linda.

It was true. Bentley allowed us a lot of license, as long as we got the job done.

"I wish I was in a combat unit," said Susan.

I stared at her in surprise.

"Really?"

"Yes, why not? I detest the Nazis as much as anyone. Just because I'm a woman doesn't mean I can't pull a trigger as well as any man."

"Well, perhaps you should join the Secret Service," I suggested. "I'm sure there's plenty of chances to kill Nazis there."

Susan shook her head.

"No, I like flying too much. I want to fly, like you … against the enemy."

I didn't know what to say. It seemed unlikely the War Office would allow it.

"You fly a lot of different planes, by all accounts," I said, moving the topic to something less contentious.

"Yes, we do. I like the Spitfire, but my favourite is the Mosquito."

We talked about planes for the remainder of lunch. The time passed pleasantly enough. Their transport came to pick them up and we watched them fly off.

"Do you think Susan has a chance of ever getting her wish?" Angelica wondered.

"I think it's highly unlikely," I replied.

"That's a shame."

"Why? Would you join up if there was a female combat unit?" I asked her.

"And leave you alone to your own devices? Not a chance," she said at once.

I set up the rota, with two pilots working in three eight-hour shifts. The two black Spitfires were kept in readiness at all times. All of M Flight were on the rota, including the two new pilots who arrived shortly after the planes. The maintenance crew were on standby too. Redwood wasn't concerned when I made the request because he often slept in the hangar in any case.

Pilot Officer Harold Jackson and Pilot Officer Stanley Turner joined the squadron. They were of a similar age, in their early twenties. Harold was quite stocky, with black hair and a moustache. Stanley was tall and thin, with blond hair. They seemed amiable enough and had come from another squadron. I didn't ask why they'd been sent to the Mavericks. I assumed they were either *persona non grata* or that they had been sent to make up the numbers. I only cared that they had some experience.

Not long after their arrival, I was on the evening shift with Harold. Angelica had remained on the base until my shift ended, and she kept us company. The conversation turned to the Mavericks squadron.

"You've been with the Mavericks a while, haven't you, Scottish?" said Harold.

"Since before the Battle of Britain," I replied.

"We heard about your squadron where I was last posted," said Harold.

"Oh, and what did you hear?"

I didn't really know what our reputation was as regards other squadrons in the Air Force.

"I heard you were a pretty good squadron in combat, but an unruly bunch otherwise."

Angelica laughed at this. "Sounds accurate," she said.

"When I was offered the chance to join your squadron, I took it. You sound like my kind of people," said Harold.

"Oh, oh right," I said, surprised to hear that someone would willingly volunteer for the Mavericks. Perhaps we weren't the Air Force pariahs I assumed we were after all.

Just then, before any of us could say anything else, I heard a telltale sound.

"Do you hear that?" I said to Harold.

"Hear what?" He looked at me blankly.

"It's a plane, coming our way."

The sound was getting louder.

"I can hear it too," said Angelica.

We quickly went outside. The sky was dark but with a bright moon. In the distance, I could just make out the shape of a plane approaching the airfield.

"Do you see it?" I said, pointing.

Harold squinted in the direction I indicated.

"Oh, yes, now I do," he said.

The plane was getting closer by the second. The hum sounded very much like the P-40. I wasn't going to wait around to find out.

"Let's scramble," I said. "Come on."

"Take care," said Angelica.

I turned and dropped a swift kiss on her lips before heading for the planes.

"Techie!" I shouted. "Techie, we're scrambling. Incoming bandit, look sharp!"

Redwood came pelting out of the darkness with another mechanic. They arrived at the planes at the same time as I did.

I jumped up onto the wing of my Spitfire, then Redwood helped me strap in.

"Good luck, sir," he said. "Hope you get him."

I gave him the thumbs up and checked Harold had got into his kite okay. We spun up the props and taxied out onto the runway. They had been placed in such a position that we could be on the runway in seconds.

"All right, Hunter Two, let's go," I said over the radio to Harold. I had chosen the codename to differentiate the two standby pilots from the rest of the flight.

"Roger that, Hunter One," he replied.

"Control, we're airborne," I said as we left the ground. "Suspected bandit."

"Roger," said the control tower.

Once in the air, the fields fanned out below us, bathed in moonlight. The incoming plane was a few hundred yards off the perimeter fence.

"The bandit is at your eight o'clock, Control, approaching fast, we're moving to intercept," I said.

"Roger, searchlights on standby," said Control.

I decided to get closer in order to make a positive identification. I took us up higher and we set a course to meet it. Within moments we were looking down on the plane.

"There! Those are the aces on the wings," said Harold.

The white symbols showed up as clear as day in the moonlight. There was no doubt of the plane's identity.

"Control, it's the Ace Assassin. We're engaging," I said. "Break Hunter Two, break, attack."

We peeled out of our pairing and bore down on the P-40, which seemed oblivious to our presence. I had wanted to be sure of my mark before firing, but a stream of tracers erupted from Harold's plane.

If the bandit had no idea about us before, he certainly did now. With expert reflexes, the pilot made a tight manoeuvre and Harold's salvo passed him by.

"Damn," said Harold. "I thought I had him."

The Ace Assassin had throttled up and was still heading for the airfield.

"Come on, let's get after him," I said to Harold. There was no time to remonstrate with him for firing too early. "Control, the bandit is coming in for an attack, we're giving chase."

"Roger," said Control.

Immediately, the searchlights came on. I hoped to God the ack-ack wouldn't fire at us. We had markings on the underwings but in the heat of the moment, who knew what might happen? No doubt air-raid warnings were sounding on the ground. Angelica would have run to her post on comms to listen in.

I pushed the throttle to maximum and Harold did the same as we screamed after the Ace Assassin. Tracers spewed up into the air from ground machine guns, and puffs of smoke from ack-ack fire as they got him in their sights.

I managed to get within range of the assassin's plane and fired. Tracers went out in a steady stream past his canopy. He banked left to avoid them.

"Keep on him, Hunter One, I am going to try and cut him off," said Harold.

I couldn't see his plane, but assumed he was somewhere to the side of me. I didn't want him to make the same mistake again.

"Hold your fire until you're close enough, Hunter Two," I said.

The assassin had turned away from the airfield. The ack-ack had stopped but the searchlights were trying to keep him illuminated. I stuck on his tail, determined not to let him get away. He weaved left and right. I fired a couple of bursts but missed each time.

"I'm almost there, Hunter One," said Harold.

From the corner of my eye, I saw his plane closing in from the side. I prayed that the assassin had not seen him. I kept up the chase, playing for time. I felt sure Harold could take him down if he managed to get a clear shot.

"I've got him in my sights," said Harold jubilantly.

He fired and the stream of tracers looked to be dead on target. However, the assassin was faster. He banked and rolled, then, unexpectedly, came out of it with Harold's plane now a sitting duck. There was definitely nothing wrong with the assassin's combat skills.

"Hunter Two, watch out!" I shouted, as the assassin opened fire.

Harold was fast, but not quite fast enough.

"I'm hit! He's hit my plane," said Harold.

I closed with the assassin and fired again to try to prevent him from pressing home his attack any further. I missed, but it proved a bridge too far for the assassin. I watched him turn his plane and start to speed away from the airfield.

"Hunter One, get after him, I'll be okay," said Harold. "You can still get him."

I ignored this. I didn't have much chance of getting him now, and my first duty was to my pilot now the assassin had disengaged.

"How badly are you hit?" I asked him.

"I don't know," he said. "I felt something go past my face."

My heart sank. This could mean that he had a superficial or even a more serious injury. Adrenaline would have had an attenuating effect. There was nothing I could do until we got him on the ground.

"He's long gone now. Try to get back down, okay?"

"Okay," said Harold.

"Control, suspected injury to Hunter Two, we may need medical assistance," I said.

"Roger, on its way," said Control.

The runway lights came on to help guide us in. I reduced speed and escorted Harold back to the airfield. Fortunately, he landed on the runway intact, which meant his plane was unlikely to have been seriously damaged. I followed suit. We taxied our kites to a stop and I jumped out, running as fast as I could over to Harold's kite. He was still sitting in the cockpit. I heard the sound of the military ambulance heading towards us.

"Everything all right?" I asked him, as I climbed up onto the wing.

"Yes … no … I don't know."

Redwood appeared beside me. He was carrying a powerful torch.

He shone the torch onto Harold. There was a streak of blood on Harold's cheek. I took the torch from Redwood and shone it onto the canopy. There was a hole on opposite sides of it, such as might be made by a passing bullet.

"You've been hit," I said.

"Have I?" said Harold, surprised. He wiped the back of his hand across his cheek and examined the blood on it. "Well, I'll be, so I have."

"Can you get out of the cockpit?" I asked him.

"Yes, sure."

By the time we had him down from the plane, Angelica was beside us.

"Oh dear," she said to Harold. "Looks like you've been grazed by a bullet."

"Another inch or two and you'd have been a goner," I told him.

The ambulance arrived and the medical team took over.

"What about the rest of the shift?" asked Harold as they took him away.

"I doubt the assassin will be back," I said. "Don't worry, I'll stay until the next crew takes over. Go and get yourself seen to."

"I'll see to the planes," said Redwood. "Unless there's anything else?"

"No, that's all Techie, thank you," I said.

Angelica and I watched the ambulance leave. I put my arm around her and she rested her head on my shoulder.

"Poor Harold," she said.

"Yes," I agreed.

"I'm glad it wasn't you…"

"I am too," I replied. "Let's go and have a cup of tea."

As we wended our way back to the hut, I reflected it could easily have been me. I had been shot before and it wasn't pleasant. Harold had got off lightly all told.

The following morning, Audrey approached as soon as we arrived on the airbase.

"Bentley…" she began.

"Wants to see me?" I finished it for her. "I don't doubt it."

The CO would want a report about the attack. We all walked together to the main building and were soon in front of the door to Bentley's office.

"See you later," I said to Angelica and kissed her.

When she had gone, Audrey opened the door and ushered me in.

Bentley was at his desk. As soon as he saw me, he picked up his pipe and began to scrape out the bowl.

"Take a seat, Angus," he said.

I waited in silence while he tamped in a fresh batch of tobacco and lit it. He puffed away for a few moments, filling the room with clouds of smoke, before speaking.

"I gather that blasted assassin had another go last night," he said, sounding rather disgruntled.

"Yes, sir. We scrambled after him and there was a bit of a skirmish."

I knew he would want to know the details, so I furnished him with a full account. He puffed away on his pipe while I told him.

"Hmm," he said at length. "Shame the blighter got away yet again, though it proves the necessity for having the standby pursuit planes. We'll keep those going for the moment and hope we get him the next time."

"Yes, sir," I said. We both thought it inevitable the assassin would try again.

Bentley sighed. There was evidently something else on his mind.

"I'm going to have to call those blasted clowns, tell them the latest news," he said finally.

I knew at once he meant the Marx Brothers. They needed to know we were still being attacked, and we had to find out if they had discovered anything about how the Ace Assassin had obtained their information.

"Might it be better if they moved Maria to a different location?" I suggested.

"No, it might bloody well not," said Bentley hotly. "I'm not having it suggested we cannot carry out the duties we've been given. I am damned if I will give the detractors of the Mavericks in Fighter Command something to complain about."

I had not realised we had detractors, or rather, I hadn't thought about it. We were, for the most part, preoccupied with fighting the war. Bentley kept the political shenanigans away from us. I must have looked surprised.

"Oh, you don't think we've got people who'd rather see this squadron disbanded?" said Bentley, continuing his theme.

"Well, I…"

Bentley leapt from his seat and started to pace the room in an agitated fashion. This was a sign that he was exceptionally annoyed.

"Believe me when I tell you that none of them expected us to do quite such a damn fine job," he continued, building up a head of steam. "So now, yes, we do have some who might prefer it if our pilots went to other squadrons after all. The bloody cheek of it. After treating us like bloody pariahs, now they want their pound of flesh. Well, no! They're not getting it!"

I waited for his wrath to subside, as I knew it would. Bentley puffed on his pipe for all it was worth, before sitting down again. He was calmer when he spoke again.

"I've worked hard for this, Angus, for all of us. You might not believe it, but we have a damn fearsome reputation. So, I'm not giving those dissenting voices an opportunity to raise any of their Johnnie Windbag objections. No, we are going to make sure that Maria — Mrs Smith — stays safe no matter what. *And* we are going to catch that bloody Ace Raider too. That would certainly shut those brass-hatted idiots up once and for all."

"I have some thoughts about a trap, sir, to catch the Ace Raider," I said, feeling this might be the time to bring it up.

"Go on," he said, leaning back in his chair and continuing to smoke his pipe.

I furnished him with the outline of our idea while he listened patiently.

"I see," he said when I'd finished. "And you actually think Churchill is going to play ball with this, do you? Come to your fete or whatever it is you're planning?"

"Well, sir, there's no harm in asking," I replied, though I hadn't much faith the Prime Minister would come either.

"Well, the plan itself sounds reasonable," said Bentley. "I'll be interested to hear the details once you've fleshed them out."

"Yes, sir."

"Very good, Angus, very good." He paused for a moment. "You will, naturally, keep my other … erm … comments to yourself…"

I knew he meant the contents of his tirade, and there was nobody apart from Angelica I would tell in any case. Audrey had no doubt heard it all before.

"Absolutely, sir," I said.

"Good, good. Well, carry on … and get that canopy mended," he added. "I assume Pilot Officer Jackson will be fit to continue flying?"

"I imagine he will, sir, yes. I'm sure Redwood is working on the canopy," I assured him.

"Excellent," he said. He turned his attention to the paperwork on his desk and I took it as a signal to leave.

Angelica waylaid me as I left Bentley's office and accompanied me to our bench.

"Were you hiding around the corner waiting?" I teased as she tucked her arm into mine.

"That would be telling."

I laughed. I couldn't imagine she'd do such a thing, but her timing was otherwise impeccable. We sat on the bench and she held my hand while I told her what Bentley had said.

"I wonder who these *detractors* are," she said.

"I've no idea, but they've got Bentley's goat that's for certain."

"Anyway," she said with determination, "it's not going to happen. They are not going to disband our squadron because you are going to save the day."

"I am?"

"Yes," she said. "You always do."

CHAPTER NINE

The following day I took my patrol up on another sortie. We were still running two or three patrols a day, partly looking for the Ace Raider but also to deter other Tip and Run bandits. Incursions were continuing, and we could not be there all the time to prevent them. However, our continued presence was hopefully some sort of a deterrent.

Harold was back on duty having sustained a graze from a bullet. Due to the demands of the standby pilot rota, I had to arrange the rest of M Flight into two six-plane patrols, using all of our pilots in turn. This meant that some pilots were now on different patrols each day. Angelica, who had a knack for organisation, was very helpful in setting up the rotas.

She certainly kept our quarters at Amberly shipshape and orderly. In fact, she was so skilful at doing it that I was hardly aware of it.

"And now that we're married, I'm busy organising you," she said with a smile.

"Isn't that what you've been doing all along?" I quipped.

"Oh yes, it's just taken you this long to realise it."

Her assistance was a godsend and I was heartily grateful for it. The administrative duties of my rank and position were not my favourite part of the job. No wonder Bentley had an adjutant. Judging by the piles of paper strewn on his desk, it was something of a nightmare. Besides which, Angelica could type extremely fast, and I was absolutely useless on a typewriter, never having learned how to type.

In this particular patrol were Jonty, Willie, Harold, Stanley and Dylan. It was the second patrol of the day and Angelica came to see me off, as usual.

"Fly safely," she said, kissing me softly.

"I will," I replied, pulling her tighter into my embrace.

"I love you," she whispered.

"I love you too."

I walked to my kite along with the others. I climbed onto the wing and Redwood strapped me in. Angelica waved as I spun up the prop and taxied onto the runway.

"Red Leader, you're clear to take off," said the control tower.

"Let's go Red Patrol," I said.

We throttled up and took off, forming up before heading for the east coast. I had decided to head south towards Cromer. It didn't do to be predictable as far as Jerry was concerned.

The sky was overcast, meaning visibility was poor and that the Germans had plenty of cloud cover were they to approach from altitude.

We reached Cromer without incident and turned south to follow the coastline. Below us were cultivated fields and the beach stretched practically all the way down the east coast. The sea was a calm grey-blue.

We soon approached Winterton-on-Sea. It was a small town with a fair few coastal defences, heathland and dunes. I couldn't imagine the Ace Raider choosing the town as a target. However, I was to be proved wrong almost as soon as I had the thought.

"Ace Raider, ten o'clock low," said Dylan, who spotted him first.

Sure enough, there was the all-too-familiar Focke-Wulf with the Ace of Spades symbols some way out to sea and streaking towards the shoreline. We were quite a distance from it and quite high up. He was unlikely to have seen us.

"Stay in formation," I told my flight. "Let's get a bit closer."

I knew that tackling the raider too early would simply mean he'd cut and run.

"Can't we get after him, Skipper?" complained Jonty.

He was obviously chafing to get into action. Based on previous encounters, I wanted to be more circumspect.

"Listen to Scottish," said Willie. "He knows what he's doing."

"I just don't want the blasted raider to get away again," said Jonty.

"Stay on course until I say we can break," I instructed the flight.

Thankfully, Jonty subsided without further argument. We closed in on the town from the north as the raider came in from the east. When I decided he'd come far enough, I gave the order.

"Break, break, let's intercept."

We peeled off at full throttle. I was optimistic that we might have a chance at him this time. However, this optimism was to prove misplaced.

Suddenly, a flak battery opened up from the coastal defences. I was rather non-plussed to see that it was aimed in our direction.

"They're firing at us!" shouted Harold.

"What the hell is wrong with them?" said Stanley. "We're British you idiots!"

Puffs of smoke filled the air and tracers streamed out from a machine-gun emplacement. There was only one thing for it.

"Take evasive action," I said.

"Shoot at the bloody Jerry not us!" Dylan shouted in frustration.

The flak was now bursting all around us. We were forced to bank away and climb higher to try and get out of range. I cursed inwardly as I narrowly avoided an explosion.

"That damned Ace Raider is still on the attack," said Harold, suddenly.

I had been too preoccupied to notice, but sure enough, the Ace Raider was continuing with his course of action undeterred. He probably couldn't be happier for the distraction, since the gunfire wasn't aimed at him.

Now we were torn between the devil and the deep blue sea. We could either go after him and risk getting shot at, or leave him to cause mayhem. I hesitated, but then the decision was taken out of my hands.

"I'm going after him, Skipper. He's not getting away," said Jonty impetuously.

Before I could say anything, he had dived back down in typical neck or nothing Jonty fashion. Inspired by his bravado, Harold followed suit. There was no point in ordering Jonty back, I knew he wouldn't obey it.

"Be careful, Jonty," I said. "The rest of us will stay out of it."

It didn't need for all of us to get shot up. God knows what Bentley would have to say in any case if one of them got shot down. I dreaded to think.

We circled around while the flak continued to fly. Jonty and Harold were heading towards the Ace Raider at high speed. The ground defences were still firing, having not yet twigged we weren't the enemy. Jonty, being the more experienced pilot, was weaving through the flak unscathed. Unfortunately, Harold wasn't quite so quick.

It appeared as though the Ace Raider would break through and attack the town as he finally crossed the shoreline. Then, miraculously, one of the machine-gunners must have spotted him and opened fire. Tracers streamed out in his direction, and he banked away sharply.

Jonty, however, was still closing in on him.

"Take that you blasted Ace Raider!" said Jonty, firing a salvo in the German's direction. I judged him to be too far away, but given the circumstances, it was better to put the Jerry off his attack.

The Ace Raider must have finally clocked he was also under fire from the air. He turned his craft tightly and headed out to sea.

Jonty looked like he was about to follow him when there was a cry from Harold.

"I'm hit. My plane's been hit by bloody flak," he said.

"Oh blast," said Jonty, turning back at once. He would never leave a fellow pilot in trouble.

"Stay calm, Harold," I said, as Harold's plane started to buck and weave about.

Jonty rapidly came alongside him to check the damage.

"It's all right, old chap, it's just a chunk out of your wing," he said.

"What!" yelled Harold in alarm.

"I'd like to go and strafe those bloody fools down there," said Dylan angrily.

"But you won't," I told him.

The flak barrage stopped as suddenly as it had started, suggesting that the ground forces had finally realised who they were shooting at.

"How did it take them so long to recognise our planes?" said Stanley.

I didn't have an answer and I was sure when Bentley found out he wasn't going to be pleased.

"You can still fly, just get yourself level," Jonty was telling Harold.

"I'm trying," said Harold, wrestling with his plane.

After a tense few moments he managed to regain control, and his Spitfire finally levelled off. Now that I knew he was not about to ditch his kite, I decided we'd better go before anything else happened.

"Form up around Harold, Red Patrol," I said. "Let's escort him home."

I set a course for Banley. The flight took up a diamond formation with Harold in the middle.

"Just keep the throttle and your kite on an even keel. Take it gently," Jonty advised him. "We'll get you home."

"But what about when I get there? How am I going to land it?" said Harold anxiously.

"It'll land all right, don't worry about that. Just take it easy and coast it in," said Willie.

It was sage advice. Willie had talked me down once when I'd run out of fuel. He had been flying from a young age and was an expert at handling his Spitfire.

Not long afterwards, Banley Airfield appeared on the horizon.

"Control," I said as we flew closer. "This is Red Patrol bringing in a damaged Spitfire."

"Roger," said the tower. "Tenders will be on standby."

I wasn't expecting anything untoward, but it was as well to be prepared.

As we readied for our final approach, I said, "Let Harold land first, we'll go in after him."

We opened up the formation and let the young pilot officer take the lead.

"Easy does it now," said Willie, following him in.

He continued to guide Harold with calm assurance until finally, Harold landed his plane without incident. The fire tenders rushed forward, but I doubted they'd be needed after all.

Soon we were all down on the ground and we taxied to the standings. As I jumped down from my kite, I could see Bentley hurrying towards us. Angelica got to me first and planted a swift kiss on my lips.

"Thank God you're safe," she said quietly.

"Wait for the fireworks," I said, "when Bentley sees Harold's plane."

We went over to inspect it and sure enough, the wing had a very large chunk taken out of it.

"Damn lucky it didn't sheer off," said Arjun, who had come out with the rest of M Flight to see the damage. Word had obviously spread fast.

"This would soon have been a different story," said Tomas. "With a bad ending."

By this time Bentley had arrived and was staring up at the shredded wing. He said nothing and instead took out his pipe. Then he methodically emptied it, scraped it out, filled it and lit it. After he had taken a few puffs, he evidently felt in a frame of mind to tackle the matter at hand.

"So," he said, pointing the stem of his pipe up at the offending wing. "How did this happen?"

"Sir, we spotted the Ace Raider coming in from the Channel to attack Winterton-on-Sea," I explained. "As we broke formation to engage him, the ack-ack battery opened fire on us."

Bentley's right eye suddenly developed something of a tick.

"They did what?" he said in a deceptively calm voice. I wasn't fooled in the slightest. An eruption was imminent, of that I was certain.

"They opened fire on our patrol —" I got no further.

"What?" he roared. "What the bloody hell are these people playing at? I'll have their guts for garters!"

Bentley started to puff on his pipe at an alarming rate, all the while looking as if he might actually explode.

"Right," he said. "Angus, come with me. The rest of you can stop gawking at the bloody plane and get on with something useful. If one of you can take some photographs of the damage, I'd be much obliged."

He strode away at a terrific rate with Audrey running to keep up. I went after him, and Angelica tagged along, unwilling to miss whatever unfolded. By the time we arrived at Bentley's office, Audrey was in the act of handing him the phone.

"Winterton-on-Sea coastal defences for you, sir," she said.

Bentley snatched the phone from her hand, still smouldering with anger.

"This is Squadron Leader Bentley from Squadron 696, I want to speak to your commanding officer," he told the person at the other end. There was a short pause and then Bentley barked, "No, I can't bloody well call back! Get him on the phone now!"

There was another pause and then Bentley erupted.

"Get your bloody commanding officer on the bloody phone now, or do I have to bloody well come down there and get him myself?" he roared.

This seemed to do the trick. Bentley handed the phone back to Audrey while he went through his pipe routine. He had just relit it when Audrey offered him the phone once more.

"Are you the commanding officer of those bloody charlatans on the coastal defences?" Bentley demanded without preamble. "I'm Squadron Leader Bentley from Squadron 696, the planes your bloody clowns nearly shot down earlier today!"

There was another pause while he listened to the CO on the other end of the line.

"A mistake? Is that what you call it? A mistake? What kind of dog and pony show are you running up there? Don't your people know a bloody Spitfire when they see one, for God's sake?"

He puffed on his pipe as he listened once more.

"Well, I've got a Spitfire here with a shredded wing no thanks to the trigger-happy cowboys on your ack-ack gun crew. I'm lucky not to have a dead pilot!"

The CO on the other end seemed to have more to say to this.

"You're sorry about it? I should bloody well hope so. You can put that in your letter to the next British pilot's family you bloody nincompoops shoot down. We're trying to defend the coast here and what are you doing? ... oh defending it too? Well, you've got a bloody fine way of showing it... Yes, well, see that it bloody well doesn't happen again... Good day to you too!"

Bentley slammed the phone back down onto the receiver with some violence.

"Bloody jumped-up arrogant popinjay of a Johnnie Windbag! Tell his colonel, will he? I'll bloody well tell his bloody colonel. Absolute bloody clowns the lot of them!"

The CO sat down heavily, his anger spent. He indicated that Angelica and I should take a seat. He set down his pipe carefully on his desk.

"Unbelievable," he said. "I don't know what kind of training they are giving these idiots but it's not good enough. I'm damn well reporting this to Fighter Command. What an absolute bloody shower."

He sighed and took up his pipe up again.

"Anyway, get Redwood onto the repairs if he hasn't started already," he said to me.

"Yes, sir," I replied. "I am sure he will have sorted it in no time."

"Indeed, but it was unnecessary, entirely and bloody well unnecessary."

I felt it incumbent upon me to mention that the Ace Raider had once more escaped.

"Needless to say, sir, the Ace Raider managed to evade us," I said.

"Yes, no doubt. I expect he was cock-a-hoop to see your own forces firing on you. Let him go back and report that to his Jerry commanders. No doubt they'll have a good laugh at our expense. Toast our stupidity with some blasted Schnapps … yes indeed," he said in acid tones. "Meanwhile that jumped-up Johnnie on the coast is no doubt complaining to his colonel that I swore at him a few times … not that he didn't deserve it."

He chuckled at the recollection and the tension eased.

"Oh well," he said. "That's that. I'll be telling Fighter Command what I think of Winterton-on-Sea's defences in no uncertain terms, you can be sure. In the meantime, carry on. Oh, and those bloody MI6 Johnnies will be here at some point no doubt. You can talk to them in the first instance. I've had enough of idiots for one day."

"Will that be all, sir?" I asked him.

"Yes, that's all," he said, turning his attention to Audrey. "Take a memo, Audrey, to Fighter Command…"

The sound of typing faded as we closed Bentley's office door.

"Goodness," said Angelica. "I've never seen the squadron leader quite so annoyed."

"I have," I said ruefully. "So has Jonty."

"Oh, Jonty, he's such a silly boy," she laughed. "Shall we go to the mess and get some tea."

"Why not?"

We found Willie in the mess nursing a cup of tea along with Jonty. Now the combat was over, Willie looked a little down in the mouth.

"What's up, Kiwi?" I asked him as we took a seat at their table.

"Woman trouble," said Jonty succinctly.

Angelica and I glanced at each other. We knew exactly what the trouble was.

"Olga?" said Angelica, prompting him.

"She won't talk to me," said Willie. "I've upset her."

Angelica was sympathetic. She reached out and squeezed his hand. He smiled a little wanly.

"Have you *tried* talking to her?" she enquired.

"Of course I have, but I can't get through the door, she just tells me to go away."

"Perhaps it will blow over soon enough," I said.

We couldn't let on that we knew the reason for their quarrel.

"Chance would be a fine thing," said Willie bitterly. "Anyway, it's all my fault."

"Just be patient," I told him. "She'll come around … eventually."

He sighed somewhat dramatically and didn't answer. Jonty put an arm around his shoulders.

"Cheer up, Kiwi, old chap," he said. "You've still got me."

They were the best of friends, and Jonty didn't like to see Willie so cut up.

"Perhaps you could compose a ballad for him," I suggested a little mendaciously.

"Jolly good idea," Jonty agreed.

It elicited no reaction from Willie, which made me think he must be in a bad way. Normally he would have risen to the bait at once.

"Don't tease him, you can see he's down in the dumps," said Angelica.

"He can do a ballad if he wants, I don't care," said Willie.

"Good Lord!" said Jonty, much struck.

I turned the conversation to the topic of the recent sortie and that at least animated our friend a little more. Soon after we left the mess, I thought about Willie's predicament and resolved to try and help him somehow if we could.

The following day Audrey met us as we arrived at Banley.

"It's either Bentley or the Marx Brothers," said Angelica as her friend walked towards us.

"I'm not taking that bet," I said. "It's too much of a dead cert."

By the time we'd jumped down from the jeep Audrey was standing in front of us.

"The Marx Brothers…" she began.

Angelica shot me a triumphant look.

"Are they in the usual place?" I asked Audrey.

"Yes."

Angelica and I accompanied her to the main building and the room where we always met the two spies. Harpo and Chico were seated almost exactly as we had left them the last time. Their trench coats and hats were on the nearby table. Both were smoking the ubiquitous cigarettes, which seemed to form an endless chain.

"Ah, the Flight Lieutenant *and* the Section Officer, how delightful," said Harpo laconically, without getting up from his seat.

"We come as a pair," quipped Angelica.

"Indeed," said Chico with a lazy smile. "We gather you've been having a few troubles."

This annoyed me immediately since they knew exactly why Bentley had asked them to come. Talking in riddles was their stock in trade.

"Bentley wants to know what progress you've made finding out how Maria's presence here has become known," I said, cutting to the chase.

Harpo took a drag on his cigarette.

"Unfortunately, none," he informed us. "But we do know that it hasn't come from us."

"Then where?" I continued.

He shrugged as if it was of no consequence. I felt Angelica bristling beside me.

"Do you think the source is at Banley?" I asked him, trying not to sound exasperated.

"We're still looking into it," said Chico.

"Meanwhile, we've still got that bloody would-be assassin coming over here trying to kill her," I replied, somewhat heatedly.

"We know and that is naturally regrettable."

"Well perhaps it's regrettable that you brought her here in the first place!" said Angelica, unable to contain herself any longer.

"That also might be the case, but what's done is done," said Chico.

I was glad Bentley wasn't present since he would have exploded with wrath by now. I'd not heard them be quite so intransigent before. In spite of their laid-back attitude, I knew they took their job extremely seriously.

"Look," said Harpo, sensing our irritation, "we understand it's not ideal, and we would like to put another operative on the ground, but currently we haven't one to spare."

"As soon as we do…" Chico trailed off, leaving the rest unsaid.

"I don't have time to look for spies on top of everything else I'm currently doing," I said, thinking perhaps that this was what was being implied.

They didn't answer, but they should have been well aware of my situation. It was true we had successfully caught more than one spy on the base, but with the burden of command came responsibilities I couldn't shirk either.

"Do you think the Germans are carrying out these attacks?" I asked them in an attempt to be reasonable.

"What do you think?" said Chico.

"We're genuinely interested in your opinion," Harpo added, noticing Angelica's infuriated expression.

"I don't think it's the Germans, no. I think it's someone who is aware of the Ace Raider's mode of operation and is trying to make us think it is," I told him.

"Yes, we tend to concur," said Harpo, taking another drag on his cigarette. "And what makes you so sure?"

"I'm not sure," I replied. "But I don't see why the Germans would attack us in an American plane when they could use a Focke-Wulf. It seems like a pointless subterfuge. I also think they would probably attempt a much heavier bombing mission than just one plane in order to be sure to try and get Maria. Also, where on earth would they have got the P-40 plane from anyway?"

"All excellent points," Chico said.

"Yes, he's very good," Harpo added.

I ignored this, as I had become inured to their way of speaking about me as if I wasn't in the room.

"Are you certain it's not the Americans?" Angelica asked them.

"As certain as we can be," said Harpo. "It's not their style, and they've nothing to gain by killing Maria."

"And everything to lose," said Chico.

"Her husband might be reluctant to continue his work if he felt his wife had not been adequately protected, is that what you mean?" I asked him.

"Something like that, yes."

"So, it could be someone in this country," I said.

"Very possibly," Harpo agreed.

"But you don't know who?"

"No."

We seemed to be going around in circles and it was getting us nowhere.

"All right, well, we will keep protecting Maria, of course," I said.

"Of course."

Harpo smiled.

"As soon as we are able to get someone else on the case here, we will," said Chico, perhaps feeling that more than just a few platitudes were required.

"Then there's the matter of setting a trap for the Ace Raider, which I asked you about last time," I said.

"Yes, we've been thinking about that," said Harpo. "Have you got any further with your plans?"

"I've some ideas, yes, but not a location as yet."

"Do tell," said Chico.

I sketched out how we intended to lure in the Ace Raider and shoot him down. The Marx Brothers listened with interest, finishing a cigarette each and lighting another almost immediately.

"Once we have a date and location," I said, "then perhaps you can put it out via your intelligence networks."

"Yes, we can do that, although I don't think it will be likely that Winston will turn up. He's far too busy and it's too risky," said Chico.

"Oh."

I must admit I was a little disappointed that Churchill couldn't be persuaded. There was evidently a limit to the strings the spies could pull.

"However," said Harpo. "He doesn't need to actually be there, does he? Jerry won't know that, will he?"

"No, I suppose that's true," I said. "I hadn't thought of it that way."

"However, there is one thing we mentioned before and we've decided that it's imperative for this plan," said Chico.

My heart sank and I glanced at Angelica. I was pretty sure they were going to present us with an impossible task once again.

"Yes," he continued. "We definitely need you to capture the Ace Raider, not kill him."

I stared at him.

"You're not serious?" I said.

"Deadly serious, old chap," said Harpo.

"I know you mentioned it before," I replied. "But I told you that it was a tall order, or did you miss that part?"

"No, we didn't, but a man of your calibre, as we said, can find a way."

Harpo shrugged as if it was a simple task. He took another pull on his cigarette and blew the smoke up into the air with a smile. Angelica looked daggers at him.

"He could be very useful to us," said Chico, trying to mollify us. "That's why we need you to capture him as opposed to simply killing him."

"And if he isn't useful?" I challenged him. "What if it's all for no result?"

"Nothing lost."

"Except maybe him when he evades our attempts to capture him," I said.

"I'm sure you will manage perfectly well, you always do," said Harpo.

"I'm obliged to you for your confidence," I said in a tone laced with sarcasm.

It was completely lost on them. As always, they appeared unmoved and maddingly affable as ever.

"Our pleasure," said Chico.

Angelica pursed her lips. A sure sign she was becoming annoyed.

I sighed, there wasn't any point in arguing with these two. There was nothing for it but to capitulate.

"All right, we'll try, but if we can't capture him then we're going to damn well shoot him down," I told him firmly.

"Certainly," said Harpo, without batting an eyelid.

There seemed little more to say.

"Right, we will let you know once we have the full details of the plan worked out," I said, standing up.

"Absolutely, we can't wait to see it," said Chico.

"Until then," I said.

"Toodle-pip," said Harpo.

"Chin-chin," said Chico.

Once we were outside the main building Angelica expressed her frustration.

"Oh God! I could happily do those two a mischief," she said crossly.

"I'm with you there," I said. "They are an exceptionally irritating pair … and now I've got to tell Bentley."

"Oh dear."

"Yes, and I can only imagine what he's going to say."

We didn't have to imagine for very long. We were soon seated in Bentley's office while he engaged upon his usual pipe routine. Having been informed of the purpose of our visit, he embarked upon it at once. The very mention of the Marx Brothers seemed to set him off. I knew his mood was not going to improve once he'd heard what they had told me.

"You've seen those blasted buffoons have you?" he said, puffing on his pipe once more.

"Yes, sir. I thought it best to report to you immediately what transpired," I replied.

"And what did transpire?"

"They have no idea where the assassin is getting their information from, but they insist it's not from their department," I said.

Bentley puffed on his pipe while he absorbed this information.

"That comes as no surprise whatsoever," he said with some acerbity. "I'm amazed they know what day of the week it is. Bloody charlatans."

This was slightly unfair, I felt, even for the Marx Brothers. They were obviously very good at what they did no matter how much it wound the rest of us up. I refrained from saying so, however.

"Well, we'll just have to continue to protect Maria as best we can," he said.

"That's what I told them," I said. "But they will put an operative in here as soon as one becomes available."

"Ha!" Bentley said sarcastically. "Chance would be a bloody fine thing. Anything else?"

I glanced at Angelica apprehensively. We both knew that he wasn't going to be happy about trapping the Ace Raider.

"Go on, spit it out," said Bentley.

"It's about the Ace Raider trap, sir. I want to shoot him down, but they insist that we have to capture him…"

"What?"

"They want us to capture the Ace Raider…"

"What the devil do these people think we're running here?" Bentley jumped up from his seat and started to pace the room. "This is the RAF, not some kind of pest control organisation. This isn't a mouse we're talking about, it's a bloody great Focke-Wulf. How on earth do they think we're supposed to capture an aircraft in full flight on the attack, answer me that! Hmm?"

The CO brandished the stem of his pipe at me as if it was all my fault entirely.

"I'm not quite sure, sir," I said. "But I plan to give it some thought."

"Not quite sure? Of course, you're not quite sure. It's the most ridiculous thing I've heard in all my life, and I've heard a few from those damned MI6 clowns."

Now that he was set against it, I found myself perversely wondering if it could really be done.

"Perhaps we could work something out, sir…" I suggested.

"Really? That's what you think, is it?" he said, returning to his chair. His tone had lost none of its acidity.

"Well, I suppose I might give it a shot first, before discarding it," I told him, inwardly cursing myself for not taking the easy way out. It would be far easier to let Bentley forbid it, which I was certain he was on the brink of doing.

"Hmm?" he said, taking a few puffs on his pipe. This seemed to calm his ire. "All right. If — and only if — you can think of a plausible way of carrying it out, then I may be prepared to sanction it. However, I will want to hear it first."

"Yes, sir."

"Those damned spies will be the death of me," said Bentley. "There seems no end to their bloody shenanigans. Every time we turn around there they are, with some blasted hare-brained scheme. The sooner this war's over and we can see the back of them, the better."

I didn't reply, though I didn't disagree with him.

"Dismissed," he said wearily.

We saluted and left the building. As soon as we did, Angelica confronted me.

"What are you doing, Angus?" she demanded. "Why on earth did you argue in favour of their ridiculous scheme?"

"I don't really know," I replied lamely.

It might have had something to do with never backing down from a challenge. A trait which had resulted in more than one trip to the local doctor in my youth.

"Oh you," she said, affectionately. "What are you like?"

"Hopeless?" I offered, helpfully.

"Don't ever change," she said, and embraced me tightly. "Just try not to get killed catching that pilot."

"I certainly don't intend to," I replied.

CHAPTER TEN

A couple of mornings later we arrived at the dispersal hut. There had been no sign of the Ace Raider or the Ace Assassin in the meantime. We continued to carry out sorties and man the two pursuit planes in the hope of catching either of them on the hop.

"You know," I said to Angelica, "it's been too damn quiet recently."

"I'm happy it's quiet," she responded.

"Well, I'm not," I said. "Usually that means something untoward is about to happen."

"Oh, don't be so stuffy, darling," she laughed.

I was about to discover that my suspicions were well-founded.

"What on earth is going on there?" I exclaimed.

"You mean that plane?" she said.

I was extremely curious to see one of our Spitfires doing circuits at some distance from the airfield. This seemed a little odd. Although our pilots did sometimes take the planes up in order to practice manoeuvres and so on, I wasn't aware of anyone wanting to do so. I couldn't quite see the markings to tell me whose plane it might be.

"Let's go and find out who it is," I said.

We were about to enter the hut when Willie came out.

"I'm sorry, Scottish," he said. "I tried to stop him."

"Tried to stop who?" I asked him, a little nonplussed.

"Jonty," he replied.

My heart sank, wondering what on earth Jonty could have done now. Willie hesitated, reluctant to continue. In the meantime, Angelica was far more perspicacious. She had taken a look inside the hut and come back out again.

"Kiwi," she said. "Percy is not in his cage."

"No," said Willie, looking suddenly shamefaced.

"Percy?" I said, confused, then, "Kiwi, has Jonty taken that parrot up in his Spitfire?"

Willie nodded.

"I'm afraid so, Scottish."

"What the deuce is he playing at?" I demanded, to his obvious discomfort.

"He insisted, Scottish. I argued with him, but he insisted that the parrot had to go for a spin…"

"It's not your fault," said Angelica, intervening. "You can't help it that Jonty is such a silly boy sometimes."

"More than just silly," I said. "There'll be absolute hell to pay if Bentley finds out."

I looked around as I said it, but Bentley was fortunately absent. It would be most inopportune of him to make one of his sudden appearances.

"How long has he been up there?" I asked Willie.

"Oh, about thirty minutes…"

"Thirty minutes? For goodness' sake!"

The longer he remained in the air, the more he was tempting fate.

"Shall I go and ask Control to get him down?" said Angelica helpfully.

"No, perhaps not. I think he's coming in for a landing," I replied, somewhat relieved.

Sure enough, the Spitfire was on its final approach to the airfield.

"All right," I said to them both. "Let's just try to keep this quiet if we can. Kiwi, does the rest of the flight know?"

"No, I don't think they noticed when Jonty slipped out with the parrot," said Willie.

"I thought you said you tried to stop him," I replied, wondering how that could have escaped everyone's notice.

"Oh, nobody bothers when we argue anymore, we do it so often."

I could well believe it. Angelica laughed. She seemed to find the whole thing rather amusing.

The Spitfire taxied to a stop. As Jonty opened the canopy, Percy spotted freedom and took off.

"Percy! Percy!" shouted Jonty. "Come back. Come back here you wretched bird!"

He jumped down from the Spitfire and broke into a run. Percy flew over our heads and was soon far out of reach. Jonty reached us and looked on helplessly as the bird became a distant spec on the horizon.

"That's one way of sorting out the problem," murmured Willie under his breath.

I turned my gaze from Percy to Jonty.

"Oh, hello, Skipper," said Jonty, trying to feign an innocent expression.

"Jonty," I said.

"Yes, Skipper?"

"What did I say about that bloody bird?"

"Remind me again, Skipper, what *did* you say?"

This only served to goad me, since he knew perfectly well.

"For God's sake, Jonty. I said you couldn't take the parrot up in your Spitfire and what did you do? You took it up in your Spitfire!" I said, annoyed at his insouciance.

Jonty looked contrite at once, in the way only Jonty could.

"Sorry, Skipper. It's just that he seemed so lonely in the hut. He needed some excitement."

I was somewhat flabbergasted at this statement, and to make matters worse, Angelica started to giggle beside me.

"Excitement?" I demanded.

"Yes."

He could be exasperating at times and this was one of those times.

"And your idea of excitement was to take him up in a plane, was it? You couldn't just sing him a song or something less contentious than taking your damn bird out for a spin?"

"Perhaps it wasn't such a good idea," said Jonty, looking suitably abashed. "He didn't enjoy it as much as I had hoped."

I wasn't about to let him off the hook so easily.

"Really? I'm so sorry to hear it, please give him my condolences," I said at my most acidic.

Angelica let out a crack of laughter.

"He squawked almost the whole time."

I turned to my wife, who was doubled up with mirth along with Willie.

"You two are not helping do you know that? Here I am trying to remonstrate with Jonty and what are you doing? Encouraging him!"

"I'm sorry, darling, it's just so funny," said Angelica, trying to look suitably apologetic.

"As for you and that parrot, Jonty," I continued, trying to sound more severe than I felt, "how bloody marvellous is that? Your blasted parrot squawking over the radio. They would have heard that up at Control and what's more, Bentley is very likely to have…"

They were destined never to find out what I thought Bentley was likely to do because just then the CO strode up to us, followed by Audrey.

What was more, Bentley appeared to have Percy the parrot sitting on his arm.

"Now we're in the basket and no mistake," murmured Willie.

"Oh Lord, I'm done for this time," said Jonty, assuming a woebegone expression.

Bentley came to a stop in front of us. The CO was just about to speak when Percy pulled Bentley's pipe from his top pocket with his beak. The parrot then proceeded to drop it onto the ground. Bentley regarded the parrot with a fulminating eye.

"Silly old pipe," squawked Percy. "Silly old pipe."

Since Bentley considered his pipe on par with a religious artefact, this pronouncement by the parrot did not go down at all well.

"Butterworth," said the CO with deceptively icy calm. "Kindly take possession of your infernal bird."

"Yes, sir," said Jonty, picking up Bentley's pipe, dusting it off with his handkerchief and handing it to him. "Sorry about that, sir. I'm sure Percy didn't mean it."

He put his arm out in order to try and coax Percy onto it.

"Come on, Percy," said Jonty. "Come to Daddy, there's a good boy."

Percy cocked his head and fixed Jonty with a beady-eyed stare.

Jonty looked disconcerted by his parrot's reluctance and tried again.

"Now come on, Percy, come to Daddy. I'll get you some nice chow-chow. Come on."

"Shut up! Jolly well shut up!" Percy squawked at him.

"I say, Percy," said Jonty. "That's very rude!"

Bentley, who had been watching this exchange with increasing impatience, decided to take matters into his own hands. He barked out an order at the parrot in his very best parade ground voice.

"Get off my bloody arm you stupid bird, or I'll have your guts for garters!"

For a moment Percy looked as if he was going to remain defiant, but under Bentley's less than friendly gaze obviously decided discretion was the better part of valour.

To everyone's relief, he hopped onto Jonty's outstretched arm and sidled up it.

"There's a good boy," crooned Jonty, stroking Percy's head. "Wherever did you find him, sir?"

"Where did I find him?" said Bentley, sounding even more annoyed. "I didn't bloody well find him anywhere. I had just gone outside for a quiet smoke when your blasted parrot decided to land on me."

Jonty's attempt to play the innocent wasn't going to wash with Bentley. It had simply served to stoke his ire even further.

"More to the point, Butterworth, why is that parrot out of his cage?" Bentley demanded.

"Well, sir … he … well, you see it's like this…" Jonty faltered, uncertain of how to proceed.

None of us could be sure if Bentley knew about Percy's joyride in the Spitfire. I wasn't about to take a bet on it, however.

"Having trouble with the explanation, are you?" said Bentley, turning the screw on Jonty's discomfort a little more.

"Well, sir —" Jonty began again.

"Let me elucidate it for you, shall I?" Bentley interrupted him.

Angelica and I glanced at each other. It was obvious what was coming next.

"I happened to be up in the control tower not long ago," Bentley continued, "when I was surprised to hear one of our pilots squawking over the radio. In fact, he sounded just like a parrot..."

None of us dared to speak. The impending Bentley storm was now brewing nicely.

"And then, surprise surprise, not long after the Spitfire lands I find myself in possession of your bloody bird!"

Jonty's expression turned stoic as he knew he was about to be the object of Bentley's wrath once again.

"It doesn't take too much deduction to work out what happened," said Bentley. "You took that parrot up in your Spitfire, didn't you, Butterworth?"

There was nothing for it but to admit it, and to his credit, Jonty owned up at once.

"Yes, sir," said Jonty. "I did."

"What on earth were you thinking?" Bentley roared. "Do you imagine this squadron is here for the express purpose of entertaining your blasted parrot?"

"No, sir... I..."

"No, sir, is bloody well right! This isn't a bloody menagerie, a circus or a zoo. What possessed you to take that bird up in your Spitfire? Have you taken leave of your senses? You have done some stupid things in your time, but this ... this takes the bloody biscuit!"

"Sir, I... I just thought he might like it," Jonty told him.

"Thought he might like it? What the hell is the matter with you? Perhaps you'd like to take him next door and give him a ride in one of their bombers? Oh, I know, we'll arrange a special tour of the countryside in one of the staff cars, especially for Percy, how about that?"

"Well, I wasn't suggesting..." Jonty began.

"Neither was I. Of all the ridiculous farragoes you have perpetrated under my command, this one takes the biscuit. Only an absolute bloody idiot would take a parrot up in a Spitfire. God knows what might have occurred, but I don't suppose you thought of that, did you?"

"I must admit, sir, I didn't, no."

"No, of course not. That is exactly the trouble — you don't bloody well think. The only reason you're still on this squadron is because you are one of the best pilots we've got. But that ice you continually skate on, Butterworth, is wearing very thin. Do I make myself clear?"

"Perfectly, sir, I'll never take the parrot up in the Spitfire again," said Jonty.

"Damn right you won't, or anywhere else for that matter. Because if that parrot gets into any more scrapes because of your idiotic shenanigans it will be exiled from this base for the rest of the war! And you will find yourself on a posting to Africa!"

Jonty blenched at this threat.

"Sir," I said, in an attempt to conciliate. "I'm sure that Pilot Officer Butterworth didn't mean to cause so much trouble."

Jonty was his own worst enemy, but I didn't want him sent away, particularly to Africa. I had heard the conditions for personnel there were dire.

"That's as may be," said Bentley. Having let off a head of steam, he seemed to have simmered down. He glared at Percy, who was snuggled up to Jonty in quite an endearing fashion. Bentley began his pipe of doom ritual. Percy watched on with interest. Once Bentley was smoking his pipe, he seemed a lot calmer.

"Sir, if I may?" I began.

"Yes?" he said, suspiciously.

"It's just that, apparently, one of the bomber crew has a dog—"

"Oh? I see nothing remarkable in that."

"He takes it up in the B-17, sir, it has an oxygen supply and everything."

Bentley puffed on his pipe, then pointed the stem at Jonty.

"That's your excuse, is it? Copying the Americans?" he said.

"Sir, I just thought if they could do it…" said Jonty.

"Perhaps, Pilot Officer Butterworth, you might try thinking less," Bentley said mildly, before he resumed smoking.

"Yes, sir."

Bentley sighed. He had spent his wrath.

"All right, that will be all. And put that blasted parrot back in his cage where he belongs," he said.

"Right away, sir."

"I never want to see him out of his cage again, is that clear?" said Bentley, reinforcing his point.

"Yes, sir, perfectly," said Jonty.

"Very well. Dismissed."

With that, Bentley turned on his heel and strode away. Audrey glanced back at us sympathetically before hurrying after him.

"Oh, Jonty," said Angelica. "What are we going to do with you?"

"That was a lucky escape," said Jonty, breathing a sigh of relief. "Reminded me of old Bagshaw that time I came down his chimney."

I could imagine that Jonty's History Master, just like Bentley, had not been amused.

"That's just the trouble, Jonty," I said. "You're not at school anymore and you need to grow up."

"I'm trying, Skipper," said Jonty.

"Well try harder, Jonty," Willie interjected.

"I'll put Percy back in his cage now," Jonty said sadly.

"Come on, you idiot, cheer up. I told you this would happen," said Willie and put his arm around Jonty's shoulder.

We watched them head back into the hut. Quite a few of the others had come out to witness Bentley's tirade. Jonty was greeted with good-humoured banter and pats on the back.

"Is Jonty ever going to learn?" Angelica said.

"I doubt it."

"Will Bentley really send him to Africa?" she asked, concerned.

"I don't suppose he will for a moment, but Jonty needs to stay out of trouble for a good while."

"It was quite funny though," she said, her mouth twitching into a smile.

"I suppose it was," I said, starting to laugh.

"Bentley's face when Percy took his pipe…"

I saw the humour in it after all and the two of us were overcome with mirth for quite some time afterwards.

Following the debacle with Percy the parrot, I felt it might be politic to avoid Bentley for the rest of the day. I saw Tomas off on the first sortie and then decided it might be a good idea to see if Gordon could offer some sage advice about trapping the Ace Raider.

"Do you know what?" I said to Angelica.

"What?" she said, eyeing me with interest.

"I think we should go for tea."

"What a splendid idea," she replied at once.

"Let's go and find Fred."

It wasn't long before we were ensconced once more at Annie's Kitchen. Annie was as pleased as ever to see us and soon brought us a tray of the treasured tea and crumpets.

"Oh, I just love these," said Angelica, taking a hot crumpet and reaching for the butter. "And this is fast becoming one of my favourite places."

"Because of the crumpets?" I asked her, buttering one of my own.

"Well, yes, but because it's also one of *your* favourite places," she said simply.

"Now *that*, sir," said Gordon with a smile, "is true love."

Angelica reached out and squeezed my hand affectionately. We all consumed the crumpets with relish before I broached the subject I wanted to consult him about. Gordon lit up a cigarette and Angelica poured us all another cup of tea.

"Something on your mind, sir?" said Gordon, after he had taken a couple of satisfied pulls on his cigarette.

"Yes," I said, "there is, and I thought you might be able to help."

"Fire away," he replied.

I took a sip of my tea and then began.

"It's about the Ace Raider," I told him. "We're trying to think of a way to trap him."

"Trap him, sir?"

I went on to explain the whole of it and also the intervention by the Marx Brothers since that wasn't confidential.

Gordon listened carefully and then extinguished his cigarette. He took a sip of his tea.

"From what you are telling me, your preference is to shoot him down," he said.

"Yes, it is," I agreed.

"But those damnable idiots want him to capture the pilot instead," Angelica added, with some irritation.

"I see the dilemma," said Gordon.

"Do you have any ideas about how we could successfully go about it?" I asked him.

"Well," said Gordon, taking another sip of tea. "The trick of any trap is for whoever is being trapped not to see it coming."

"Right."

"It obviously can't look like a trap until it becomes one."

"Yes, I see," I said, but Gordon wasn't finished.

"The Ace Raider will be approaching over the sea, am I right?" he said.

"Yes, he will."

Gordon cleared a space on the table and placed a knife down on it. Then he took a teaspoon and placed that down too.

"Here is the coastline," he said, indicating the knife. "And here is the Ace Raider."

He began to move the spoon over the imaginary coastline as he spoke.

"Now, over here, well out of sight, you'll have a squadron — or several planes at least — lying in wait and one here too, further up the coast."

More items were brought into play as he continued his demonstration.

"Timing is everything, you see," he said. "This squadron up the coast will fly out to sea and then come in behind him unseen, like this. In the meantime, the other squadron will come at him from the front, and possibly some from the side."

The various accoutrements of the tea were pressed into service to illustrate his point.

"Then," he said, "you box him in, like this."

He moved all of the items into a formation, with the teaspoon representing the Ace Raider in the middle. I must admit I was impressed although I had some questions.

"What if he won't be boxed in?" I asked.

"Hmm," said Gordon. "Well, he's got a choice, hasn't he? Either to try to shoot his way out, in which case he's going to die very quickly, or cooperate, in which case he isn't."

"Right," I said. "But which will it be?"

Gordon sat back in his seat, took out another cigarette and lit it.

"Who knows?" He shrugged as he took a drag on his cigarette. "The cornered rat becomes a lion or a mouse depending on their makeup. We know he's a showman, but in a pinch, we don't know how he will react. The trick is to be ready for anything and respond accordingly."

"He could just fly straight up and escape that way," Angelica pointed out.

Gordon had a ready answer.

"Yes, and that is why you need to have some planes above him to negate that possibility."

I sighed, thinking about the sheer size of the operation.

"Twenty-four planes just to catch one bloody plane," I said, feeling a little frustrated.

"But as you yourself have said," Gordon replied, "he's evaded you several times already."

I couldn't disagree with that statement. The Ace Raider had outsmarted us on each occasion we'd met him.

"Yes, he's remarkably quick."

"Then your best hope lies in outnumbering him by a large margin."

"You're right," I said. "And thank you, perhaps it really could work."

"If anyone can make it work, sir, you can," said Gordon.

"Now you're sounding like those blasted Marx Brothers."

We all laughed. I couldn't imagine anyone less like Harpo and Chico.

"You're a wizard at tactics, Fred," said Angelica admiringly.

"I wouldn't say that," Gordon demurred. "But perhaps I have learned something from my time in the Great War. More about what *not* to do, than what to do..." He trailed off.

Most of us knew that the Great War had been a disaster, with millions of lives wasted. Outdated tactics saw the infantry fed to the machine guns like cannon fodder by generals who didn't seem to care.

"Anyway," said Gordon brightly. "How about another round? My shout."

"Yes, please," said Angelica at once.

We spent a pleasant half an hour talking of this and that. I told Gordon about the parrot incident, which he thought was a capital joke. Gordon filled us in on some of the latest gossip. He said that the mess had served a rather good rabbit pie the other day. There seemed to be quite a lot of game on the menu of late, and I wondered where it was all coming from. I knew the mess engaged in bartering with the Americans. I bit into my crumpet and put it out of my mind. How the mess got their fare was the least of my worries.

Gordon dropped us back at the base. I had to run a patrol.

"I suppose you have to go," said Angelica, taking my hands in hers.

"Yes, I'm afraid so."

"I'll be glad when you catch that blighter, you won't have to run so many patrols."

"Let's hope so."

I didn't feel entirely optimistic about our chances.

"Fly safe," she said, kissing me softly.

"I will."

"I love you."

"I love you too."

We parted slowly and I walked with the other pilots on the patrol to my plane. I wondered if we would encounter the Ace Raider today. Tomas hadn't seen him on his morning sortie.

"What-ho, Skipper," said Jonty as I caught up to him.

"I hope Percy is safely in his cage, Jonty," I said.

It did no harm to make sure he was minding the stricture Bentley had laid on him.

"Absolutely, Skipper, safe as houses. In any case, I don't think he wants another trip in a Spitfire."

"He isn't getting one either," I said meaningfully.

"Yes, of course, most definitely not," said Jonty, contrite.

"I'll make sure he doesn't," shouted Willie from the cockpit of his plane.

"Let's get up and away then," I said.

Jonty gave me the thumbs up and climbed onto the wing of his kite. I did likewise and Redwood strapped me in.

"Take care out there, sir," said Redwood. "It's a bit windy today."

"I will, Techie, never fear," I told him.

It was unusual for him to be concerned but it was true, the wind had certainly picked up. We taxied out onto the runway. This time I was taking Willie, Jonty, Arjun, Harold and Stanley. I was trying my best to give everyone a fair go. Harold and Stanley needed to get more hours under their belts. Dylan had just come off the pursuit plane shift along with Jean.

"Red Patrol, you're clear for take-off," said the control tower.

"Roger, Control," I replied, throttling up.

The power of the Merlin engines kicked in and we were soon airborne. There was quite a bit of buffeting from the wind, but I managed to keep the kite steady. I set a course for Felixstowe.

We flew reasonably low since there was little point in subterfuge. If nothing else, we needed to deter the Ace Raider or any other Jerry from attacking our towns. I secretly hoped we might still shoot him down, thus negating the need for an elaborate trap.

Once we were over Felixstowe, I turned the patrol northwards, following the coastline. The wind was coming in at a fair lick off the sea. You could see the white tops of the waves.

"Oh blast, this bloody wind is a damnable nuisance," complained Jonty.

"I'll say," Harold agreed. "Hard to keep her steady."

"Try to hold formation," I said. "And keep your eyes peeled."

There was cloud cover above us. It was fairly scudding across the sky, and I wondered if perhaps it might deter the Ace Raider from coming.

We flew over Felixstowe and headed towards Bawdsey.

"Can't we just go home, Skipper?" Jonty complained, as if reading my mind. "I bet that Ace Raider isn't going to come."

"No!" Willie complained at once. "You've jinxed it again!"

"I have not," Jonty shot back.

"Yes, you have, you always do this!"

Right on cue, Harold suddenly shouted, "It's the Ace Raider. He's coming in low at two o'clock!"

"I told you this would happen," said Willie triumphantly.

I looked over to the right. The Ace Raider was skimming as low as he could and streaking towards the small town ahead.

"Why is he attacking Bawdsey of all places?" said Jonty. "There's nothing *at* Bawdsey."

"He's heading for the church," said Stanley.

"All right, break, break, let's try and take him before he gets there," I said.

We peeled off and flew down on the attack. The Ace Raider was now halfway between the Martello tower and the town. I assumed he'd picked the target because it wasn't well defended. There was possibly an emplacement on the tower, but it appeared they had been caught napping.

Arjun managed to get ahead of us all and dropped low behind the Ace Raider before the German spotted him. He opened fire and a stream of tracers emanated from his guns. At the last moment, the Ace Raider flipped to the side and avoided the salvo. He started to fly south but Stanley and Harold were on a course to cut him off. He must have seen them and started to climb but Jonty had managed to get above him. Willie had circled around to one side of him, and I was somehow on the other.

"We've got him surrounded," I said. "Let's take him down."

Faced with no escape, the Ace Raider decided to take us on. Jonty fired as the German pilot flew directly at Harold and Stanley.

The salvo missed but the Ace Raider had to turn away sharply, straight into the path of Willie. Willie's Spitfire sent out another salvo and the Ace Raider had to turn again. As I closed in on his tail, I got him in my sights and my finger hovered over the button. Unfortunately, I waited one second too long.

A gust of wind suddenly hit my plane and before I could do anything it had pulled me off target.

"Damn!" I said in frustration, wrestling with the joystick.

"It's all right," said Stanley. "I've got him, I've —"

He was cut short. The wind had also hit him and his Spitfire pitched up, exposing the underbelly. The Ace Raider saw his chance. He fired and bullets raked across Stanley's plane. Smoke began pouring from the engine.

"I'm hit," said Stanley. "I've been hit!"

"Blast that Jerry, I'm going to get him, he's not getting away," said Jonty, trying to get on the Ace Raider's tail.

But the Ace Raider had seen an opening and he'd taken it. He flew up almost vertically and disappeared into the clouds. In the meantime, Stanley had managed to control his plane, but the engine was still smoking.

"I've got it," said Stanley. "I think it's all right."

"Let's head for Banley," I told him. "But if it starts to catch fire, you need to bale out."

"Aye, aye, Scottish," said Stanley.

We formed up around him and I kept an anxious eye on his plane in the mirror. Fortunately, although there were a few odd spurts of flame it seemed for a while as if it was all going to be okay. As we approached the airfield I saw flames suddenly starting to shoot out from the sides. I didn't hesitate, Stanley was my responsibility.

"Stanley," I said. "Bale out, that's an order."

"But Scottish!" he protested.

"Bale out, for God's sake, before it's too late."

Stanley's canopy went back. His kite dropped away to earth while he engaged his chute. I was relieved to see him safely out of his craft. And not a moment too soon. Seconds later his Spitfire exploded.

"That was close," said Arjun.

"Control," I said. "One of our patrol had to bale out. Can someone go and pick him up?"

"We've seen it, Red Leader, we're on our way."

As we landed, I could see in the distance that Stanley had made it safely to the ground. Angelica hurtled over the field to greet me as I jumped down from my kite.

"Oof!" I said, as she flung herself into my arms.

"I'm glad Stanley got out in time," she said, kissing me. "And you're all back safe. Especially you."

"Me too," I agreed.

Naturally, Bentley had hot-footed it over to us and was waiting patiently to speak to me. Angelica detached herself and stood beside me. Bentley finished his pipe routine and lit it.

"What happened?" he asked me.

"We almost had the Ace Raider penned in," I said. "But for the wind…"

"Oh, really?" he said.

"Yes, sir, it was damned unfortunate." I went on to describe to scene while Bentley listened without comment.

"Blasted Jerry and his antics," he said crossly when I'd finished. "I'm getting sick and tired of his bloody shenanigans."

"I think we all are, sir," I said.

"And we nearly lost a pilot to that bloody hooligan. Enough is enough. It's time to get serious about that trap, Angus."

I had had the same thought.

"Yes, sir," I said. "If nothing else, this encounter has taught us a valuable lesson."

"And that is?"

Bentley puffed on his pipe and waited for my answer with interest.

"The lesson is, sir, that with the right tactics, the Ace Raider can be caught."

"Right, very good."

He gave a perfunctory salute and I returned it. We watched him stride away along with Audrey.

"Will you feel better once you've done your duty and caught this Jerry?" Angelica enquired.

"This is no longer just about duty," I told her. "He nearly killed one of my pilots. Now it's personal."

CHAPTER ELEVEN

There was now one objective on my mind and that was catching the Ace Raider. I meant it when I told Angelica it was personal. That's how it felt. He had evaded us too many times. He would know that we were the Mavericks. It was painted on our planes. Up until now, it had been rather like a game of cat and mouse. However, when cornered, like the rat Gordon had mentioned, he had tried to shoot his way out. We had only been six planes. I wanted to see him try it when we were twenty-four. The trouble was that I needed another squadron. Rather than ask Flight Lieutenant Judd, who led the other Maverick's squadron, I decided I'd ask Sandford. I was sure he'd be more than happy to help. After all, we had assisted him on several bombing missions and I'd let his pilots fly with us. First, though, I had to finalise the details of the plan.

Gordon had given me the shell of an idea, but I needed to work it out on paper. In our rooms at Amberly one evening, I enlisted Angelica's help.

"I'm thinking of Cromer," I said. "We'll call it a fete, something like that."

"Why Cromer?" she asked, playing devil's advocate.

"It's not too far from RAF Langham and it's got a suitable park where we could hold the event."

"All right, that makes sense," she said.

We examined the map in front of us.

"M Flight and Captain Booker's flight can wait at Langham," I continued. "We'll time it so that his flight is in the air and out to sea before the appointed time. They can sweep in behind the Ace Raider. M Flight will scramble once the Ace Raider has been sighted. They will come in from the land side. Together we will box him in and force him to land."

"And if he does what he did before?"

"We'll shoot him down without hesitation."

I had already made that decision. There wouldn't be time to procrastinate. If the Ace Raider wasn't going to cooperate, then he would pay the ultimate price.

Angelica watched as I pencilled in the intended approaches of the various planes.

"What about the people attending, won't they be in danger?" she asked.

It was true that we were going to have the local populace there to make it look authentic. We also would not be able to tell them what had been planned.

"They could well be," I said. "But our presence should minimise the risk. In any case, they are in danger every day from possible raids."

"That's true," she acknowledged. "But what if he brings others and you have them to deal with too?"

This was a fair point. However, all the times we'd encountered him bar one, he'd been alone. I had a strong impression this was how he liked it.

"I don't think he will," I said. "In fact, I'd put money on him being by himself. But if he does come with a couple more planes then I imagine we will have to abandon the plan to capture him and just shoot them all down. It will still accomplish the same result of removing him as a threat."

Angelica sighed and I slipped my arm around her waist.

"It seems as if there are quite a few things which could go wrong," she said.

I hastened to reassure her. What she said was true, but with very careful planning I actually thought we had a chance.

"There are," I said. "But it's a gamble we have to take. Either way, we will get him, as long as we can get the timing right."

"Yes," she agreed. "It's all about the timing. It's a matter of all those little details."

I smiled. I needed someone to figure those details out properly. I wasn't sure who the best person would be. Unfortunately, we didn't have anyone like the Mosquito crew that helped us on the missions to do all the navigation. I didn't have an immediate solution to hand. I wanted Angelica's endorsement nevertheless because her opinion mattered to me very much.

"All right," I said. "But in principle, what do you think?"

I saw her lips curve into a smile.

"I think it's marvellous, darling, and I think it can certainly work. And now I think, in principle, you should come to bed."

I laid down the pencil and took her into my arms.

"Then in principle, I suppose I ought to kiss you," I said softly.

"Yes, you should."

I forgot about the plan and instead surrendered my lips to hers.

The following day I decided we should check up on Maria. She hadn't been much in evidence lately and I assumed she was keeping to her house. It was probably safer. We had a brief chat with the sergeant on the ack-ack battery on the way.

"Anything to report, Sergeant?" I asked him.

"Not really, sir, no. It's been remarkably quiet. We're remaining vigilant as ever though," he replied with a smile.

"The assassin could attack at any time," I said. "So, it's just as well to do so."

"Never fear, sir. We're on the ball, right lads?"

His gun crew signified their agreement with a chorus of "Yes, Sarge."

"Strange though isn't it, sir, that one plane attacking us with the Ace of Spades on its wings. I wonder where it comes from?"

"That's what we'd all like to know," I told him.

We chatted for a few moments more, then I saluted and approached Maria's front door with Angelica. I noticed that the house now had sandbags piled up around the walls, excluding the windows. The door was opened by Olga before we could knock.

"Hello," she said. "Nice to see you."

"We thought we'd just come and see how you are both faring," I said.

"That's kind, come in, Maria will be pleased to have some visitors. I'll make some tea."

She ushered us into the living room. It was looking more homely with some pictures on the walls. There were houseplants on the windowsill too. Maria stood up as we entered.

I noticed she was now wearing an RAF uniform and looked like an ordinary WAAF. This was all to the good since she couldn't be singled out if she went out onto the base. Olga was similarly clothed. I presumed her pistol was concealed within easy reach on her person.

"How are you doing?" I asked her. "You seem to be making yourself at home."

"Olga very kindly obtained a few things," she said. "to make the place feel a bit more comfortable. For the most part, we're not doing much. Reading, playing cards…"

I noticed a bookcase now populated with several books, a pack of cards and a chess set too. This made me think of Willie with a slight pang. I knew he and Jonty were keen chess players.

Olga returned with some tea and homemade Victoria sponge cake. She cut us all a slice and poured the tea.

"She's chafing for something to do," said Olga who had overheard the tail end of the conversation.

"I wouldn't say chafing," Maria demurred.

"So, pacing up and down the living room isn't chafing?" said Olga with a teasing tone.

I could see they were getting along very well by the easy manner in which they spoke to each other. Just like old friends.

"How about you, Angus?" Maria asked me, turning the subject.

"We're still trying to catch the Ace Raider. He nearly shot down one of my pilots recently," I said. She knew of the Ace Raider from previous conversations.

"Oh dear," she said. "He's proving to be a difficult adversary then?"

"Yes," I said, conversationally. "We have a plan though to put an end to his activities. I just need to find someone with decent navigation skills to figure out the finer points. It's not my forte at all."

"I could help, if you like?" Maria said tentatively, a sudden spark of interest in her eyes.

"You?" I said, surprised.

"Is that so strange?" she replied with a laugh. "I took navigation as part of my degree. As a matter of fact, I studied aeronautics."

"Aeronautics?" I said, slightly flabbergasted.

"Yes, of course, I had hoped to become a pilot one day. That was before Hitler..." She trailed off, then said, "Did you think that a woman couldn't do such things?"

Her tone was a little defensive.

"Of course, he doesn't," Angelica cut in. "We have women pilots here transporting planes all over the place. Perhaps it's just that when you first came you seemed so sophisticated."

Maria acknowledged this with a slight incline of her head.

"Ah, well, you can't always judge a book by its cover. Just because I am fashionable, it doesn't mean I am also empty-headed," she said lightly.

"I was not suggesting it," I told her. "But perhaps you *can* help. It's a matter of getting the logistics right for an operation involving several planes."

"I would like to help, if I can," she replied. "You've done so much for me."

"The plan is obviously secret," I told her.

"Of course," she smiled. "Who am I going to tell? It's just me and Olga."

"I think it's a splendid idea," said Angelica. "You're like the cavalry coming over the hill at just the right time."

Angelica would always have my best interests at heart. Apart from anything else, it was her personal mission to see that I survived the war intact, as she had informed me on more than one occasion.

I outlined the gist of the plan to capture the Ace Raider while Maria listened carefully. I drew a sketch on some paper thoughtfully provided by Olga.

"Yes, I see," said Maria when I had finished. "It's all about the timings. I can work this out for sure. I will need a map, a scale rule, and some figures about the airspeed of your Spitfires. I'll write a list."

She picked up another piece of paper and began to make some notes.

"Well, this is a turn-up for the books," said Angelica, finishing off her slice of cake. "Delicious cake by the way."

"Yes, it certainly is," I agreed.

"Olga made it," said Maria. "She is a brilliant cook."

"You flatter me."

Olga blushed. I drank my tea and thanked whatever providence had brought about the happy coincidence of Maria being trained in navigation.

"How is the reinforcement of the bedroom going?" I asked Olga, since she had mentioned it the last time.

"It's fine, would you like to see it?"

"Why not?"

We followed her into the main bedroom. I noticed it now contained twin beds. The walls did look as if there was now an extra layer of concrete blocks.

"The ceiling is reinforced from above," Olga told us.

She noticed us looking curiously at the beds.

"I sleep in here now," she said. "Maria feels safer that way, and we are both protected. If there's a raid, we get under the beds too. They have sheet steel under the mattress. It's a bit uncomfortable, but will afford the best protection. The frames are also steel and very sturdy."

"You seem to have thought of everything," Angelica remarked.

"It's my job."

Olga shrugged. I mused that there was certainly no expense spared to protect Maria. Her husband must be incredibly important to the war effort.

"Olga," said Angelica suddenly. "Might I be a little forward and ask you something?"

"Of course."

"It's about Willie ... you and he don't seem to be getting along."

Olga sighed. She sat down heavily on the bed. Angelica went to sit beside her and took her hand.

"Do you want to talk about it?"

"There's not much to talk about," said Olga frankly. "He wants to marry me and I, well, I want to wait."

This was pretty much the gist of what we'd already heard when they were arguing. We didn't let on, however.

"Why do you want to wait?" Angelica asked her.

"It's the war," said Olga. "I might be killed, he might be killed, we can't be together for much of the time because I'll be on missions — you know how it goes in the Secret Service."

Angelica squeezed her hand sympathetically.

"But do you love him?" she asked gently.

Olga's expression softened at once.

"Love him? Of course, I love him so much. He's such an idiot, he can't see that."

A solitary tear trickled down her cheek.

"Look," said Angelica, who had agonised over our marriage for different reasons. "I do understand how you feel. I had similar fears. After all, Angus is a pilot too. I led him quite the merry dance over getting engaged and married, didn't I, darling?"

She flashed me a smile and I smiled back.

"It was frustrating, yes," I agreed.

Olga looked from one to the other of us and laughed.

"You did get married after all, then?"

"Yes," said Angelica.

"And?" Olga prompted her.

"None of us can know the future," said Angelica, "particularly in wartime. I realised that I was worrying about things which might never happen. I also knew that we had faced so much and overcome it. I felt that, with Angus, I could overcome anything. Besides, I wanted to be with him all the time and not just some of the time. Our relationship is so much better now."

"But I'll still have to go away," said Olga. The sadness crept back into her voice.

"Yes, but you can make the most of the time when you *can* be together," said Angelica. "It is so much sweeter, I promise, when you're married."

"Is it really?" I said, not because I was surprised but because I was happy to hear it.

"Yes, darling, don't you feel it too?"

"I do," I agreed. "And she's right, Olga. If you do love him as much as you say, then why not just tie the knot if it's what you both want and let the future take care of itself."

Olga was silent for a while.

"I'll think about it," she said at length.

"Do you think you might at least see Willie?" Angelica asked her. "The poor man is pining away."

"Is he?" Olga looked contrite.

"I can vouch for it. He's not his usual self at all," I said.

"Oh, I've been too hard on him. I was angry with him and I shouldn't have been. After all, he might be killed any time … and he would die thinking … thinking…"

She didn't finish the sentence but we both knew what she meant. He would die thinking she thought badly of him or worse … perhaps even hated him.

"Look," I said. "Could I perhaps suggest he comes to call on you? You could … talk. Talking things out does seem to help."

Angelica flashed me a smile. We had had many talks together, some of them more difficult than others.

"Perhaps he won't want to see me after I was so horrible to him," said Olga.

"Listen, Olga," said Angelica, "I flung my engagement ring at Angus in a fit of temper once and he still wanted to see me again afterwards, so…"

Olga's eyes widened.

"You did that?"

"She did," I said ruefully. "It was pretty much my fault."

"I shouldn't have lost my temper," said Angelica, determined not to allow me to take all the blame.

"Okay," said Olga, laughing. "Tell Willie to come and see me."

"All right, we will."

"Come on," she said, standing up. "Maria will be wondering what we're doing in here all this time."

"We'd best be going," I said to Maria, when we returned to the living room. "I've patrols to organise. Give me your list and I'll bring you what you need. Then you can work out the details."

She handed me the list and we said our goodbyes. As we strolled back towards the hut, Angelica slid her hand into mine.

"Willie will be pleased," she said.

"I certainly hope so," I replied.

She stopped and wound her arms around my neck.

"I'm glad you gave me back the ring, after I threw it at you."

"I'm glad I did too."

"How glad?"

My reply was lost in a long passionate kiss.

"I've got some news for you, old chap," I said to Willie upon arrival at the dispersal hut. I had resolved to tell him as soon as possible about Olga.

"Oh?"

"You'll like it, Kiwi," said Angelica. "I promise."

"Go on then, what is it?" he said, sounding rather sceptical.

"We saw Olga just now…" I began.

"Yes?"

Given his demeanour, I didn't want to keep him in suspense any longer, so I came straight out with it.

"She wants you to go and see her."

He stared at us both open-mouthed.

"What?"

"Go and see her," Angelica assured him. "She wants you to."

I'd rarely seen someone's expression change so quickly from despair to hope.

"Right," he said. "Right, well … I'll be off then … okay…"

He practically leapt from his seat and was out the door in a matter of moments.

"What-ho, Skipper," said Jonty, coming up to us just in time to Willie disappearing from sight. "Where's old Friday Face off to?"

"Friday Face? Is that what you've been calling him?" I enquired, amused.

Jonty rolled his eyes.

"Well, he is a blasted Friday Face, Skipper, and no mistake. He's been casting a damper on everything for days," he said.

"He's in love, Jonty," said Angelica.

Jonty wasn't mollified by this statement.

"That's as may be, but he's been a rotten companion all the same."

"He won't be soon enough," I told him. "I think he and Olga are about to kiss and make up."

"Thank the Lord for that," said Jonty. "I won't have to see him mooning around the place like a lost sheep anymore."

I tried not to smile. I knew very well that he cared immensely for his friend.

Just then I heard the sound of Spitfires in the distance. Tomas was returning from his sortie. I went outside to greet them. The planes taxied to a stop and soon Tomas strolled towards us. As it happened, he had returned with nothing to report.

"No bandits anywhere, Scottish," he informed me when he reached us.

"Oh well," I said. "Things will hopefully change soon."

"Ah," he said, picking up on this at once. "You have a plan, no?"

"I do and very shortly I'll be in a position to share it," I said.

Surprisingly, he didn't enquire further.

"Yes, I will look forward to this, but now I'm tired and it's time for tea."

He clapped me on the back and headed for the hut.

"Shall we get some lunch at the mess?" I asked Angelica. "There's time before my patrol."

"Why not?"

Sandford's squadron was taking the patrol after Tomas', and then I would fly the final patrol of the day. As we walked over to the mess, a flight of six Spitfires roared overhead, dipping their wings. We waved as they passed over us and then they were gone.

In the mess we discovered Olga, Willie and Maria seated at a table. We went over to join them. Willie was looking the happiest I'd seen him since their quarrel.

"Everything all right?" I asked as we sat down.

"Yes, thank you," replied Olga. "Everything is just fine."

She glanced at Willie and he broke into a grin. I concluded they had settled their differences and turned my mind to the matter of lunch.

"What's that you're eating?" I asked Willie.

He had a plate of mashed potatoes, meat pie and cabbage in front of him.

"This is venison pie," said Willie. "And jolly good it is too."

"Rabbit stew," said Olga, pointing at her plate.

"And the trout is nice," added Maria.

I was somewhat surprised to hear that such a variety of food was on the menu, particularly in wartime.

"Where on earth is all this coming from?" I asked them. "Venison? Rabbit stew? Trout? Where did they get it?"

Olga laughed at my incredulous expression.

"It's from the American base," she said.

"But where did the Americans get it?" I replied. "This is surely not part of their normal supplies."

Olga took a forkful of stew and ate it with evident relish before answering.

"I'm not sure. I think it might be from some local source. Is it important? I can find out?"

I considered this. Did it matter? It just seemed highly unusual, and after all the recent spying capers I had become suspicious of anything strange or unusual. I couldn't imagine the significance of this particularly though. Perhaps they were bartering with someone.

"Don't worry," I said. "I'll ask Gordon, he's bound to know."

Olga laughed. "I would have asked him myself, anyway."

We all chuckled at this. Gordon evidently had something of a reputation. In any event, I put the matter to the back of my mind and ordered the venison pie. Angelica followed suit and we spent a happy lunch hour talking of other things.

After lunch, Angelica and I returned to the hut. She tucked her arm into mine as we walked.

"Is it important?" she asked me. "The sudden appearance of all this game in the mess."

"I don't know," I said, honestly. "It just seems odd."

"Well," she continued, "if you're concerned, then we'll ask Gordon just as you said."

"All right," I agreed.

I couldn't put my finger on why it niggled me so much, but it did. However, there was no more time to ponder it then as I had a sortie to fly.

CHAPTER TWELVE

The plan came together satisfactorily. Maria proved to be an asset in that regard, producing the timings I needed. There were a lot of assumptions and the biggest one was whether or not the Ace Raider would actually take the bait. If he did, then I was determined to be ready for him one way or another. First, I needed to take the plan to Bentley. I went to his office accompanied by Angelica. After we had been ushered in by Audrey, we sat watching him conduct his pipe of doom ritual before he sat back and puffed away with great satisfaction.

"So, Angus," he said. "What have you got for me?"

I went over the details of the operation while he listened without comment.

"These timings are pretty exact, how did you work them out?" he asked, eyeing me with some scepticism. I wasn't known for my navigational acumen.

"Maria did the calculations, sir," I said.

"Maria?" He raised an eyebrow at this.

"She's a graduate in aeronautics. She studied navigation."

He received this news with some surprise.

"Well, wonders will never cease, will they," he said. "Aeronautics? What made her want to study aeronautics?"

"Apparently she wanted to be a pilot," I told him.

"I see. Perhaps when the war is over, I suppose," he mused. "Anyway, what are the next steps? I suppose you want to get those bloody reprobate spies down here."

"I will have to do that, yes," I said. "I also need to brief my squadron and also Captain Booker's once I've asked him."

He seemed happy enough with this. "Jolly good, don't let me keep you."

Bentley turned his attention back to his desk and I left with Angelica. Now we had effectively been given the go-ahead, there was much to do.

I enlisted Gordon's services to drive us over to the American base. As we drove, I decided to ask him about the sudden appearance of game at the mess.

"Fred," I said as we bowled along. "Have you eaten at the mess lately?"

"Yes, sir, very good it has been too."

"Did you notice there's been a fair bit of game on the menu?"

"I did indeed. I had some rather nice pheasant the other day as it goes."

"Doesn't it strike you as odd?"

He shot me a quick look before returning his gaze to the road.

"Odd, sir?"

"Well, have you wondered where's it all coming from?"

He was silent for a few moments as we approached the American base and were admitted by the sentries. Gordon drove us towards the offices where Sandford worked.

"Would you like me to enquire, sir?" he asked me.

Gordon knew me pretty well by now and if I wanted some information there would be a good reason for it.

"Yes, if you wouldn't mind. Olga says it's from the American mess."

"Then this is most opportune," he said, smiling. "I'll see what I can find out."

He parked up and Angelica and I alighted from the jeep. Gordon took out a packet of cigarettes, removed one and returned the packet to his pocket. He lit it and sat back in his seat, smoking it with satisfaction. He would no doubt tackle the question of food in the mess in due course.

Angelica and I arrived at Sandford's office and he smiled as soon as he saw us. He'd been expecting us, as I had phoned in advance. He stood up as we entered and motioned for us to sit.

"Hello, good to see you both," he said. "Let me order you some refreshments."

"I was hoping you'd say that," said Angelica.

He laughed and asked his corporal to obtain the ubiquitous Coca-Cola which seemed to be part of the American Forces' way of life.

"What brings you here?" he asked with interest.

"A joint operation," I said. "If you're game for it."

"Game for it?" He smiled. "Of course I'm game for it."

"Then let me explain…"

I went over the plan in essence. The corporal reappeared with three Cokes, which he duly poured into glasses containing some ice cubes. It seemed that ice was essential, even in winter. Angelica sipped her drink with relish. When I had finished outlining the plan, I waited for Sandford to comment.

"Wow," he said. "That's quite an undertaking."

I sighed.

"Meaning you don't think it's going to work?"

"No, I mean it's a hell of a damn operation. If you can pull it off … if *we* can pull it off. Everything has to go just right though…" He trailed off.

"Are you in?" I asked him, wanting to be sure since he seemed to hesitate.

"Oh, I'm in all right, just try keeping me away. The boys are sick of bomber escort missions, they'll love this for sure. There's just one thing though…"

He hesitated again.

"What's that?" I prompted him.

"The CO will want some quid pro quo, you know … like if we need you on a bombing run afterwards, that kind of thing."

"That goes without saying," I told him. "We're all on the same side here and besides, weren't we pledged to cooperation?"

"Sure, of course," he said. "But things change, or should I say… might have changed… I don't like to presume."

I was grateful for his circumspection but as far as I was concerned, we were going to continue working together for the good of the war.

"I'm sure I can speak for Bentley and say that if you need our help, we'll provide it."

"All right, well then, just tell me when you need us and we'll be there."

"I imagine we will have a full briefing shortly," I said. "And then perhaps some practice runs."

"Okay, you're on."

We finished our drinks and returned to the jeep. Gordon was there smoking a cigarette, almost exactly as we had left him.

"Successful mission, sir?" Gordon asked me, putting the jeep into gear and setting off.

"Absolutely, Fred," I said. "Things are moving ahead on the plan we discussed."

"Glad to hear it."

"And did *you* have a successful mission?" I enquired.

"Ah, as to that, it wasn't too hard to discover," he replied.

"Which was?"

"Apparently, it's all coming from a local estate not far from here. The gamekeeper is supplying the base with their surplus game."

"And why would he do that?" I asked him.

"The story goes that they've too much and can't get rid of it. Recently they've been culling deer and so on. They're running on a skeleton staff, so to speak, and not so many grand events due to the war, meaning there's plenty to spare. I suppose it's also to help the war effort," he explained.

"Do you know which estate it is?" I asked.

"No, but if it's important, I can find out if you wish," he said.

I thought about it and decided we had enough to contend with for the moment. It sounded plausible, although I wondered why the gamekeeper had picked the American base to trade his goods, rather than the RAF base. I suspected the estate was getting something in return, financial or otherwise. Perhaps the Americans were a better bet.

"Let's leave it for now," I told him. "We've got this mission to accomplish, and I need to focus my attention on that."

Having got Sandford on board, the Marx Brothers were next on my list. Angelica asked Audrey to get in touch with them, and the following day they were once more ensconced in their usual place in what would once more become our mission room.

"Ah, Flight Lieutenant *and* Section Officer," said Harpo, taking a drag from his ever-present cigarette. "Do we divine correctly that you have something to discuss?"

"Yes, we do," I told him, taking a seat alongside Angelica.

I resolved this time not to allow their manner to rile me up, which it usually did.

"Have you come to some conclusion about your plan to capture the Ace Raider?" asked Chico, who seemed the more conciliatory of the pair.

"Absolutely," I replied.

"Then we are all ears."

I went over the intended operation while they listened carefully and smoked their cigarettes.

"You've certainly thought of everything," said Harpo.

"He certainly has," said Chico.

"Maria was very helpful. In case you didn't know, she has a degree in aeronautics," I told him.

"Oh yes, we knew," said Harpo.

"We certainly did," said Chico.

I was minded to let this pass, but Angelica wasn't as patient.

"Then why on earth didn't you tell us?" she erupted. "Didn't you think it might be helpful to know that?"

Harpo shrugged, as if it was of no consequence.

"You discovered it anyway…" he said laconically.

"Oh, you two are impossible!" Angelica exclaimed in exasperation.

"If we'd thought it might be relevant then we would have told you," said Chico, opting to placate her. "Everything was done rather in haste in any case."

I glanced at my wife to see her pursing her lips.

"Anyway, we have some good news that you might like," said Harpo, changing the subject.

"Is Churchill coming after all?" I asked him, since it was the first thing which sprung to mind.

"Not quite, no," he replied. "But we do have someone who will act as his double."

"Oh, right. That's good." It seemed better than not having him at all.

"It took some doing, I can tell you," said Chico.

"This mission must be important to someone, then," said Angelica, still annoyed.

"It most certainly is," said Harpo. "A definite coup if we can pull it off, or rather if *you* can pull it off."

"We can only try," I said. "But we need you to do your part and put out the intelligence. Plus, I was also hoping you would manage the organisation of the event, if you would."

Decoy or not, we had to make sure the event appeared to be real. This would require advertising it locally. I was relying on the Marx Brothers to play their part in making that happen.

"It will all be in hand. Just concentrate on getting the Ace Raider back here and we'll do the rest," Harpo said.

"We'll need ack-ack and machine-gun defences on alert too," I said. "As a precaution."

"It will be taken care of," said Chico with a dismissive sweep of his hand. "Just keep the real reason under wraps."

"Of course," I said. "Then it seems there's no more to be discussed."

"Well, there is just one more thing," said Chico. "We should have a codename for the mission."

I must admit I had not thought of it, but Angelica was more awake on that suit.

"How about Operation Octopus?" she suggested.

"Octopus?" I said, surprised.

"Yes … we are ensnaring the Ace Raider within multiple arms, or planes in this case, so it makes sense," she said brightly.

"An excellent notion," said Harpo.

"She's hit it," said Chico.

"All right," I agreed. "Operation Octopus it is."

Since this was quite a tricky mission, I elected to hold a full briefing early on. I gathered both M Flight and Sandford's squadron in the mission room. Angelica sat in the front row along with Audrey, Bentley and the two MI6 spies.

"I've assembled you all here today for a top-secret mission," I said. "At least, the part you all have to play in it is top secret. The other part is not. Let me explain."

I paused, taking in some puzzled glances. Angelica smiled at me encouragingly.

"I'm sure you all know about the Ace Raider," I began.

"Oh, that guy!" said Second Lieutenant Joe McClusky, a pilot from Sandford's squadron. He was a little loud but had proven himself to be dependable in combat.

There was laughter at this.

"Yes, McClusky," I said. "*That* guy. The Ace Raider has been causing us a lot of problems as you know. He's dropped bombs, strafed high streets. In short, he's an infernal nuisance and we're going to put a stop to his antics. We've come up with a plan to lure him out," I continued. "Operation Octopus."

"Better than Operation Fish Bait," remarked Bentley caustically.

This had been the codename of a previous mission to which he'd taken great exception.

"A winter fete is going to be held in Cromer," I said.

"Oh no, not Cromer," said Jonty, causing everyone to laugh again.

I noticed Willie digging him in the ribs.

"Yes," I said, "Cromer, due to its location and various other suitable factors. That is the not so secret part. The other part, which is secret, is that this entire event is a decoy to capture the Ace Raider and bring him back to Banley."

There was silence at this, and indeed one or two people were staring at me open-mouthed. I wasn't in the least surprised.

"I know it's a tall order," I continued. "But here's how we plan to accomplish it…"

I went through the details of the plan, indicating flight paths and so forth on a map behind me. Once I had finished, I waited for questions.

"What happens if he won't cooperate?" asked Arjun at once. He could be relied on to look at the practicalities of any situation.

"Then we go to plan B," I said.

"Which is?"

"We shoot him down."

There were some other questions related to the timing, formation and logistics which I was able to answer.

"We will be conducting rehearsals," I explained, "to try and give us the best chance of success. It goes without saying that none of this information leaves this room. The date of the event is set. We will have a final briefing on the morning of the operation, fly up to Langham airfield and then wait until the appointed hour. We will take-off from there to carry out Operation Octopus."

When there were no more queries, I called an end to the proceedings.

The Marx Brothers came up and took their leave, as did Bentley.

"Well done, Angus," he said. "Hopefully it will all go swimmingly, rather in the manner of its codename."

He smiled at his own joke.

"I hope so too, sir," I told him.

Some of the Americans came up to say hello, notably McClusky and Second Lieutenant Larry Washington.

"Good to be flying another mission with you, Scottish," said Larry.

"Good to see you, Larry."

"I hope we can nail this Ace Raider, Chief," said McClusky, using the nickname he alone had assigned me.

"We'll do our best," I told him.

"Is Jonty going to make up one of those songs about it?" McClusky asked me. "I like them."

"Why don't you suggest it?" I said mendaciously.

"All right, I will."

Angelica sniggered beside me. I could well imagine what Willie would say. My prediction came true as a rather loud argument broke out at the other end of the room between Willie and Jonty.

Between patrols and rehearsals for Operation Octopus the days were soon filled. Part of me couldn't wait for the appointed day to arrive, and part of me was dreading it. With a mission there was always so much which could go wrong in spite of all the careful planning and rehearsing.

In the meantime the Ace Raider had been spotted on a couple of patrols. We had a little collection of his cards since word had spread about them, and they all found their way to Banley.

Of the Ace Assassin, on the other hand, there was no sign. This in itself was perturbing because I wondered where on earth he was and when he might attack again. I was leaving two pilots to cover the pursuit planes when we carried out the mission. Those two pilots would not be happy they weren't going to take part.

The day before the mission I gathered M Flight together in the hut after all the patrols were done.

"I am sorry but a couple of you are going to disappointed," I said. "I only need twelve pilots on this mission including myself. I have to choose the most experienced pilots first. So that's myself, Willie, Jonty, Arjun, Tomas and Jean."

I paused while the others looked at me expectantly.

"I'm also taking Dylan and Olek," I said.

These two, although newer than the veterans of our flight, were proving to be excellent pilots. Dylan smiled to hear he was included.

"That leaves four spots," I said. "Angelica here has six straws. The two short straws will stay here on pursuit duty. It's the best I can do to make things fair."

Patrick, Harold, Stanley, Berek, Arthur and Clive stepped forward. Each took a straw in turn. Berek and Clive drew the short straws. I could tell they were a little downhearted, but they hid it well.

"Berek and Clive," I said. "You'll stay on pursuit duty while we are away. The rest of us will reconvene in the morning."

There would be no patrols the following day since we were all hoping our mission would succeed.

That night I found it difficult to sleep, as I often did before a mission. This one was different in that we were not going into combat *per se*. However, it was still fraught with difficulty no matter how much planning we'd done.

I felt Angelica's arms go around me. She hugged me tightly.

"What's wrong?" she asked me softly.

"Oh, you know … the mission…" I sighed.

"You've every chance of success and you know it," she murmured. "It's not as if you haven't practiced it enough times."

I let out a low laugh. That much was true.

"And then there's the two pilots I had to leave behind."

"That's what happens when you are in command, darling," she reasoned. "You make the best decisions you can and every one of them respects you for it."

"Doesn't make it any easier," I said quietly.

"Let me see if I can help make it easier," she said.

"And how do you propose to do that?" I whispered.

Angelica laughed and pulled me into her embrace.

The morning arrived soon enough. Angelica and I opted to go down to the main dining room at Amberly Manor for breakfast. Jonty and Willie were already there, tucking into eggs and beans on toast. I was surprised more of the new pilots were not billeted at Amberly, but it seemed for the moment that the RAF had found places elsewhere.

"What-ho, Skipper," said Jonty. "Looks like a nice day for it."

The weather was indeed quite clement, I was happy to see. That would have been the one thing which could mar the whole proceedings. The other would be if the Ace Raider didn't show. The Marx Brothers had assured me that the word had gone out through their intelligence channels.

"Just as well," said Willie.

"Shame we can't go to this fete ourselves, it looks rather fun," said Jonty.

We'd seen the posters — the Marx Brothers had pushed the boat out. There was to be a military band, a few stalls, a march past of local soldiery and the rumoured appearance of Winston Churchill. That this was going to be a double was known only to myself, the Marx Brothers, Angelica and Bentley.

"We're not there to have fun," said Willie. "You know very well. Besides, you said Cromer was rather a dull place."

"That's before they organised a fete," said Jonty.

"Jonty," said Angelica, taking a bite of her eggs on toast. "You really are hopeless."

We all laughed.

"Let's just hope it all goes off without a hitch," I said.

"What about the … you know who?" said Jonty in a staged whisper. "What happens if he doesn't turn up?"

"Then it'll all be for nothing, I suppose," said Willie.

"I'm hoping the temptation will be too great," I said. "And in any case, we will find out soon enough, won't we."

"Here's to a successful mission then," said Jonty, raising his mug of tea in salute.

"I second that," said Willie with a grin.

After breakfast Gordon drove Angelica and me to Banley. Willie and Jonty went in Jonty's Morgan.

"Today the day is it, sir?" said Gordon.

He would have seen the poster for the fete. It was common knowledge. However, since he was privy to the plan, he would have put two and two together.

"Yes," I said. "It's today."

"Let me be the first to wish you success then."

"Here's hoping," I replied, with more optimism than I felt.

"It will be all right, darling. Tell him, Fred," said Angelica.

"I'm sure your good lady wife has the right of it, sir," said Gordon.

"Thanks," I told him.

I couldn't help the sinking feeling. But then I had felt the same on other missions too. You just could never tell if things were going to go your way, and that was inevitable.

We arrived at the airfield and headed to the hut. The flight was assembled and soon ready for the off. With a few minutes to go, Bentley appeared, striding towards us with Audrey. When he arrived, he stopped and took out his pipe. He had evidently already filled it with tobacco because he put it straight in his mouth and lit it.

"Just came to wish you chaps good luck," he said puffing away on his pipe. "Do your damnedest to bring that blasted Jerry back here."

"We will, sir," I told him.

"Jolly good, jolly good, well … carry on."

With that he left. I turned to Angelica. I took her in my arms and kissed her.

"Be safe," she said. "I hope you get him."

"So do I," I said.

"I love you."

"I love you too."

She was smiling as I made my way to my Spitfire with the others. Redwood strapped me in and I spun up the prop. The sound of twelve Merlin engines made an impressive roar as we taxied to the runway. Angelica would watch us leave before hurrying to her post on the comms.

"Kestrel One, you are clear for take-off," said the control tower.

'Kestrels' was the codename I had picked for M Flight for this mission. 'Catchers' was the codename for Sandford's squadron, which I think he had picked partly because it's a baseball term, and partly because it was appropriate considering the mission objective.

"Kestrels let's get airborne," I said, opening up the throttle.

We took off and I set a heading for Langham airbase. All of the Spitfires were fully loaded with ammo and had extra fuel just in case. I sincerely hoped we wouldn't have to use any ammo or much fuel. The radio crackled to life.

"Kestrel One, this is Catcher One, we're right behind you."

Right on cue we were joined by Sandford's squadron. They flew beside us in their own formation and together we made our way to Langham.

"Langham Control," I said, as we approached the airbase. "Kestrels and Catchers seeking permission to land."

"Go ahead," said Langham Control.

"Roger," I acknowledged and took us onto a final approach.

RAF Langham was used primarily by Coastal Command. It had concrete runways and hangars. Various protocols had to be gone through to allow us to land there.

Once down on the ground, we taxied to the part of the airbase we'd been told to go to. I killed my engine and the others did likewise. It was now a matter of waiting it out. Cromer lay due east of Langham. At the appointed hour, Sandford's squadron would take off first and head out into the Channel.

The fete was due to start around midday and Churchill's speech was well advertised at around half an hour after that. I figured that the Ace Raider would time it so that he arrived when this was taking place, if he was going to attack at all.

The waiting was the worst part. Various members of the crew went to use the facilities, but otherwise we were just hanging around. The minutes crawled by and then suddenly it was time. I felt the adrenaline start to kick in.

"It's showtime folks," said Sandford to his crew.

"Cometh the hour, cometh the man, aye, Skipper?" said Jonty.

"Let's hope he does then," I said.

"He will, Skipper, I can feel it."

Sandford's crew climbed back into their Spitfires. They were fired up once more and taxied out onto the runway. In short order they took off.

"Let's get set," I said to the others, jumping up onto the wing of my plane. I spun up the prop and sat there idling with the rest of the flight.

Sandford's squadron was to fly out to sea at altitude and then sweep back around. Hopefully, by that time, they would be behind the Ace Raider. We had figured how long it would take him to reach the site of the fete from where we wanted to intercept him. We had practised it and now we were just waiting for the word.

"Kestrel One, this is Catcher One, we're at waypoint one, ready to turn," said Sandford.

This meant they'd reached the point out to sea where they needed to fly parallel to the coast.

"Roger, Catcher One, any sign of the Rabbit?" I asked him.

The 'Rabbit' was the codename for the Ace Raider.

"Negative," replied Sandford.

My heart sank a little. If all was to go to plan, the German pilot had to be in sight shortly or he'd end up behind Sandford's squadron, where we didn't want him to be. Even worse, he may not turn up at all. The minutes ticked by. It wouldn't be long before the squadron were due to turn back to Cromer. There was no word. I watched the second-hand crawling around my watch face with trepidation. Then, just as I'd given up hope, the call came through.

"There he is. There's the Rabbit!"

It was McClusky. The Ace Raider had been spotted. I felt my heart start to beat faster. It was now or never.

"Roger, Kestrel One, we are tracking the Rabbit, ready to drop down to backstop position," said Sandford.

"Roger, Catcher One, we copy. We're about to join the party. Kestrels let's go," I said.

"Kestrel One, you are clear for take-off," said Langham Control.

That was the signal I needed. I throttled up and soon we were airborne once more. I tried to remain calm. Could we really do this?

We headed for Cromer and then I split the flight. Six planes flying in from each side at an angle to close the net around the Ace Raider.

"Kestrels, it's time for the two-step," I said. This was the codeword for me to take one half of the flight to the left, with Tomas leading the other half to the right.

I banked away and dropped down a little lower as we came at Cromer from the left-hand side. Tomas came at the town from the right. We spread out into the formation we had practised.

As we closed on the town, I could see crowds of people in the North Lodge Park. There was bunting, tents and a podium, upon which there appeared to be someone making a speech. I presumed this was the fake Churchill, arranged by the Marx Brothers. There wasn't time to take much in. It was all about to happen in short order.

"The Rabbit is almost at the coast," said Sandford.

"Roger," I said.

Timing was everything. If we'd worked it out right, we would intercept him before he was able to start firing at the crowd. That situation had to be avoided at all costs.

"Catcher One, go low, get in behind him," I said.

This manoeuvre was designed to spook him; he would try to turn and escape, but we'd be there to cut him off.

I saw the raider's plane streaking in. Sandford's squadron fanned out. Some of them dropped low and the others remained higher in case he started to climb. For a moment he kept going towards the waiting crowd. Faces turned as they heard the roar of the aircraft. There would be no friendly fire this time. The ack-ack battery and machine-gunners had been properly briefed. They would only open fire on the Ace Raider as a last resort.

Then it all happened at once. The pilot must have suddenly clocked the Spitfires in his mirror. Perhaps he had become a little blasé, having got away with his antics for so long. Just as he had done before, he tried to climb whilst pulling a tight turn.

"He's trying to get away," said McClusky.

"We've got him, don't worry," I said.

Four of us had come in from the left in a stretched-out line. We had his exit covered. He saw us and immediately turned to go the other way. He found his exit blocked there too. The only way out was inland or upwards.

We'd already thought of that. Some of Sandford's planes were in a position which negated the possibility of him gaining altitude without being caught. We had deliberately left him with one real option and that was the one he took. He gained some height and headed inland, just as we had planned.

"Kestrels, close the net," I said.

This would be the *pièce de résistance*. If this went well, then we had him where we wanted him. Two planes on either side of him were going to create the box.

I watched as they executed it perfectly. The Ace Raider wouldn't have had time to think about it. His attention would have been on the large number of planes at his back. He would be distracted and hopefully feeling outnumbered. I was counting on it.

"I've got him, Skipper," said Jonty.

In the prearranged manoeuvre, he pulled up alongside the Ace Raider on one side, Dylan on the other.

"I'm in position," said Willie, arriving above him.

"Me too," said Tomas, who had managed to get underneath.

In the meantime, I had shifted position and was now flying behind the Ace Raider. The rest of our planes moved into their designated positions to support us. He hadn't had time to realise what we were doing. The fact we had not opened fire would have disconcerted him. He would have expected us to shoot him down, not surround him the way we had.

"I'll just give him a wave, Skipper," said Jonty.

From my position, I could see him doing so. The Ace Raider looked at him for a moment. This was the moment when I thought he might attempt to run, and I was right. All of a sudden, he throttled up his kite. Unfortunately for him, I was ready for it. I fired a burst of tracers over him. He couldn't have failed to see it. The Ace Raider slowed down and settled back into his box.

"Well done, Skipper," said Jonty.

"Don't count your chickens," I replied.

I suspected the Ace Raider might try again. He was as wily as a fox. I kept my finger poised on the trigger. Jonty pointed in the direction we wanted him to go. The Ace Raider turned his plane as directed. We all turned with him, keeping him in our box.

As I suspected, he hadn't completely abandoned the idea of escaping. As we headed due south and started a course for Banley, he throttled up his plane once more and tried to flip sideways. I was ready for that too. This time I fired a burst at his wing.

"You've hit him, Scottish," said Willie.

I fired again. Just a short burst, as I didn't want to shoot him down. I just wanted to show him that we meant business. He got the message and his plane started to slow. I wondered if, perhaps, I had hit a control line, but he was able to keep flying. We adjusted our speed accordingly. I wasn't taking any chances. By now the Ace Raider would have figured out that he couldn't get out of this situation alive. I felt it was safe to completely enclose him.

"Kestrel Four, take up a forward position," I said to Arjun.

"Roger."

I had not wanted him there before in case I had to fire, or in case the Ace Raider had fired on him. Arjun's plane dropped in front of the Ace Raider. He was now truly boxed in.

"Caught like a rat in a trap," said McClusky with satisfaction.

"Yep, we got him," said Larry.

After all the times that he had evaded us, the Ace Raider was finally captured. We still had to get him home, but I sincerely doubted he would attempt to escape. He could be under no illusions that he'd be shot down at once. It was time to give Banley the prearranged coded phrase for a successful outcome.

"Control," I said, as Banley Airfield came in sight. "We're bringing home the bacon."

"Roger," said the tower. "We have an escort standing by."

Jonty began to sing, "A-hunting we will go, a-hunting we will go, we'll catch a fox and put him in a box, and never let him go…"

CHAPTER THIRTEEN

It was with a sense of jubilation that we landed. I could hardly believe we'd actually achieved what we had set out to do. We had done the impossible and caught the Ace Raider.

As we taxied to a stop, all the other planes were coming in too, including Sandford's squadron. Nobody wanted to miss out on the finale to our successful mission. Even better, apart from a couple of salvos, not a shot was fired.

As we came to a standstill, the Ace Raider's plane was immediately surrounded by armed soldiers. He casually opened his canopy and got down from the wing. He was checked for weapons and then kept under guard. The sergeant in charge offered him a cigarette, which he accepted, and stood there smoking as if he hadn't a care in the world. In truth, perhaps he hadn't, since the war was effectively over for him.

To my surprise, there was a film crew filming the entire event and also cameramen taking photos. In fact, I now noticed there was a large press contingent. In amongst them I spotted the Marx Brothers.

Before I could do anything else, Angelica came running out from the crowd of reporters. She jumped into my arms while I whirled her around.

"You did it, darling, you did it," she said jubilantly.

"*We* did it, all of us," I replied, smiling.

"Yes, of course, but you're the leader, it was your show. I'm so proud of you."

There were hearty congratulations going on all around us. All the other pilots were shaking hands and talking in excited voices. It was, after all, something of an unusual occasion.

As expected, Bentley and Audrey were soon standing beside us. Bentley was finishing his pipe routine and soon had it alight. He seemed in a sunny mood as he puffed away.

"Well done, Angus, that was a damn fine show," he said.

"Thank you, sir," I replied, shaking his hand.

"You've no doubt noticed that those blasted spies have arranged a bloody circus. Typical, bloody clowns," he said, pointing the stem of his pipe at the camera crew and newsmen.

"I did wonder, sir."

He took a few more puffs before continuing.

"Oh, you know, the usual flannel about helping the war effort. I suppose it will. Catching that blighter might boost morale for a while. It's sorely needed, but really, I think we could have done without a bloody stampede of reporters," he said.

"Yes, sir."

"Oh well, I see those damn fools approaching, no doubt they want to talk to you, the hero of the hour. We'll debrief later," he said, making a hasty exit.

The objects of his scorn, the Marx Brothers, appeared moments later. They seemed rather animated for once.

"Well done, Flight Lieutenant," said Harpo, holding out his hand.

"Precisely," said Chico.

I shook hands with both of them. They then immediately lit up a cigarette each.

"We'd like you and your chaps to be photographed with the captured pilot, if you don't mind," said Harpo.

"Really?"

"Yes, you know, for the war effort, that sort of thing."

"Okay," I said, seeing nothing against it.

I glanced at Angelica and her eyes twinkled mischievously. She seemed to find the idea amusing. She and I accompanied the Marx Brothers to where the rest of the crew were already being arranged into a group. The Ace Raider was placed in the centre as if he was some kind of hunting trophy.

"We'd like you to help us interrogate the Ace Raider," said Chico, as we walked towards them.

"Me? Why?"

"We think he might relate to you as a fellow pilot; you might be able to soften him up a little, get some information out of him," said Harpo.

"But I'm not an interrogator," I protested.

"We just want you to talk to him, that's all. There are limits, obviously, to how much we can try to persuade him to tell us anything," said Chico.

I didn't like to imagine how they might go about persuading someone to talk. There seemed no harm in me talking to the Ace Raider, however, so I agreed.

"All right," I said. "Tell me where and when."

"Perhaps tomorrow," said Harpo. "Once this little shindig is over."

The Ace Raider seemed happy enough to be photographed with the rest of us. Perhaps it suited his personality to be made the centre of attention. I was sure that while it was news of the moment, it would soon be forgotten in the grand scheme of things. I doubted it would even be remembered five years hence. However, today was a triumph and we all enjoyed our part in it.

The Ace Raider was eventually removed and taken into custody. The reporters dispersed after canvassing a few lines about the operation from the rest of us. Sandford's crew took off and returned to their base.

"That's that then, Skipper," said Jonty as we walked back to the dispersal hut.

"Yes, that's one problem solved," I said. "But there's still the Ace Assassin and we haven't solved that."

"Not to worry, Skipper, I'm sure something will turn up."

"That's what you always say," said Willie.

"And it's true!" Jonty retorted.

"Oh boys, don't you ever stop?" Angelica said, laughing.

"I'll stop when he does," said Jonty.

"Oh no you won't…" Willie shot back.

I burst out laughing too. Some things never changed.

The following morning, I expected to see Audrey waiting for us when we arrived at the airbase. I wasn't disappointed in that assumption. As soon as Gordon parked the jeep, she came running up to us.

"Let me guess," I said. "The Marx Brothers want me to talk to the German pilot."

"Yes," she said. "That's right."

"Lead on," I told her.

Angelica accompanied us to the main building and our erstwhile mission room. The Marx Brothers were sitting leisurely smoking cigarettes in their usual fashion.

"Ah, Flight Lieutenant Mackennelly," said Harpo. "Glad you can help us with this little … problem."

I sat down and Angelica took a seat beside me.

"What exactly do you want me to do?" I asked them.

"Just talk to him, see if you can get him to loosen up," said Chico. "We can't obviously put too much pressure on him … the Geneva Convention, that sort of thing."

"Right."

The Geneva Convention had been put in place for a reason. It applied as much to the Germans as it did to us. However, I wondered if the Germans would still adhere to it if they won the war. I didn't like to think about it too much. In any case, I was determined to play my part to ensure they did not.

"See if you can get anything useful from him, that's all," said Harpo.

"What do you call, useful?" I asked him.

He took a pull on his cigarette and let the smoke float up to the ceiling.

"His unit, his *raison d'être*, why he's doing what he's doing, how many of them are there, that sort of thing. We can find all that out in time, but it's far easier if he will tell us."

"I'll try, though I don't really see why he will be willing to do so. After all, in his position, I wouldn't."

"Give it a go," said Chico.

"All right, and where will you be?" I asked him.

"We'll be listening in the room next door. We've set up a recording device." He turned to Angelica. "Come and listen with us if you like, Section Officer."

"Yes, I will," she said.

As they didn't seem disposed to move, I chivvied them a little.

"Shall we get on with it then?" I asked them.

"As you wish," said Chico.

This was the type of thing that annoyed me immensely about them. They'd ask me to do something and then make it seem as if I was the one who had initiated it.

"Yes," I said, barely containing my impatience. "Yes, let's do that."

"Follow us then," said Harpo, getting up.

We accompanied them to another part of the building. There was a door with two armed guards outside it.

"In there," said Chico. "When you've finished, knock on the door. Oh, and you'll need these."

He handed me a packet of cigarettes and a box of matches.

"Let him smoke, but don't leave the matches with him," he said.

"Okay."

I put them in my pocket and waited while they opened the door. I entered a windowless room lit by a single bulb hanging from the ceiling. It was sparse except for a table and two chairs. I supposed this was deliberate. A little discomfort might make a person disposed to talk.

The Ace Raider sat in one of the chairs. He looked to be in his late twenties, with blond hair, blue eyes and a square jaw. He was wearing a leather jacket over his tunic, the uniform trousers which flared out at the sides, and high black boots.

"I'm Flight Lieutenant Angus Mackennelly," I told him.

He stood up and clicked his heels.

"Hauptmann Edgar Neumann at your service," he said.

His rank was the Luftwaffe equivalent of mine. I motioned him to sit while I took the seat opposite him. I took out the packet of cigarettes and offered him one. He took it and I lit it for him. I carefully put the cigarettes and matches back in my pocket.

He waited for me to say something, observing me with interest while taking a long drag on the cigarette, then blowing out the smoke with satisfaction.

"Are you being treated well?" I asked him, trying to think of how best to start.

"Yes, for sure. I was given a room, a bed, food. It's what I would hope to expect," he replied.

His English was accomplished. I thought I would begin there.

"Where did you learn such good English?" I asked him.

"I studied it before the war," he told me. "I was planning to go into business as a banker. But the war…" He trailed off.

"So, you became a pilot. Why did you choose to do that?"

I hoped that by engaging him in less contentious issues he might let slip something a little more confidential. At least that was my plan.

"Why did *you*?" he asked me instead.

"I always wanted to fly, I suppose. When the war started it was natural for me to want to join the RAF."

"Well, then you see we are not so different. I was the same. It seemed perhaps something of a glorious profession. To soar above in the sky like a bird."

It sounded quite poetic. He said it with some passion.

"You seem to imply it was something of a calling," I replied with a smile.

"Yes, of course. Also, it seemed the best way to serve the Führer," he told me.

Perhaps he was a zealot after all, I thought. If he was, then he probably wouldn't be particularly forthcoming. I decided to test that theory.

"And now?" I said lightly.

"Now, I don't serve him anymore … unless, of course, you lose the war."

He laughed and continued to smoke his cigarette. I pushed the point a little further.

"So, it was more than just for the glory of the Third Reich then? This urge to fly?" I asked him.

"Glory, it's something all of us want, *ja?* To excel, to be the best, to do extraordinary things. Things that others cannot do. For me, this was to be the best flier in the Luftwaffe."

"These raids you've been carrying out, is that what you mean?" I asked him.

"For sure, a single fighter against many, and still to escape… to come by stealth and go again without being challenged. That's something special. Don't you think?"

Gordon had been right. He was certainly a showman.

"These calling cards you left behind, why did you do that? Why do you have the Ace of Spades painted on your Focke-Wulf?"

"So, you found them?" he said, looking pleased. "I wasn't sure."

I capitalised on this topic a little.

"Yes, we have a nickname for you. We call you the Ace Raider."

I wondered if flattery would work. It was worth a try. He tipped his head back and laughed.

"That's funny. I wish I could tell them back at the unit about this. They would say 'Edgar, you are famous now in Britain'. Edgar the Ace Raider. That's very funny."

"So, you had a few people in your unit? How many?" I asked, seizing the opening.

He stopped laughing and wagged his finger at me in mock admonishment.

"Ah … no … I see what you are doing, but you won't trick me so easily."

This irritated me more than perhaps it should. I decided to go on the offensive.

"I was just curious," I replied, ignoring this. "Why did you pick coastal towns to attack? Why were you bombing civilians and strafing the streets?"

"Your bombers are doing the same in my country," he retorted.

"Yes, but not our fighters. We attack military targets, other fighters, not defenceless towns. Who gave the orders to do that?"

"I did," he said, to my surprise. "It was my idea, all mine. Why not? This is how we disrupt the enemy — keep them busy, no? Look at how many planes you needed to capture me. Which was, by the way, well done. You executed that trap extremely well. I'm impressed."

"So how many more are there in your unit?" I shot back.

"You will find out, of course, when they attack you like I did. But I was the best ... I wanted to be the best. I even have the Iron Cross. Hitler gave it to me himself."

I noticed it, now he mentioned it. It sat in the centre of his tunic at the top, near the collar. I began to feel I wasn't getting anywhere. It seemed almost like a game to him.

"You know," he continued, "we've heard of your unit too. The Mavericks, am I right?"

There seemed no point in hiding it. We had the badge on our planes. I had one on my uniform.

"Yes, you're right."

"We respect good pilots," he said. "You have some very good pilots. Some of us ... others ... don't want to fly against the Mavericks. But me, I will fly against anyone and try to win, always."

He was certainly full of himself, that much was clear.

"Thank you," I said.

He finished his cigarette. I offered him another and went through the same routine.

"*Danke,*" he said smoking it with relish.

"Do you really believe in all that? Hitler's thousand-year Reich? The master race?" I asked him, thinking I might as well see what his true feelings were.

"Do I believe it?" he said, leaning back in his chair once more. "It's easy, you know, to become taken up by the ocean, swallowed in the tide of popular enthusiasm. Besides, those who don't believe it…"

He didn't finish the sentence, but I knew exactly what he meant. They wouldn't fare too well under Hitler's regime. He had told me a lot without saying much. He was an opportunist going with the tide, using it to his advantage. Perhaps the profession of a banker would have suited him. He believed what he had to in order to get by. Many others in Germany probably did the same.

"Then why, if you don't really believe it, don't you tell us what we need to know?" I asked him curiously.

"Because I'm also loyal to my comrades. I mean my people, in my unit. We are brothers in arms. I took an oath. No matter what I believe, or what you think of me, I'm still an honourable man."

I could understand that, to a degree. I would probably be the same. However, I also believed in a just cause. I didn't believe Hitler's regime was a just cause. Toppling it, however, certainly was.

"Your pilot," he added. "That one I shot recently … did he…?"

"He made it back to base," I said.

"I'm glad."

There was often fellow feeling among pilots if you met them in the flesh. Enemies or not. In a plane they were faceless but like this, it was somehow different.

There seemed nothing more to say. He was unlikely to tell me anything useful after all. Hopefully, the Marx Brothers would fare better, although I did not think so. I stood up.

"Thank you for your time," I said.

"As you can see, I am a man of leisure now. After the war, then perhaps I can still become a banker."

"Perhaps you can," I replied.

"*Auf wiedersehen*. Good luck with the rest of the war," he said, tipping me a salute.

I returned the salute and knocked on the door to be let out. Back in the corridor, the Marx Brothers and Angelica were waiting.

"Well done," said Harpo.

"Yes, excellent work," said Chico.

"He didn't really tell me anything," I demurred.

"Oh, but he did. We now know it's his unit and he's the one who made the plans. We will gather a little more intelligence to see if we can't persuade him to talk a little more."

"What will happen to him?" I asked them.

"He'll be sent to a POW camp in due course," said Chico.

"When we're done," said Harpo.

"Well, the main thing was to stop him and that's been accomplished," I said.

"Indeed," said Chico.

I waited because Harpo seemed disposed to say something further.

"The fete was a great success, by the way, according to reports from our people. Churchill's double inspired them all. By all accounts, the crowd had an excellent time. They hardly noticed the operation you carried out with such success. Some people thought it was a flypast, apparently," he told me.

"It's a good job we didn't shoot him down then, with all those people there."

"Not to worry if you had," said Harpo. "We'd simply have made up a story of your heroics, and had your pictures taken anyway."

I might have guessed they had an answer. They always did.

"All's well that ends well then," I said, since there was nothing further to say.

"Indeed, in which case I guess this is toodle-pip," said Harpo.

"And chin-chin," said Chico.

Angelica and I left them to it and went outside.

"Come and sit on the bench with me," she said, tucking her arm into mine.

"All right."

We made our way towards our favourite spot at the edge of the field.

"You did wonderfully well, darling," she told me.

"Do you really think so?"

"Yes, of course."

"I think I'm a better pilot than an interrogator," I said.

"You must be glad it's over, darling. At least you can cut down on the patrols," she said.

"Yes," I agreed.

The high number of patrols I had organised was due mostly to the Ace Raider's incursions. Now I would have to reorganise things. Angelica rested her head against my shoulder.

"I love this," she said. "Just you and me, it makes me feel so content, even for a few moments."

"I do too," I said, absently, and then thinking out loud, "but there is still the matter of the Ace Assassin. We haven't solved that problem."

"Must you?" Angelica said in a teasing tone.

"I can't help it," I replied. "It's on my mind. He could attack at any time."

"I know that, of course," she said. "But can't you just stop worrying about it, just for a moment?"

"All right, I'll try…"

"You know," she said playfully, "you could just kiss me, that will take your mind off it."

It was her remedy for everything. I was about to oblige her when there was a discreet cough beside me. It was Audrey.

"I'm sorry to interrupt," said Audrey. "It's just that, well, I've got orders here for a sortie."

"It's all right," I said and took the sheet of paper from her.

"What is it?" asked Angelica.

"We're to fly as a bomber escort this afternoon along with Sandford's squadron," I said.

"Oh, well, I guess he's called in the favour then," said Angelica.

"I guess he has," I replied.

Once I had the orders, there was nothing for it but to return with Angelica to the hut and round up the rest of the crew. The mission was to take place around midday. I decided I would leave Dylan and Patrick behind, manning the pursuit planes.

Angelica and I took an early lunch. Olga was in the mess with Maria, it seemed they often ate there now that Maria had her uniform. Nobody paid her much attention, which was all to the good.

"Listen," I told her in a low voice as I consumed a plate of rabbit stew with potatoes. "I suggest you lie low after lunch. The Mavericks have been called away to escort the Americans."

"All right," said Maria.

"The two pursuit planes will remain in place," I said. "Nevertheless, it is sensible to be careful."

"Yes," she agreed.

After lunch, Angelica and I headed back to the hut. I gathered M Flight together and briefed them on the mission details. Then I wrapped things up.

"So, as I said, the target is some suspected armaments factories in Rotterdam. We're flying escort along with Flight Lieutenant Judd's squadron. It's been a while since we've done one of these, but just keep it tight and try not to get shot down."

"I thought we were done with these missions, Skipper," Jonty complained.

"Apparently, they've not enough of their own escorts for this one, so we have to oblige. Besides, Captain Booker has helped us out plenty of times in the past," I told him.

"Not to mention the Ace Raider one we just flew, or did you forget?" said Willie.

"True, I suppose. Anyway, Skipper, I'll make sure I come back, don't you worry. Percy would miss me otherwise."

There was general laughter at this. Jonty certainly seemed to have become inordinately fond of his parrot. Percy also liked to watch with great interest as Jonty and Willie played chess.

"All right," I said, "let's get to it. Our codename for the mission is Wildcats."

The crew filed out, leaving Dylan and Patrick, who would remain behind.

"I'm counting on you both," I told them. "If that assassin appears, do your damnedest to shoot him down."

"We won't let you down, Scottish, never fear," said Dylan.

Outside the hut, I turned to Angelica and took her in my arms.

"Duty calls," I said with a smile.

"I know, I'll be waiting for you."

"I'll be back."

I kissed her for a long moment before letting go slowly, as we always did.

"I love you," she said.

"I love you too."

I walked to my Spitfire and Redwood helped me strap in. I could hear Judd's squadron firing up their engines. I spun up the prop on my kite and the air was filled with the roar of twenty-four Merlins. It was one of the sweetest sounds a pilot could hear. I taxied my Spitfire out to take-off position.

"Zebras airborne," said Judd as their squadron took off first.

"Wildcat Leader, you're clear for take-off," said the control tower.

"Roger, Control. Wildcats let's go," I said, throttling up.

The Spitfire responded immediately and in moments we were airborne too. I set a heading for the rendezvous with the bombers due east.

It was a straight hop across the Channel to Rotterdam. Within moments I sighted the massive flights of B-17s. This was to be a big bombing raid, hence the need for the extra fighter cover. I settled the squadron into position to the left of the main phalanx of bombers.

"Big Bear Leader, this is Wildcat Leader on station," I told the lead bomber.

"Roger, Wildcat Leader, welcome aboard. Looks like a nice day."

"Roger," I replied.

It was a clear and sunny day, which would be good for visibility on the bombing run, but at the same time make the job of the flak batteries a lot easier.

"Wildcat Leader, this is Moose Leader, glad you could make it." It was Sandford.

"Wouldn't miss it for the world, Moose Leader," I said with a laugh.

"Let's hope it goes like clockwork," said Sandford.

"You and me both," I replied.

We relapsed into silence. Pretty soon we were over the Channel. The blue water below us was flecked with white and I could make out a convoy of ships heading northwards. I didn't envy the Navy their lot, although they would probably say the same about us.

The coastline of Holland loomed up ahead. It wouldn't be long before the flak started up, then we'd need to keep on the alert for enemy fighters. Many of the bombers and their crews would not return to Blighty. I didn't aim for M Flight to be of their number.

It did not take long to make landfall over the Dutch coast.

"Wildcats here we go," I said. "Watch the flak and keep your eyes peeled for bandits."

Rotterdam is a little south of the Hague. Puffs of exploding flak started to fill the air as the batteries opened fire. It was now just a matter of engaging any incoming fighters. I was certain they would arrive in short order. Our presence was some deterrent, but the enemy liked to try and pick off the bombers which were hit by flak and started to falter.

I noticed right away that more than one bomber had already been hit. A B-17 with flaming engines started to dive towards the earth. The crew baled out — the pilot last. I wondered if he would make it. However, my attention was claimed by a cry from Jean.

"Bandits, twelve o'clock high, coming in fast."

"Break, Wildcats, break, engage," I said.

There was a bevy of Focke-Wulfs heading for the bombers. The flak had diminished somewhat so they could get in closer.

"Five minutes to target," said the lead bomber.

We split up and flew against the incoming planes. Tracers streamed out from the B-17 gunners as the German fighters flew by taking potshots.

I closed on a Wulf whose attention was on a bomber which had just been hit by flak. For a second, he was in my sights. I fired.

The salvo raked his fuselage. I was sure I'd got him as his kite fell away. I had no time to think about it further as there were too many others. I turned back into the pack. The air was filled with ammunition and radio chatter from the fighter pilots.

"Get him off my tail," said Arjun, weaving left and right in frustration. A Wulf was chasing him down.

"I've got you," Tomas told him.

He swooped in from the side like an avenging angel and fired. The Wulf's engine started to smoke.

"Thanks," said Arjun, returning to the fray.

"I'm hit, I'm hit," came a shout from Second Lieutenant Clement Floyd, a member of Sandford's squadron.

"Get the hell away if you can," Sandford told him.

"I'm trying."

His engine was smoking. I hoped he'd make it, Clement was a likeable guy. I turned my attention to another Wulf which was circling in for an attack. He saw me and turned away as soon as I fired. The bullets passed him harmlessly by.

"Bad luck, Skipper," said Jonty, who appeared on my wing. "Isn't this a jolly wheeze?"

"Not exactly what I'd call it, no," I replied, pulling a tight turn to avoid a salvo from another Jerry fighter.

"Take that," said Willie.

In my mirror, I saw the Wulf explode into flames. Willie always seemed to have my back.

"Thanks, Kiwi," I said.

I could see several bombers were either in the throes of going down or with disabled engines. The others flew on to the target regardless. Then came the words we were all waiting for.

"Bombs away," said the lead bomber to my relief.

The B-17s were finally over the target and their deadly cargo rained down to earth. The inevitable explosions came not long after. The ground below us was filled with smoke and flames.

"Big Bears, let's go home," said the lead bomber as soon as their ordinance had been dropped.

"Wildcats, we're heading back," I said to M Flight.

However, there was no time for jubilation. The Germans would harry the bombers for as long as they could. I circled around over the main phalanx of bombers looking for enemy fighters.

A couple of Wulfs decided to attack the bombers from the rear, I turned to meet them.

"I'm with you, Skipper, never fear," said Jonty, as I fired a burst at the leading plane.

The Jerry banked away. Olek came in from the side and fired at the other plane. He shattered the German's canopy. The Wulf went into a dive.

"That's another one down," said Tomas with satisfaction.

In the periphery of my vision, I saw Harold and Jean chasing down another Jerry. They were firing while he tried to avoid them. He went into a steep dive and they sensibly broke contact.

In the meantime, we continued to weave over the flight without further incident. It seemed that the Germans had decided enough was enough. Their fighters retreated and the flak started up again, hoping to catch a few more tail-end bombers as they departed. Once we had crossed the coastline, I decided it was safe to return to our escort position.

"Wildcats form up," I said.

The rest of M Flight — who were thankfully intact — took up our usual formation once more.

"That was a bun fight," said Jonty, settling on my wing.

He enjoyed aerial combat, it seemed, and took to it with relish.

"What is wrong with you?" Willie asked him, arriving on my other wing.

"Just taking pleasure where I can, Kiwi," said Jonty. "Can't go hunting, so this is second best."

"I would hardly compare this to hunting," I told him.

I wasn't fond of blood sports myself, but the upper classes would do what they would do. Jonty was born into that life. I was, too, but my father didn't indulge in such pastimes unless it was to hunt for the dinner table.

"Hey, Jonty," said McClusky. "Give us one of your tunes."

"No!" cried Willie in despair.

With such encouragement, Jonty naturally felt obligated to comply.

"Oh, the Brits and Yanks they went out on a mission, and we took down some Wulfs, just like going fishing. The bombers hit their target and the fighters hit their mark. It was a jolly shindig and we kicked up quite a lark…" sang Jonty lustily, to barely stifled moans from Willie.

I didn't quell Jonty's enthusiasm for once and to Willie's annoyance, I let Jonty serenade us all the way home.

"Wildcat One, we're signing off," said Sandford as we saw Banley in the distance.

"Roger," I replied.

"That was a great song," McClusky said. "I'd love to hear it again sometime."

"I say, good show," said Jonty.

As opposed to Willie, McClusky genuinely seemed to like Jonty's ballads.

As we got closer to Banley, something caught my eye. A flicker in the sun off a canopy in the distance. I squinted to get a better look. It was the familiar shape of a black plane, a P-40, and it was streaking in low towards the airbase.

"That's the Ace Assassin!" cried Jonty, who had seen it too.

"Break," I said frantically. "Break, let's get him, shoot him down at all costs!"

We dropped out of formation and fanned out on the attack. The assassin continued on, almost oblivious to our approach. I saw two figures running for the pursuit planes. Dylan and Patrick were on the ball. The assassin had been spotted.

Just as we were closing in on him, he must have seen us because he turned away abruptly.

"Don't let him out of your sight," I said, throttling up in pursuit.

I dropped down low, followed by the others. I was determined that this time the assassin would not get away from us.

CHAPTER FOURTEEN

Now began quite a chase. The assassin's plane had a head start, but our Spitfire Mark IXs had a marginally higher top speed if we could keep it up. The assassin was an expert flier, hugging the ground, skimming over trees and largely leading us a merry dance.

Nevertheless, we started to gain on the fighter little by little.

"We're behind you, Scottish," said Dylan.

"Thanks, Dylan," I said.

He and Patrick had taken off and were catching us up. I was sure I still had ammo but not certain if we all did. However, regardless of that, the assassin could not outrun us all.

"We'll get that blighter this time for sure," said Jonty. "Tally-ho! What fun!"

I was too busy concentrating to answer. The assassin was relying on outmanoeuvring us. He must know he could not otherwise escape us. A huge bank of trees was looming in front of him. I felt he must surely have to pop up a bit higher, but instead, he banked sharply, with his wing almost touching the ground. On instinct, I fired, and the shots went wide.

His plane streaked along the edge of the woods and then around the side. We temporarily lost sight of him. I took us up higher over the wood, looking in the direction he had gone. He wasn't there. Cursing the fact he'd eluded us again I throttled back a little, with the intention of circling around.

"There he is!" shouted Arjun. "On your nine o'clock."

The assassin had cut around the back of the woods unseen and was trying to make a getaway.

"Come on, let's get after him," I said, turning my kite towards the assassin and throttling up to maximum.

The others followed suit. He'd gained some distance, but we would soon make that up. I dropped low again and continued to pursue him over the open ground.

"Surely he knows the game is up," said Tomas. "We are going to get him in the end."

The assassin was like a cornered rat and twice as wily. I figured he wouldn't be giving up any time soon, unless he ran out of fuel. There was a danger he might turn and try to fire at us. We outnumbered him by a large margin and he would surely die.

We continued to close in and this time there was no cover. He was flying over open fields and even though he was low, it was just a matter of time before we caught him.

Up ahead loomed a country estate with a large manor house. I had no idea exactly where we were, being too intent on going after the assassin. Suddenly, the Ace Assassin gained height. Following suit, I noticed what looked like a long level open area just behind the house. The assassin flew over the house and started to lose height rapidly.

"He's going to land," said Dylan.

"But whose house is that?" said Patrick.

I didn't answer; I was too intent on putting paid to the assassin's antics. I finally saw my chance. I had closed the distance between us. The P-40 was in my sights. I opened fire and the tracers streaked out towards it, hitting the assassin's plane in the wing and the tail. It rocked as the bullets found their mark. I prepared to fire another salvo when the P-40 dropped abruptly to the ground without warning. It skidded on its belly on what at second glance appeared to be some kind of runway.

I overshot the plane and pulled a tight turn. In the meantime, the pilot was opening the cockpit. As I flew back towards him, he set off at a run. There was absolutely no chance I would let him escape. As he pelted at top speed away from his plane, I fired. The bullets kicked up divots in the ground. The line of fire was almost perfect as the bullets took the assassin amidships. His body was lifted up in air by the impact and then spun sideways. As I passed over him once more, he lay stock still on the runway. The assassin was dead.

"You got him, Scottish, you got him!" shouted Dylan with jubilation.

I thought fast. We would need some ground reinforcements as soon as possible. I had no idea where the estate was or whose it was, but I didn't think that the pilot had landed there by chance. That meant that whoever owned the estate might be somewhat hostile. The rest of M Flight had been circling the estate while the drama unfolded beneath them.

"Jonty, Willie and Dylan," I said. "You stay with me. We're going to land. Tomas, take the rest of the flight back to Banley. Get a bearing on this place and bring some ground forces pronto."

"Wilco, Scottish," said Tomas. "Form up on me, M Flight, let's go."

The main body of M Flight dispersed with Tomas, while I banked around so that the rest of us could land on the airstrip.

Within a few moments we were all on the ground and I killed the engine. The others followed suit. I climbed out of the cockpit, jumped down from the wing and pulled out my revolver. Willie, Jonty and Dylan did the same. Warily we advanced on the pilot. He did not move.

"Shall we find out who he really is, Skipper?" said Jonty.

"Go ahead," I told him.

We stayed back and levelled our pistols, just in case the pilot wasn't really dead. It seemed unlikely but you could never be sure. Considering the crafty nature of this assassin, I wasn't taking any chances. Jonty reached the pilot and gingerly put his foot out. He prodded the body with the toe of his boot but there was no reaction.

"He's definitely dead, Skipper," said Jonty.

"See who it is then," I replied.

Jonty squatted down and pulled off the pilot's leather helmet. He gasped.

"It's a woman," he said in surprise.

"What?" I said, coming nearer for a better look.

"The pilot is a woman, Skipper. See for yourself."

I could hardly believe it. It seemed so unlikely. We all looked down at the prone body of the dead pilot. Sure enough, the pilot was definitely female. Her long blonde hair spilled out around her head on the ground. Her blue eyes were open and staring vacantly upwards. She was also wearing red lipstick which, for a pilot, seemed incongruous. The earth beneath her was now stained red to match her lipstick as was the white shirt under her sheepskin jacket.

"Do we know who she is?" asked Willie.

"I've no idea," I replied. "Nor do I know who this estate belongs to."

"Maybe we should find out?" said Dylan.

"Perhaps you're right," I said. "Leave her for the moment, she's not going anywhere. We'll go to the main house, but be careful."

We approached the house with trepidation. There wasn't any sign of activity, which seemed a tad unusual. The manor house was quite a large edifice of two storeys. It was made of stone and seemed to be a square-shaped building from the back.

French doors opened out onto a stone terrace and thence to what might once have been a back lawn, but had since been fashioned into an airstrip, considering the distance it stretched out from the house.

"There's a hangar over there," said Dylan, whose sharp eyes had spotted a large open-sided building under cover of the trees which lined the runway. The hangar was painted green and appeared to be camouflaged. It looked like there was another plane inside it. A Tiger Moth or similar. Having a Tiger Moth may not have been unusual for someone in the upper classes, but the possession of a P-40 certainly was.

We couldn't see anyone moving about inside the house.

"Shall we go inside, Scottish?" asked Dylan.

"No," I said. "We don't know what we're walking into. Let's go round to the front."

My instinct was to exercise as much caution as possible. After my previous experiences with Lord Buchanan, I didn't want to take any chances. If the proprietor of this estate was a Nazi sympathiser, then being inside their domain wasn't a good place to be.

The side of the house had a few windows which looked out onto some ornate gardens. The house was, however, quite wide, which spoke of generational wealth probably going back centuries. As we rounded the corner, the vista opened up into a large gravel turning circle with a fountain in the middle. A long driveway lined with trees stretched off into the distance.

There was an open-topped Rolls-Royce in the driveway with the engine running. A man was sitting at the wheel and there was another man in the back. Since they hadn't seen us, I was inclined to be circumspect.

However, before I could do anything, Jonty decided to take matters into his own hands.

"Stop!" He levelled his pistol and shouted at the men in the car. "You are under arrest!"

Things suddenly took a dramatic turn for the worse. The man in the back pulled out what looked remarkably like a Bren gun and opened fire. Our reflexes kicked in as we hit the deck, diving left and right.

The Rolls took off at high speed, with the man in the back firing randomly as they went.

"You bloody idiot, Jonty," said Willie. "You nearly got us all killed!"

"Sorry, Skipper," said Jonty, most contrite.

"Never mind that," I said. "Let's get to the planes, we've got to stop them!"

The Rolls had disappeared from view. We struggled to our feet and ran for the Spitfires.

"He won't get far," I said as we ran. "We'll split up and find them."

"And then?" said Dylan.

"Shoot them dead, obviously," said Willie.

I made it back to my kite, holstered my weapon and climbed into the cockpit. I spun up the prop while the others did the same. In short order I taxied into position, gunned the throttle and was soon airborne.

From the air there were only two possible ways the Rolls could have gone. There was a road going past the driveway, so it would either have gone left or right.

"Jonty come with me," I said. "You two go the other way. If you see the car then shoot it."

"Wilco, Scottish," said Willie. "Come on, Dylan."

They banked away and started to follow the road. We did the same in the opposite direction.

"I hope we get them, Skipper," said Jonty. "Sorry about earlier."

"No matter," I told him. "We just need to stop them now, that's all. We can't let them get away."

The road was flanked by hedges on either side. It was quite narrow, as some of the country roads often are. I was beginning to think we'd gone the wrong way when Jonty let out a triumphant shout.

"There they are Skipper, up ahead!"

Sure enough, the Rolls was bowling along at a tremendous rate, weaving this way and that along the road.

"Let's get after them," I said.

It wouldn't take long to close the distance, but we were flying quite low. This would render us vulnerable to small arms fire.

"He's in my sights, Skipper," said Jonty. "Oh damn, look out!"

The rear gunner had spotted us and fired. Jonty banked left and I banked right to avoid him.

I pulled a tight turn around and fired at the car. The bullets kicked up the dirt but missed.

"Bad luck, Skipper, let me try."

Jonty fired but he too was also unsuccessful. The car was now weaving crazily from side to side. We continued to follow but the gunner managed to keep us at bay. Then, up ahead, I saw some woods made up of very tall trees. They formed a narrow avenue along the road, not quite wide enough for a Spitfire's wingspan. Once in there the Rolls would be out of reach.

"We've got to get them before they reach the woods, Jonty," I said.

"Not to worry, Skipper," said Jonty. "I've got it covered."

I tried a couple more bursts but couldn't hit the car. Then, just as I had a beautiful shot lined up, I clicked the fire button and nothing happened. My guns were empty.

"I'm out of ammo, Jonty," I said, pulling up and out of range.

"I've got some, Skipper, not to worry," he informed me.

"Willie, Dylan, we're due west of you, we've found the fugitives," I said, calling them up as reinforcements. "I'm out of ammo."

"Yes, we heard, Scottish," said Willie. "We are on our way."

In the distance I saw their planes closing with us fast, but not quite fast enough. The avenue loomed up and within seconds the Rolls would be inside it.

"Jonty, what the hell are you doing?" I said, as he dropped his kite down low.

"They're not getting away, Skipper!" said Jonty.

Before I could do anything sensible, the Rolls made the woods and was speeding down the avenue of trees. Jonty flipped his Spitfire sideways and started flying down it after them.

"Jonty, you've lost your bloody marbles!" I told him, following from a distance above him.

The Rolls was driving at a furious pace, spurred on by Jonty's pursuit. In the meantime, the Bren gunner couldn't draw a bead on Jonty because the car kept rocking from side to side.

"What's he doing?" said Willie, drawing up alongside me.

"Don't ask!" I said helplessly.

"It's all right, Skipper, I've got this covered," said Jonty, completely oblivious to the danger he was putting himself in.

The road was also very winding, but Jonty handled his Spitfire with impressive ease, particularly since he was flying sideways.

"We can't get a shot in this way because of Jonty," said Willie. "Dylan and I will circle around and get them from the front when they come of out the woods."

"Good thinking," I told him.

Willie and Dylan peeled off, throttled up, and overtook the crazy car chase going on below. There was a large bend in the avenue coming up. I was pretty sure even Jonty couldn't make it.

"Jonty," I said. "Watch out!"

My heart was in my mouth. Part of me wanted to order him to break off contact. The other part told me to have faith. Jonty somehow managed to pull off some of the most outrageous manoeuvres I had ever seen. I said nothing and hoped for the best.

The Rolls began to slow for the bend and Jonty took advantage of this. He opened fire and this time his bullets found the target. They raked across the Rolls which suddenly pulled wildly to the right. It hit a bump in the road and cartwheeled. Jonty pulled up at the last minute just before the bend. His Spitfire roared up into the air and he levelled it off.

"I'll just make sure of the kill, Skipper," he said, turning tightly.

The Rolls-Royce was upside down with its wheels still turning. Jonty fired once more, and the engine caught fire. There was an explosion as the fuel tank went up. I was pretty sure nobody could have survived it.

"Let's head back to base," I said. "We need to report in and make sure they've sent some ground forces to the estate."

"Roger," said Jonty, forming up on my wing.

"Well done, Jonty," I said.

I had to acknowledge that he'd saved the day.

"You've done some crazy things, Jonty," said Willie, arriving on the other wing. "But that pretty much beats all."

"Well, I was bloody impressed," said Dylan. "That was quite a flying display. I wish I could do that."

"For God's sake don't encourage him," I said. "One Jonty on the squadron is more than enough."

"I second that," said Willie.

"Let's go home," I said, laughing.

It wasn't long until we arrived back at Banley. It turned out that the estate was far closer than we thought. As I taxied to a stop, I could see Bentley and Audrey waiting for us along with Angelica, who started pelting towards us.

"Oh Lord," said Jonty. "I'll be on the carpet again, no doubt."

"Not if you let me do the talking," I told him.

"I'll be as silent as the grave, Skipper," he said.

I turned off the engine and climbed out of the cockpit. As soon as I jumped down from the wing Angelica threw herself into my arms.

"Thank God you're back," she said. "And in one piece."

She kissed me, effectively silencing any response I might have made. By the time we had celebrated our little reunion, Bentley had arrived. Angelica detached herself and stood beside me.

Bentley was in the act of tamping some new tobacco into his pipe. He lit it and puffed on it for a few moments.

"Sounds like you've all had something of a rum do," he said at length.

"Yes, sir," I said. "But Jonty here is the hero of the hour."

"Butterworth?" he said with surprise. "Hmm, in that case let's hear it from the beginning. Better still, might as well go to the mess, they do a tolerable cup of tea. You can enlighten me further there."

We accompanied Bentley and Audrey to the mess, with Willie, Jonty and Dylan tagging along. Bentley would probably have heard some of the story already from Tomas. He indicated a table in the corner, ordered tea for everyone and then we all took a seat while he smoked his pipe.

"So?" he said as the mugs of tea were brought over, along with some slices of fruit cake.

"After the bombing sortie, sir, we spotted the Ace Assassin's plane…" I began. I went on to furnish him with a full account. Bentley alternated between smoking his pipe, sipping his of tea and eating a slice of cake without commenting.

Once I had finished, he puffed on his pipe for a long while.

"So this blasted assassin," he said, "turns out to be a woman, and then a man, presumably her husband, takes off in his bloody Rolls-Royce… And his accomplice, no doubt the butler considering the farcical nature of this farrago, starts shooting at you."

"Yes, sir," I said. "That's about the size of it."

"Then Butterworth here, pulls one of his bloody half-baked stunts, flying sideways down a road lined with trees and manages to shoot the Rolls-Royce…" He trailed off.

"Yes, sir, that's what happened."

"Well, it's a damn good job you pulled it off then, Butterworth, isn't it? Otherwise, it might have been a different story altogether," Bentley said with his usual acidity.

"Yes, sir," said Jonty, no doubt happy he'd got off lightly so far.

"What I can't quite work out, Butterworth," Bentley said, "is whether you go looking for trouble, or if trouble just finds you?"

"I don't know, sir," said Jonty.

"Yes, well…" Bentley took another puff on his pipe. "On this occasion I will say, well done. However, do not under any circumstances take that as a carte blanche to go around committing all the folly you are normally capable of, do I make myself clear?"

"Perfectly, sir," said Jonty.

"Good. Your tomfoolery might pay off once in a blue moon, however…" Bentley left the rest unsaid.

He puffed on his pipe a little longer before speaking again.

"We've despatched plenty of chaps over to the house," he said. "To round up the staff and whatnot. I've sent word to those blasted spies and no doubt they'll be showing their faces around here pretty soon. I believe they'll be leading the investigation at the house into what on earth went on there. I suggest we all sit tight until we have some word. In the meantime, stand down. I think you've all done enough for one day."

With that he stood up and left the mess along with Audrey.

"What should we do now?" asked Angelica.

"I think we'll wait, like Bentley said, until we get word from the Marx Brothers," I replied.

"Yes, good idea. Willie, darling, why don't you go and tell Maria and Olga that the assassin is dead," Angelica suggested.

"All right," said Willie, getting up at once.

"Well, I'm off to tell Percy the good news," said Jonty.

Willie rolled his eyes.

When they had gone, Angelica turned to me.

"So," she said. "We're stood down, so that means I get you all to myself."

"Yes," I replied with a smile.

"Then let's go home…"

Although part of me was chafing to discover the mystery of the occupants of the assassin's manor, the other part was quite content to spend the evening with Angelica. We took dinner in our rooms and then she disappeared into the bathroom.

When she reemerged, she was wearing a sheer black negligee.

"I thought it was time for something special," she informed me with that all too familiar smile. "Do you like it?"

"Is it new?" I enquired, enfolding her into my embrace.

"Yes…"

Her lips were now less than an inch from mine.

"How many of these … surprises … do you have?" I said softly.

"That is for me to know and for you to find out."

"Is it?"

"I aim to keep surprising you for as long as I live," she whispered.

"Is that a fact?"

"Kiss me…" she breathed and naturally I wasn't able to resist her. I lost myself gladly in her caress and forgot about the troubles of the day.

We met Jonty and Willie for breakfast. Also, Dylan, Stanley and Harold, who had just been moved to Amberly Manor from their previous billet.

"What-ho, Skipper," said Jonty.

"I say, this is a posh kind of place," said Dylan, tucking into his eggs and beans.

"The food's pretty good too," said Stanley. "Compared to the last place."

They had apparently been put up at a boarding house. However, after numerous complaints about the landlady, the RAF had relocated their personnel. Amberly Manor was able to accommodate a fair few pilots and I was glad to have some more of M Flight staying there.

I accepted a plate of eggs, bacon and beans on toast from one of the staff and Angelica did the same. I took a sip from my mug of tea.

"What do you think is going to happen today, Skipper? Will we find out who those traitors were?" Jonty asked me.

"I hope so," I said. "No doubt we will discover more when we get to Banley."

"That was a hell of chase, yesterday," said Dylan.

"A hell of a day all round," agreed Stanley.

"Don't expect every day to be like that," I told him.

"I know, but wasn't it fun, Scottish?" said Dylan.

I smiled and ate my breakfast. Angelica shot me a look brimming with amusement at his enthusiasm. It was good, in a way, the newer pilots hadn't lost that. Some of us were a little more jaded, having been through the Battle of Britain. The fresh faces reminded me of my own exuberance when I started to fly.

We finished our breakfast and Gordon drove us into Banley. As soon as we alighted from the jeep, Audrey appeared.

"The Marx Brothers…" she began.

"Yes, I've been expecting them," I replied.

Angelica and I followed her to the mission room. The Marx Brothers were seated as usual, leisurely smoking cigarettes. This time, however, there seemed to be an air of purpose about them.

"Ah, Flight Lieutenant and Section Officer," said Harpo, taking a drag on his cigarette.

"We've discovered the identity of your mystery pilot," said Chico. "And her husband."

We sat down and waited a little impatiently for them to elucidate further.

"Lord Kevin McLinton and his wife, Lady Anthea," said Harpo. "We've had our suspicions about them for a while. Been keeping them under scrutiny, as it were."

"Obviously not enough scrutiny," said Angelica.

"Indeed, that's one of the failings of being stretched a little thin," said Chico, completely unfazed by this remark. "If you'd care to join our department, of course…"

"You know my feelings on that score," she replied. "I'm perfectly happy here with my *husband*."

Angelica emphasised the word 'husband' and Chico smiled.

"Ah, well," he said. "The offer's there."

"Who was the chap in the back of the Rolls-Royce?" I asked them, steering the conversation to less contentious matters.

"Ah, apparently that was the butler," said Harpo with a wry smile.

I laughed and so did Angelica.

"Bentley said so," I explained.

"Yes, as much as it does sound rather like a lurid crime novel," said Chico, "unfortunately, it's all too real."

"Where on earth did they get a P-40 from?" I asked them. The question had been niggling me for quite a while.

"When you have money — and McLinton had a considerable amount," said Chico, "then the ability to obtain things you probably shouldn't have is unfortunately multiplied. We shall naturally have our people investigate it, since we can't have military equipment falling into the hands of the gentry — or anyone else for that matter — who aren't part of the armed forces."

I would have to be content with that answer. They didn't know. I imagined the McLintons must have had contacts and somehow smuggled the aeroplane to England from America, or had it flown here. In the grand scheme of things, it wasn't important. What was important was that two traitors to our country were dead. Unfortunate as this was for their relations, it was a time of war. The impact of such people on the war effort could be great.

"What about Maria? What happens to her now?" asked Angelica.

"As to that," said Chico with a shrug, "she stays until such time as we decide to move her."

"At least she will no longer be under threat of assassination," Harpo added.

I had no more questions and neither did Angelica. The two spies continued to smoke their cigarettes. I wondered if there was something else they wanted so I asked them.

"So, what now?"

"You could come and see their manor if you like. It's quite … enlightening," said Harpo.

I glanced at Angelica and she nodded.

"All right," I said. "Then, yes. We'll find Sergeant Gordon and follow you there."

"Certainly," said Harpo. "I'm sure you'll find it suitably entertaining."

This wasn't the first word which sprang to mind in connection with the house of Nazi sympathisers, but I held my peace.

A short while later we pulled up the long driveway of the now deceased Lord and Lady McLinton's manor. It was all too familiar from the previous day's chase. There were quite a number of personnel including police in evidence. I imagined there was a fair bit to investigate.

We drew up at the front of the house in the gravel turning circle along with the Marx Brothers.

"Come and take a look," I said to Gordon, who was in the act of lighting a cigarette.

"Why not?" he said.

The three of us jumped down from the jeep and joined the Marx Brothers at the entrance to the house. It was a vast pile and the entrance portico sported a canopy held up by ornate fluted columns. The place was obviously several centuries old.

"Come on in," said Harpo. "We'll show you something interesting."

We followed them into an exceptionally large hallway which had a central staircase sweeping up and a gallery above. This formed an atrium from which sunlight filtered down through a dome high above us.

"As you can see," said Chico, "the McLintons were not short of a bob or two."

There were various people taking notes and talking in hushed tones to the staff. I assumed these were detectives or agents from MI6.

We continued to walk with the Marx Brothers down a corridor and into what was apparently the library. Bookshelves lined the walls. My parents had a similar one at home in Scotland. There was no time, however, to admire the McLinton's penchant for reading.

Harpo led us to a small opening in one of the bookcases. It looked rather as if it was a secret door. I was not prepared for what was behind it.

It was a reasonably sized room with wooden wainscoting and panelling. That was unremarkable. The contents were a different matter. The large portrait of Adolf Hitler on the wall was definitely out of place in a British household, along with the Nazi flags. There appeared to be Nazi regalia everywhere one looked and even some uniforms hanging up. There was a desk covered in paperwork which was being photographed. A Luger and other weapons including a Nazi-style dagger with a swastika carved into the hilt lay on the desktop.

Among the numerous pictures on the walls was one depicting a man and woman beside Hitler.

"The McLintons," said Chico helpfully. "With Hitler ... presumably before the war."

"Good God," I said, unable to help myself.

"Leaves something of a nasty taste in the mouth," said Gordon.

"Yes, indeed," agreed Harpo. "You are to be congratulated, Flight Lieutenant, for eliminating an embarrassment to this country."

I smiled. They hadn't been too happy about the spies we'd shot on other occasions.

"What's going to happen about their ... demise?" I asked him.

"Oh, a flying accident. A car accident ... that sort of thing."

I was incredulous. How on earth could they keep it all hushed up with the number of people involved?

"Oh, don't worry," said Chico, divining my thoughts and taking a pull on his cigarette. "Nobody leaves here without signing the Official Secrets Act... Breaking it has serious consequences."

"Is this ... all?" I asked him as I gestured around the room, wondering if there was more to see.

"Oh, by no means. Come along and take a look at the rest," he said cryptically.

After a fair walk around the manor house, we descended into what were a set of tunnels which made up the cellars. Many similar houses had them installed for storing food and wine, among other things. They were cold and with good reason. There was a fair quantity of game hanging from hooks along the length of one of the tunnels. This brought back to my mind the fare at the mess.

Before I could ask the obvious question about that, we arrived at an iron door. Chico swung it open. Gordon let out a low whistle. It was filled with armaments and ammunition boxes.

"Good God," I said. "There's enough here for a small army."

"Certainly more than a gamekeeper needs," agreed Harpo.

In the meantime, Gordon was examining an open box quite closely. It seemed to have contained grenades, except it was almost empty.

"Where do you think all these grenades have gone?" he enquired with interest.

I picked up his thought at once.

"Where's the gamekeeper?" I said to Chico.

"I don't know. I'm not sure if we've seen him, or even enquired about him," Chico replied.

This was something of an oversight in my opinion, but then they weren't privy to the suspicions I had been harbouring.

"Well perhaps we ought to find out?" suggested Angelica.

"Yes, perhaps we should. Come on, let's go!" said Harpo.

CHAPTER FIFTEEN

In a short space of time, we were standing talking to a uniformed housemaid whose name was apparently Betsy. The Marx Brothers appreciated the urgency of the situation without needing to have it spelt out. The empty box of grenades spoke volumes.

The gamekeeper had been somehow overlooked. However, we were assured by one of the operatives that Betsy was well acquainted with him. Gordon suggested Angelica might be best talking to the housemaid, since being questioned by a female might be less intimidating.

"Tell us about the gamekeeper, Betsy," said Angelica. "What's his name?"

"His name is Hans," Betsy said in a strong West Country accent. "Hans Sheaffer."

"What?" I exclaimed.

"He's German..." Betsy trailed off.

"How do you know he's German, Betsy?" Angelica said gently.

"Because he told me. I didn't ... I didn't think anything of it," she said defensively. "He said he didn't like Hitler ... he was against them Nazis... I thought..." She started to cry.

"Don't cry, Betsy, we understand how you might have been taken in," she said.

"It's not that," said Betsy. "It's not just that..."

The Marx Brothers remained silent throughout this exchange, allowing Angelica to draw her out.

"What is it then, Betsy?" Angelica asked her.

"He ... I ... we..." Betsy couldn't get the words out.

Angelica looked at me. I imagine we were both thinking the same thing.

"You were lovers, is that what you're trying to tell us?"

Betsy nodded miserably.

"And you didn't know that Lord McLinton was a Nazi sympathiser, nor his wife?" Angelica asked, just to make sure.

"No, I didn't … I swear. None of us were allowed into that room. None of us except Matlock … he was the butler and … and Hans."

She broke into a fresh fit of tears. We waited a little more impatiently this time, until these subsided. Angelica pulled a handkerchief from her pocket. Betsy accepted it and blew her nose.

"Keep it," said Angelica. "So, you had no idea what was in there. That Hans was really a Nazi sympathiser too?"

"No, I didn't. He made me care about him. I loved him and now he's done this… I'm so ashamed … just so terribly ashamed."

"It's all right, nobody here blames you, do we?" Angelica said, looking at us.

We all averred at once that Betsy was the innocent party.

"Where is Hans now?" I asked Betsy.

"I don't know. I haven't seen him," she said. "I was looking for him."

"Where *might* he be?" Angelica asked her.

Betsy thought for a moment. Now she felt complicit in his betrayal it was clear she wanted to help us as much as possible.

"Lord McLinton has some motorbikes in a hangar," she said. "He quite often used to go there … *we* used to go there…"

"Oh?"

"There's a bed…" she murmured.

The implication was obvious; they had used it for a secret rendezvous.

"And where is this hangar?" Angelica asked her.

"Out the back…"

We all glanced at each other. There was no time to lose. Probably nobody had thought to look in the hangar what with everything going on.

"Betsy, you've been very helpful, thank you," said Angelica kindly. "You stay here in the house. I'm sure these gentlemen will want to ask you more questions later, okay?"

"Yes," said Betsy in a small voice. "I'm sorry … I'm so sorry."

"We need to go," I said urgently. "Come on."

We left Betsy standing and hurried out to the back of the house.

"Where's the hangar?" said Harpo.

"It's over there."

I pointed out the concealed structure we had seen when we'd landed the day before. The remains of the P-40 were still on the airstrip, but the body of Lady McLinton had since been removed.

"All right, let's approach it with caution," said Chico.

We drew our guns. I kept Angelica behind me for safety as we neared the entrance. The hangar was large. The interior was dim. It was hard to see all the way in. A Tiger Moth stood close to the entrance. There were benches of tools and machines against the walls. I could see a couple of motorbikes.

"Do you think he's in there?" I said, as Harpo motioned us to stop.

"Hard to tell, but best to be cautious," he said.

"Let's see if we can flush him out," said Chico.

He raised his weapon. I did the same, along with Gordon and Harpo.

"Hans Sheaffer, we know you're in there," said Harpo loudly. "Come out with your hands up."

There was silence. Harpo tried again.

"It's no use, old man. The game's up. Give yourself up."

For a moment or two there was no response. Then suddenly there was the sound of a motorbike being kick-started and an engine roared to life. Without warning, the motorbike burst out from around the side of the building and sped straight towards us.

I grabbed hold of Angelica and flung us both aside. We scrambled up to see the motorbike heading off around the side of the house at speed.

"Come on!" shouted Gordon. "Let's get after him."

We ran at full pelt to the front. I could hear the sound of the bike's engine as it headed off down the drive. Angelica, Gordon and I jumped into the jeep. The Marx Brothers dived into their car after shouting at a couple of others to follow.

"Hang on," said Gordon, letting out the clutch.

The jeep spun the gravel as we took off in hot pursuit of the bike.

"Where do you think he's going?" asked Angelica.

"I've a shrewd idea," replied Gordon, who executed a perfect turn onto the main road with tyres squealing.

"The American base," I said.

"Bingo," said Gordon.

He drove the jeep at high speed and with incredible expertise. I dreaded to think what would happen if we met something coming the other way along the narrow road. There wasn't time to think about it, though, just hang on for dear life.

The Marx Brothers and two more cars were keeping pace behind us. We made quite a convoy. For a while there was no sign of the gamekeeper on the motorbike and then we hit a straight stretch of road. We spied him in the distance.

"That's him!" shouted Angelica triumphantly.

"Let's see if we can catch him!" said Gordon, accelerating as fast as he could.

"There's the American base up ahead," said Angelica. "You were right."

I wondered what would happen next. Was the gamekeeper really going there? For what purpose?

The first question was rapidly answered as the bike continued towards the sentries at the gate at a tremendous pace. There was a wooden barrier which they had put down to stop people from proceeding. The sentries spotted the bike and one of them stood in the road. He put his hand up, indicating the bike should stop. It didn't.

The next moment the sentries were diving left and right. The motorbike smashed through the flimsy barrier and pieces of wood went flying. Our convoy continued without stopping either, hell-bent on catching him. The gamekeeper seemed to be heading somewhere with a deadly purpose. I suddenly recalled he was carrying a large number of grenades. No doubt he intended to use them.

"Where's he going?" I said to Gordon.

"Not sure, sir," he replied, without slowing down. Then he said. "Oh no, I think he's headed for the munitions storage where they keep all the bombs."

"What?" I shouted. "But he's got all those grenades."

"Never fear, sir," said Gordon calmly. "It's just up ahead."

I didn't quite share his confidence, but the bike suddenly slowed in front of a series of large humps in the earth. These were underground facilities where they kept all the bombs. There were USAAF personnel walking about, but they seemed to pay him no mind. The gamekeeper stopped near the entrance to one of the bunkers and got off the bike.

Gordon screeched the jeep to a halt and jumped down. In one swift move, he pulled a rifle from its housing on the side of the jeep. He rapidly breached a round and aimed it.

Meanwhile, the gamekeeper was walking swiftly towards the entrance with something in his hand. I dreaded to think what would happen if several grenades went off in those bunkers.

The next instant, Gordon pulled the trigger. A shot rang out and the gamekeeper dropped like a stone. Seconds later there was a tremendous explosion as the grenade in his hand went off and the others concealed on his person blew up too. Gordon was blown off his feet, along with a number of others nearby.

The Marx Brothers helped him up and Harpo offered him a cigarette.

"Good shot," said Harpo.

"Indeed, quite a feat of driving too," said Chico, admiringly.

The three of them stood smoking cigarettes without a care in the world as pandemonium broke loose all around us.

Sometime later we were all seated in the mission room at Banley. Along with Bentley, the group consisted of me, Angelica, Gordon, the Marx Brothers and Audrey.

There had been a long and involved inquest at the American base into what had occurred, which the Marx Brothers had dealt with for the most part. When we had returned to our own base, Bentley had insisted on having a personal briefing and so here we were.

We waited while he emptied his pipe, scraped it out, filled the bowl with fresh tobacco and lit it. The Marx Brothers and Gordon were smoking cigarettes and the air was filled with a light haze.

"If someone would like to explain from the beginning just what went on today," said Bentley, "I'd be much obliged."

I decided that it might be politic if it was me, particularly as the Marx Brothers would very likely wind him up. So, I began a long explanation from the moment we'd arrived at the McLinton's manor house to the point where Gordon had shot the gamekeeper.

Bentley listened patiently and without comment, until I had finished.

"I see," he said at length. "So it seems these blasted people were traitors and your lot knew nothing about it."

He pointed the stem of his pipe accusingly at Harpo.

"We were monitoring them," said Chico. "But we were not aware of the full extent of their allegiance to the Third Reich."

"Well, it's a damn shame you didn't," said Bentley. "We might have been spared what appears to have become an unbelievable farrago."

"Yes," said Harpo. "We are looking at our intelligence network to see how we can tighten things up."

The Marx Brothers knew better than to rile Bentley up and so opted to placate him by agreeing with him.

"I should bloody well think so," said Bentley, irascibly. "Yes, indeed."

He paused for a long moment before speaking again.

"In any case, how does this blasted gamekeeper enter into it?" he said.

"He was supplying the American mess with game," said Chico. "According to American Military Intelligence who have questioned the staff at the mess, he hung around quite a lot and so possibly gleaned information, gossip and so forth that way. We are looking into his background. It's very possible he was planted here by German Intelligence."

"You don't say," said Bentley with some acidity. "Well, perhaps our friends next door won't be so damned naïve in future."

"No," said Harpo. "I believe the Americans may well tighten their own security up on their base after this."

"Ridiculous letting any damn Tom, Dick or Harry in just because they've got some pheasants," said Bentley.

"I suppose they saw it as a bonus, sir, from which we've all benefited," I said, trying to defend our American allies.

"That's as may be," said Bentley. "But let him drop it off and go, not hang around chewing the fat like it's a blasted knitting circle. Whatever next? Perhaps they'll just hand over all their secret documents to any bloody clown that wanders in."

It seemed that it was the human element which would often fail us as much as anything. No doubt the mess crew thought the gamekeeper was just someone trying to help them out and perhaps make a few pennies in the process. They had no idea he and his employers were working for the Germans.

"Anyway," Bentley continued, turning his attention to Gordon. "I gather you're the hero of the hour, Sergeant. Where did you learn to shoot like that?"

"I was a sniper, sir, in the trenches," said Gordon.

"The Great War?" said Bentley. He looked suitably impressed by this information.

"Yes, sir," said Gordon.

"Right, well, I think there's hopefully been some lessons learned from this," said Bentley. "We can get back to normal duties — if anything happening in this bloody squadron could be classed as normal. It gets more like a farce every blasted day."

We let the sarcasm pass. Bentley was inordinately fond of the Mavericks and would defend the squadron to the hilt against all comers.

"Anyway, Maria should be safer by all accounts," suggested Harpo.

"As to that," said Bentley, "I'm taking nothing for granted. We will be retaining our air defence around her house and the pursuit team on standby until such time as she's no longer with us. Doubtless, you can't tell us when that will be, can you?"

"I'm afraid not, no," said Chico.

"I thought as much. Not that I haven't come to expect anything else."

Bentley's tone was acidic. I decided to lighten the mood if I could.

"I suppose that's the end of rabbit or venison stew at the mess," I said. "A pity, since the McLintons had a large amount of game hanging in their cellars."

"Oh, did they, indeed. It happens I rather liked the venison pie," said Bentley, suddenly becoming decisive. "Well, that's where you're wrong. I'll be writing orders to requisition it immediately. Perhaps, Sergeant, you can make arrangements to go and collect it and bring it back to Banley. Might as well try and make a silk purse out of a sow's ear."

"I will do so with pleasure, sir," said Gordon.

"An excellent notion," added Harpo.

"Indeed," said Chico.

"Right, well, if that's all then we can put this all behind us," said Bentley. "It's not as if I don't have other things to do than get involved in these blasted ridiculous antics. Sergeant, you can come with me. Audrey will type up the requisition orders right away. Take some men and whatever trucks you need."

Nobody demurred and shortly afterwards the meeting broke up. Angelica and I were left alone once more.

"What shall we do now?" I asked her, feeling at something of a loose end.

"We should go and have dinner."

"And then?" I said, standing up.

She wound her arms around me.

"Then you can kiss me ... a lot."

"Why not now?"

"Oh, well," she murmured, "if that's what you want to do, then don't let me stop you, Flight Lieutenant Mackennelly."

"I don't intend to, Section Officer Mackennelly," I whispered back.

A NOTE TO THE READER

Dear Reader,

I hope you enjoyed this latest episode of the Mavericks. You'd be interested to know that the 'Tip and Run' raids were indeed a real thing where lone wolf raiders would bomb and strafe coastal towns in Britain. They became more than something of a nuisance for quite a while. I thought it would be interesting to write a story about it, and about a German pilot who was a little obsessive in that particular mission.

Truth is stranger than fiction and there really was a dog who went up with his owner in a B-17 and had his own oxygen mask, which was the inspiration for Jonty's parrot escapade.

I would be very grateful if you could spare the time to write a review on **Amazon** and **Goodreads**. As an author, these reviews are hugely important, and always appreciated.

You can connect with me in other ways too, via my **website**, **Facebook**, **Twitter**, **Instagram**, and a special **Spitfire Mavericks Page**.

I very much hope you were entertained enough to read the next book in the Spitfire Mavericks series.

Warmest regards,

D. R. Bailey

Sapere Books is an exciting new publisher of brilliant fiction and popular history.

To find out more about our latest releases and our monthly bargain books visit our website:
saperebooks.com